Impossible Bliss

For Don —
This warning to
avoid sand traps.

Lee Shel

Impossible Bliss

Lee Sheldon

iUniverse Star
New York Lincoln Shanghai

Impossible Bliss

iUniverse Star
an iUniverse, Inc. imprint

For information address:
iUniverse, Inc.
2021 Pine Lake Road, Suite 100
Lincoln, NE 68512
www.iuniverse.com

ISBN: 1-58348-021-8

Printed in the United States of America

For Tara

CHAPTER ONE

Herman de Portola Bliss sat on a steeply sloping hillside, improving on nature. Well over six feet of Bliss hung over his easel, applying oils with lavish strokes. He felt like a vulture, one of his favorite birds, perched high above Carmel Bay Country Club, all-seeing, patient as the grave.

From the hill he could look across the seventh fairway to the very brink of the cliff that dropped to the ocean beyond. Mist hung in the sharp April air. Dew lay on the grass. The rocks and sky and wild surf demanded his attention in the early morning light, compelling him to capture it.

The picture taking shape on his canvas however sprang from a palette unknown to nature. Bold swirls of color competed enthusiastically for attention, lifting the sea's rough beauty into the realm of statement and significance.

Bliss half heard the sound of many approaching feet crushing ice plants and snapping pine branches, but his art consumed the vast bulk of his consciousness. Crucial moments passed before the danger of his position struck him. Looking around in dismay, his hand worried at the week's growth of whiskers on his chin. He knew he sat on property protected by guards and wire fencing in addition to astronomical greens' fees and long waiting lists. He knew also he sat there uninvited.

A brigade of uniformed police officers and security personnel emerged from the trees on his left. To his relief the forces of law and order didn't look in his direction. They navigated a gully between his hill and the next. Crossing beneath his vantage point, they made their way toward a trio of golfers standing on the seventh green nearly a hundred yards away.

The men waiting there, dressed in the latest golfing fashion, had inspired Bliss to elevate the landscape in front of him to a higher plane. Their presence had cried out to him to paint the intrusion of man upon nature. So the natural rich greens, grays and blues of the scene before him mutated into puce, magenta, fuchsia, clashing with Venetian red and yellow ochre, and Day-Glo's of pink and lime, a transformation that filled Bliss with pride.

His sausage nose quivered, aggressive chin jutting further out. Someone had once called his hair, mud brown streaked with mouse gray, a garden gone to seed. The furrows of flesh that fifty-six years had carved into his face added to the image, but Bliss no longer minded. If he needed to nurture his love of beauty, he looked at his art, not in the mirror.

He watched as the official party reached the green. Soon after the first cold sunlight cleared the trees, and began nudging the previous night's fog away, the golfers, riding in two electric carts, had appeared at the seventh tee. There had been four of them then. Bliss, knowing little of the game, counted himself lucky that they lingered near the green while others, always in quartet, eventually came along, then passed them by.

One golfer had trotted off for a while. Bliss had wanted to duplicate the utterly unique shade of green of the man's shirt. Busily swirling colors on his palette, he looked up to catch a glimpse of the golfer trudging into the trees near where the police would later make their entrance. The correct mix of oils still eluded Bliss, so his subject's sudden absence caused the painter no end of consternation. The golfer returned before Bliss went in search of him, to drag him by his neck back to his place in the grand composition.

Bliss knew little of the subtleties of golf, but he sensed something strange in the scene he painted. Up until this moment the strangeness failed to distract him from giving life to his vision. It took the appearance of the authorities, decked out in the crisp khaki uniforms of the Carmel, California Police Department, and escorted by the club's security men, to steal his concentration from his latest masterpiece.

He now watched with interest as the officers conferred with the trio of golfers in the distance. These three, with much shrugging and head shaking, appeared to be describing an occurrence of more than usual significance. They pointed in the direction of the hole, then turned to wave their arms at a sand trap some twenty yards away.

Gulls cawed at one another in the pale blue morning sky. The air carried the unmistakable edge of salt and decomposing marine life. Bliss tried to ignore it all, concentrating on his favorite sense: sight.

The men below walked to the deep scar of the sand trap near the cliff's edge. Two of the uniformed police officers moved off in different directions, apparently looking for something. Bliss felt pretty certain no one called them in to search for a lost ball. His interest rose.

Bliss rose with it to get a better look, shuffling forward, straining over his easel. All of a sudden he felt his right foot hook beneath a loop of root. He twisted to pull it free, weight shifting. Misjudging the force required by a factor of ten, he felt the root give way, severely over-balancing him.

He toppled into his easel. It, the paints, the stool, and Bliss, cart wheeled down the hillside in an avalanche of dust, loose earth and stone and paint. Day-Glo pinks and limes splattered everywhere. Improving on nature.

*　　　　　*　　　　　*

An insistent melody that Carmel Police Chief Dan Shepard had awakened with that morning teased around the edges of his mind. A phrase or two tantalized him, threatening to fade forever, a few stray bars, not enough to commit to paper yet. Whenever he concentrated, it came wafting back to him like the hint of a departed lover's perfume. He ran his fingers over his receding hair, cut close to the scalp, a style cultivated during his years as an M.P., pushing the snippet of melody aside.

Shepard looked across the green at the pin, its flag fluttering bravely in the offshore breeze, then down at the sand trap beneath his feet. He listened to the story the three men before him had to tell, his pleasant face, a rich coffee color, creased with thought. Their story annoyed him like a stain on his uniform.

In his early forties, Shepard had worn a uniform of one kind or another most of his life from scouting to the army to law enforcement. He liked uniforms. They gave him a sense of order in a disorderly world. Wrinkles cut to the heart of him. Stains soiled his soul.

The sound of the avalanche made Shepard jump. On the far side of the fairway he could see a cloud of dust plummeting comet-like down a hill. The shapes tumbling within the dust exploded at the bottom. A scream of outrage rose from the cloud, immediately echoed by dozens of terrified seabirds.

"Charlie." Shepard turned to one of his officers. Charlie Revere, a young man with red hair, and a severe crop of freckles, moved to his side. "Invite whoever that is to join the party, if he hasn't broken his neck." He nodded to the shorter of his two men, an easy-going older officer named Stan Durbin, to go along.

The dust cloud began to clear, and Shepard could see a figure rising shakily to its feet in the center. His men reached the scene of the cataclysm. Shepard saw a stoop-shouldered man wave imperiously at his scattered belongings. To Shepard's amazement his officers scurried to collect them all. They then followed behind the man like court retainers. When Shepard saw they were carrying artist paraphernalia, he realized with a jolt who the owner of it must be.

The man approached with a pigeon-toed, shambling gait. Most of the dust he'd picked up on his plunge down the hill still clung to him, little puffs rising from the tattered tennis shoes, soiled flannel shirt, and paint-stained, rumpled pants. One of the characters drawn by Charles Shultz sprang to mind: Pigpen come to life, but so ungracefully aged. Shepard had only held his job for a few short weeks, but he knew this must be Bliss stumbling toward him, grousing at the officers who struggled with easel, canvas, palette, brushes and assorted tubes of paints.

"Who are you?" Bliss demanded as he approached. "You the new Chief of Police?"

"Yes, sir," Shepard responded. "Dan Shepard."

"You're black," Bliss shot back, peering at him keenly from beneath impossibly bushy eyebrows.

"Yes, sir," Shepard continued politely, "I am."

"I have a heightened sense of color," Bliss snapped at him.

Shepard tried to figure if Bliss was joking, actually defining some artistic insight, or just being nasty. Stanley MacGregor, Chief of the Carmel Bay Company's security force, interrupted.

"Sir," he said. "This is private property. What were you doing up on that hill?"

Bliss brought his face around ninety degrees to glare at MacGregor.

"Stealing ball washers," Bliss snarled, looking him up and down. This didn't take long since MacGregor stood only somewhat over five feet four inches in height. Strategically built-up heels didn't help much, sunk as they were in the spongy grass.

Shepard saw Bliss take in the slicked back, razor-cut hair, starched cuffs, dark green blazer with its security logo and the light green trousers.

"What are you?" the artist asked in a pleasant voice. "Some sort of fascist leprechaun?"

Shepard decided Bliss certainly lived up to his advance press. Warned about the man by every official he'd met since arriving on the Monterey

Peninsula, Shepard had taken the time to read the extensive file the Carmel Police maintained on him in preparation for their inevitable meeting. Now, faced with the reality, he realized no amount of study would have been sufficient.

Shepard knew every law enforcement agency in the county had arrested Bliss on numerous misdemeanors such as trespassing, loitering, public nuisance, inciting to riot, even public indecency. Minor blemishes on the face of a world cratered by malignant evil maybe, but the list of complaints numbered close to four hundred. Surely Bliss held some kind of record for petty criminality.

The oddest thing about that distinctly odd file had struck Shepard as he leafed through it. Everyone who lodged a complaint against the man dropped it before the case reached a court of law.

Shepard could see MacGregor building a head of steam that could only inflame Bliss to new heights of disagreeableness. Noting the canvas carried by one of his officers, he had an inspiration.

"What is your name, sir?" Shepard asked Bliss with all the pleasantry he could muster.

"Bliss," came the grudging reply.

"And you're an artist?"

Bliss gave a short honk of laughter. "You'll go far in law enforcement with deductions like that, Chief. What gave me away? Was there a stray dab of burnt umber under one of my fingernails?"

Shepard took a deep breath, allowing the wayward melody to rise within him again, calming him like a mantra. He prided himself on how well he could keep himself controlled and professional in the face of any provocation. The artist appeared to have no inhibitions at all.

"Mr. Bliss, something kind of peculiar has happened here. You may be able to help us."

This seemed to disconcert Bliss for a moment.

"Peculiar?" he asked, a trace of interest creeping into his voice.

"How long were you up on that hill?"

Bliss' mouth scrunched up. It looked, thought Shepard, like the edge of a clamshell. He'd seen something like it in cartoons, but he hadn't realized a human mouth could do that.

"Ha!" Bliss exclaimed. "If I admit I was on that hill, I'd be admitting I was trespassing. Are you trying to force me to incriminate myself?"

"You fell down the hill!" MacGregor sputtered. "We all saw you!"

"I'm a law-abiding citizen," Bliss replied without a hint of irony.

"I know who you are, Bliss!" MacGregor continued. "You've been cited for trespassing on every golf course on this peninsula! You're the one who gave that deer a heart attack over at Spyglass!"

Shepard stared at MacGregor. He'd missed this particular charge while skimming Bliss' file. How did you give a deer a heart attack anyway? Not about to let himself be drawn into battle, Shepard played the peacemaker.

"Mr. MacGregor, please. Mr. Bliss is an artist. If he was up on that hill, painting for some time, he may have seen something that can clear up this mystery."

The oldest of the three brightly clad golfers gave a snort of derision, looking elaborately out over the ocean to show how little he thought of this idea.

"Mystery?" Bliss licked his lips.

Shepard realized that he'd struck a chord. "Yes, sir." He indicated the golfers. "Mr. Romaine there and Mr. Webb and Mr. Holly were part of a foursome that arrived at the seventh tee about, what? Forty? Forty-five minutes ago?" He looked toward the three men. One of them, heavy-set, of average height, and florid complexion, nodded. The other two followed suit. Shepard turned back to Bliss.

"Were you up there forty-five minutes ago, Mr. Bliss?"

Bliss scowled. "I might have been."

"Which direction were you facing?"

Bliss made a vague gesture toward the ocean.

"Did you see anything unusual?"

"Unusual? Of course I did! I put it all in my painting!"

Shepard allowed himself a flicker of hope. "May I see the painting?"

Bliss looked around, spotted the canvas held by Charlie Revere, and yanked it from the young man's grasp. He held it out for Shepard's inspection.

Shepard recoiled, then hoped Bliss had missed his instinctive first reaction. Beneath the twigs, leaves, pine needles and raw earth added by the hill, lurked a monstrous creation. Colors abraded each other as they lay on the canvas. They assaulted the eyes. One line appeared to be the cliff edge. A kidney-shaped wound might even be the sand trap, but it could just as easily have been the front view of a dead fish with an American flag in its mouth. Shepard knew Bliss' fall must have smeared some of the painting, but not all of it. No, most of what Shepard held in his hands the artist had put there on purpose.

"I see," he managed to get out.

"Of course you do," Bliss beamed, his smile almost ghastly in its childlike pleasure. "It's one of the more accessible works in my current series of seascapes. The coastline primeval flattened, twisted and pounded into synthetic shapes by the clumsy hands of avarice. A sterile wasteland perpetrated by men who can't see beyond the balance sheet expressly for men with senses so deadened, they can wear clothes like that without vomiting."

Here he gestured at the three golfers. The third, a good-looking brown-haired man in his late thirties, Shepard judged, sported various shades of designer green. What Robin Hood might look like if he lived in Palm Springs.

A pink shirt and maroon trousers hung from the thin, frail-looking frame of the first man, clearly the elder of the three by quite a few years. Shepard knew his name: Loren Holly, one of the peninsula's leading developers. The young man in green, Ben Webb, worked for Holly as his vice president of something or other. Webb had been the one who telephoned the police.

The red-faced golfer, maybe fifty years of age, wore a lemon yellow knit shirt and red trousers with a spandex waistband and white shoes. Beyond his name, Leonard Romaine, Shepard knew nothing about him.

Shepard admitted privately to himself that Bliss had a point. The color combinations did seem a bit much even for golfers, but the idea, translated to paint on canvas, may have been too successful. Shepard could barely bring himself to look at it.

"Mr. Webb, would you mind telling Mr. Bliss what you told me? Maybe it will help him to remember something he saw that can explain...this..." He gestured at the green, then back at the sand trap.

Bliss squinted at Webb with an almost obscene intensity of concentration. Obviously ill at ease, Webb cleared his throat, and began.

"Mr. Holly, Mr. Romaine and I were part of a foursome with a gentleman named Alex Wagner. This is a regular match for us every Wednesday morning. We tee off at six o'clock precisely. Except in the winter," he added somewhat unnecessarily. "In the winter we tee off an hour later. Because of the light."

Bliss nodded. "I understand light."

"Everything proceeded pretty much as usual," Webb said. "I was up a stroke coming to the seventh tee. Our second shots all landed on the fairway."

He pointed to a spot that dipped down in a shallow bowl forty yards across. Dew glistened there, still protected from the morning sun, but trampled by cleated feet.

"My third shot landed on the front part of the green," Webb continued. "Mr. Romaine's carried over the back apron, and rolled down that little hill. Mr. Holly's you can see there in the fairway on the upslope just short of the green. Alex's shot landed in this bunker."

Webb stopped talking, an irritated look on his face. Bliss had turned away. He walked across the green, scuffed with his shoe at something in the sponge-like grass that looked to Shepard like a runny bird dropping from the gulls overhead. Bliss glanced back down the seventh fairway, a

slight dogleg, running roughly south to north. The cliff bordering the
western edge of the fairway fell in places as much as thirty feet to the
surf that hammered steadily against the rocks. Then the artist swiveled
around to peer into the bunker.

Shepard turned to follow Bliss' gaze. The bunker lay parallel to the
cliff. Shepard gauged it to be about twenty-five feet in length and half
again as wide for the most part. It seemed fairly deep, maybe four feet
nearest the fairway, gradually sloping down to only three feet or so on
the cliff side. The thickly woven grass here still wore a heavy rime of
dew. Several small rocks dotted the area, with more near the cliff's edge
some thirty feet away.

Bliss rejoined them; his eyes scanning from side to side like a security
camera.

One pair of footprints scuffed through the wet grass from the fairway
to the shallow western edge of the bunker. Where they reached it, the
turf at the lip of the trap seemed chewed up a little, probably by the
golfer climbing down inside, Shepard supposed. The single set of tracks,
now clearly made by golf cleats, continued across the sand to a spot
closer to the green. There the sand looked somewhat kicked about. A
rake lay on the ocean side of the bunker. A few feet from the disturbed
patch of sand a golf club rested, its head caked with wet sand. Bliss
pointed at it.

"What kind of club is that?" he asked.

"A sand wedge." Holly's lips curled in contempt.

Shepard saw Bliss' eyes narrow. There's some history here, he
thought, and filed it away. He prompted, "Go on, Mr. Webb."

"Well, like I said. Alex…Mr. Wagner's shot landed in the bunker. He
was away, so he played first. He took his sand wedge from his bag there
on the cart, went over and climbed inside the trap. We stayed down
there in the fairway."

"Why?" Bliss interrupted again.

Webb appeared momentarily at a loss. "It's what you do. You don't walk into the line of a man's shot."

"Then what happened?" Shepard prodded.

"After a little while his ball came sailing out of the trap, and…Well, it was a miraculous shot. It hit the green about eight feet from the pin and rolled right into the cup for his par."

"He's never parred the seventh in his entire life," Holly interrupted with a scowl. "In five years he's landed in that bunker more times than I can count. He's always chipped short and two-putted for a bogey. Always!"

Webb nodded. "Like I said. Miraculous."

"Miraculous, nothing!" Holly glared at him. "He cheated. You know it. I know it. He was a cheat! Somehow he cheated!"

Bliss threw up his hands. "And that's why you called the police? Is cheating at golf a felony or a misdemeanor?"

Romaine spoke for the first time. His voice sounded deep, and as cool as the sea spray that occasionally drifted over them. "If it *were* a crime, the jails around here would be bursting at the rivets."

"We are wasting our time!" Holly complained.

"Go on, Mr. Webb, please," Shepard replied calmly.

"Well, so we came up here to see where the ball went. And sure enough, there it was in the cup. I almost fell down. We all began talking at once, shouting to Alex. We expected him to climb out of the bunker so he could gloat like he always did when he managed to make a decent shot, and pretend it had been skill instead of luck. We waited, but he didn't climb out."

Bliss had a glimmer of what happened, Shepard realized. The artist's crooked smile grew broader, but he said nothing, waiting for Webb to finish.

"After a few moments, when he didn't appear, we looked at each other."

"I thought he wanted us to go over to congratulate him," volunteered Romaine.

"So we did," Webb continued. "We walked over here and stood just about where Chief Shepard is standing now. We could clearly see every inch of the bunker."

"And Wagner wasn't in it," Bliss finished for him.

"No," Webb chimed in with something approaching awe. "He'd vanished. Into thin air."

CHAPTER TWO

The words hung in the thin air Alex Wagner had vanished into, along with a few remaining traces of mist. Shepard watched Bliss wrestle with the problem. He realized that an artist, even a bad artist like Bliss, might spot something a policeman overlooked. He also could tell by the way Bliss concentrated that the man apparently felt the same way.

"We looked around," Webb concluded. "But there was no sign of Alex. I mean he was out of our sight for less than five minutes tops. Finally I cut through the trees to the clubhouse to call the police."

As presented, the situation sounded impossible. The sand trap appeared to have swallowed a man whole. If he'd walked away from it, his three companions, and probably the painter up on the hill, would have all seen him. Shepard turned it over in his mind, listened to the insistent melody that accompanied it.

"You didn't happen to see anybody climb out of this bunker while you were up on that hill, did you, sir?" he asked Bliss.

Bliss sighed and shook his head, looking down the fairway toward the tee, some four hundred yards distant. A mass of agitated golfers, kept at bay by a couple of security guards, grew steadily like a backed-up drain.

"Then I'm sorry to have troubled you." Shepard handed the painting back to Bliss, and indicated his men were to give Bliss his belongings.

Bliss made no move to depart. "You know anything about art, Chief?"

For one horrific moment Shepard thought he would be forced to give his opinion on the monstrosity Bliss had shown him.

"Well, not a lot…"

Bliss studied him. "You think this is all about perspective, don't you? Sight lines?"

"I'm sure there's more to it than that."

Bliss agreed with a belligerent nod. "There sure as hell is."

"There's color, of course, and light," Shepard went on, growing in confidence. "Choice of subject matter…" His voice trailed off when he saw Bliss' expression sink to one of outright disgust.

"What are you going on about?" Bliss growled at him.

"Art," Shepard replied.

"Art? Art? I'm talking about murder!"

The last word rose and echoed. Those gathered around seemed to have turned to stone. Even the distant golfers stopped their impatient pacing and flailing of arms. The waves still boomed against the rocks. The gulls still wheeled raucously in the air above their heads. All else was a still life.

"Murder?" Shepard repeated, the soothing melody banished from his mind in an instant.

"What do you think happened here, Chief?"

Shepard hesitated, then saw that MacGregor, the three golfers, even his own men were gazing at him expectantly. Shepard took a deep breath.

"Okay. I think Mr. Wagner decided to play a little joke on his friends. You mentioned perspective and sight lines. Even though this bunker is only four feet deep, it's situated above that low area in the fairway where Mr. Webb said he, Mr. Romaine and Mr. Holly were standing. I suspect from there it would be difficult to see someone in it even if he stood completely upright."

"Bravo," Bliss muttered. "I'm on pins and needles."

Shepard plowed ahead, refusing to let Bliss get to him. "Since my men didn't find him hiding in the shrubbery, I figure after he made his shot, Mr. Wagner crawled over to the cliff's edge, keeping the rise of the bunker between him and the other three. Then he climbed down the rocks, and went off somewhere. Maybe he made his way back to the clubhouse. He's probably there now, having a good chuckle, and wondering what's keeping his golfing buddies."

Shepard turned to Webb. "What was he wearing?"

Webb thought for a moment. "Red shirt...light blue pants and shoes..."

"White socks," Holly added in an impatient voice.

Shepard nodded. "Mr. Wagner was quite a practical joker, I'll bet."

"Yes, he was," Webb agreed.

Holly broke in. "Yes! Yes! Yes! But his ego would've filled Carmel Bay out there, with plenty left over for Monterey Bay and Elkhorn Slough!"

Shepard shook his head. "I don't quite follow.

Holly gestured in the direction of the pin. "The ball went in the cup! However Wagner managed that, he would've stood his ground, and basked in the glory! He wouldn't have crawled off on his hands and knees to play hide and seek like some pre-adolescent!"

Shepard saw the valleys in Bliss' face re-arrange themselves into a look of triumph. "Besides," Bliss said, "he couldn't have done it anyway."

"Why not?" Shepard protested, feeling things getting way out of control. "You yourself were talking about sight lines!"

"Of course!" Bliss wagged his head up and down. "The sight lines meant it was possible that whatever happened in this bunker would not have been seen by those down in the fairway. But use your eyes, man! Observe! Your profession has at least that in common with mine! You must observe!"

"Observe what?" Shepard shot back.

"The dew! Down there in the hollow of the fairway the golfers and your men have tracked through it like a herd of sheep, but look at the dew on the grass between the bunker and the cliff's edge! Not a mark on it! There would've been some trace if a man walked across it, let alone crawled on all fours!"

Shepard studied the broad band of glistening gray moisture only now beginning to dry in the rising sun. How could he have missed it? Not a mark stained it, not a bird track. That awful man, squinting at him from beneath eyebrows that looked like two caterpillars smooching, was right.

"And then of course, there's the weapon…" Bliss added with surprisingly little rancor.

Shepard could hardly bring himself to reply. "The weapon?"

Bliss indicated the sand trap. "That club. What was it? A sand wedge?" The three golfers nodded in unison. "Well look at it! The head is plainly caked with sand." Bliss held out his hands, as if presenting the obvious to Shepard on a silver tea tray.

"It's a damp morning," Shepard began. "The sand in that trap—"

"—is granular, and drier than the grass," Bliss concluded. "It isn't even clinging to the rake!"

Shepard started to reply, thought better of it, and instead fought silently to recover his composure. Without a word he walked to the rim of the trap, gazed down at it for a long moment. Reaching a decision, he carefully moved along the cut. Finding an unmarked spot near where the lip of the trap looked damaged, he stepped gingerly down inside. His shoes leaving distinct prints, he crossed to the sand wedge.

The others moved to the very edge of the trap, and watched in silence. Shepard stopped two feet from the sand wedge, settled down on his haunches and frowned at it. He ran his hand over his hair. Another melody, low and ominous, insinuated itself into his thoughts.

"Yeah," he said slowly. "Yeah, there's something on the head of the club all right. It's soaked down into the sand a bit, too. It's dark enough to be blood. Okay." He looked up at Durbin. "Stan, call it in. I want a crime scene team here ASAP. Rope off this whole area from that dip in the fairway across the green then out to the cliff on both sides."

"Wait a minute!" MacGregor cried. "That would prevent play on this hole!"

"Yeah," Shepard agreed, straightening. "It would."

He nodded to Durbin. The man carefully placed his share of Bliss' art supplies on the grass, and trotted off at a good clip toward the tree line.

"But we have over three hundred golfers lining up to play the most famous course in the world!" the security man exclaimed.

"I'm sorry, MacGregor. That's the way it's going to be."

MacGregor shook his head in wonder. "You don't play golf, do you?"

"No," Shepard said."

"You can't ask a golfer to skip a hole, particularly on this course! Some people wait their whole lifetime to get a chance to play Carmel!"

Shepard failed to keep the annoyance from his voice. "I don't care if they skip, hop or jump over the hole. Nobody else is parading through here until we get a better fix on what happened."

MacGregor opened his mouth to continue the debate, but apparently thought of a better tack. "All right," he said, his lip curving into a smirk, "This club pays a whopping share of Carmel city taxes. You'll be hearing from the manager."

Shepard shrugged. "You can drag the ghost of Bing Crosby out here to threaten me if you want. The seventh hole stays closed until further notice."

MacGregor nodded at his two men. The trio headed off toward the seventh tee. Shepard hoped the crowd, when it learned the tragic news, might turn on the messenger.

Taking a last look at the sand wedge, Shepard climbed back up out of the trap. He avoided the smug expression he knew must be firmly fixed on Bliss' face.

The three remaining members of Wagner's foursome moved forward. Holly spoke first.

"See here, Chief. There must be some mistake. Alex couldn't have been murdered! The idea is preposterous!"

"I didn't say Wagner was the victim. Maybe he was the murderer!" Bliss snapped at him.

"Nonsense!" Holly retorted. He stopped, momentarily distracted by the outcry that rose from the crowd at the seventh tee. MacGregor had delivered the news. Shouted threats reached them even here. Shepard saw somebody throw a golf club against a tree.

Holly brought his attention back to the issue at hand. "We've gone from one man sneaking out of that trap for no good reason. Now we're to believe there was someone else in there with him? Why only two? Why not three? Or four? Perhaps the Bach Festival Orchestra and Chorus hunkered down in there for a quick rehearsal of *The Passion of St. Matthew!*"

"The breeze is from offshore," Bliss pointed out. "I would've heard them."

"You are a raving lunatic, and everybody knows it!" Holly yelled.

"How do we know for sure you're telling the truth?" Bliss continued, undaunted.

"Chief," Holly said. "You are new to the peninsula. This man's reputation is infamous!"

"Not as infamous as the man who crushed half a mile of magnificent sand dunes and cypress with that resort complex near the point!" Bliss shot back, then turned to Shepard. "It was supposed to blend into the surrounding landscape. It's pink! Have you ever seen a pink tree, Chief Shepard?"

Shepard glanced involuntarily at Bliss' painting, then caught himself, and looked quickly away.

"No, but—"

Bliss wheeled around on Holly again. "Luckily I managed to capture the purity of the land on canvas before you smothered it in steel and stucco!"

"Chief!" Holly exclaimed. "Ask him how many times he's been arrested as a public nuisance!"

"Ask him about that other condo project of his up by Moss Landing!" Bliss countered. "How fast are the units sinking back into the sand, Holly? Four inches a year? The water supply's already undrinkable. The next earthquake'll probably bring the whole place down!"

"He exposed himself to a group of congressmen meeting at Asilomar!" Holly fired back.

Bliss shrugged. "They were Republicans."

Things were careening out of control again. Shepard held up his hand. "Gentlemen!"

Bliss continued, inexorable. "How do we know the three of you didn't see Wagner make that shot, realize the gloating you'd have to endure, and scurry over here to shut him up once and for all?"

The color drained from Holly's face. Webb hurried to his side, muttering something about his heart.

Romaine looked amused. "And how did we then dispose of the body?" he asked Bliss in his calm, bass voice. "You've pointed out that no one approached the cliff. I doubt that even the three of us combined could fling the body the thirty feet necessary to clear the edge. Maybe you'd better check our golf bags. Maybe we chopped Alex up with nine irons and hid chunks of him in each of them."

Shepard looked at Romaine with interest. "That's quite an imagination you've got there, sir, but if you were all in it together, two of you could've carried the body into the woods while the third raked away any telltale traces in the sand."

Bliss sighed. "Unfortunately they didn't. I would have noticed them lugging a body into the trees or hacking it to pieces, I promise you. For example I did see the young one there going off by himself."

"To call the police!" Webb retorted.

"I wondered about that," Shepard said. "You then notified MacGregor, is that correct?" Webb nodded. "Why did you call us first? Did you already suspect a crime had been committed?"

Webb looked momentarily at a loss for words, but Holly leaped into the breach.

"It was my idea, Chief Shepard," Holly said softly. He leaned very slightly on Webb, but the color was seeping back into his face.

"I...there were certain things about Mr. Wagner that led me to believe it was something more than a simple practical joke."

"Such as?"

"There are a lot of people who may have wished him harm."

"What was he?" Bliss interjected. "A dentist?"

"He was an attorney." Holly said.

Bliss nodded. "That explains it."

"I'm an attorney," Romaine told him without a hint of ill will.

Holly went on. "Besides being a cheat, as I've mentioned, he was also a liar, a fraud, and very likely a thief."

Bliss nodded. "I'm surprised he hadn't made judge."

"Chief," Holly went on, "I am answering your questions as plainly as I can. I will be happy to give you a fuller account, but—" Here he looked Bliss squarely in the eyes. "—not while that hoodlum is present."

Bliss took an angry step toward the older man.

Shepard stepped between them. "Mr. Bliss, thank you for your cooperation. I'll have one of my men escort you off the course. I'd appreciate it if you'd provide him with an address and phone number. We'll need to take a formal statement."

Bliss fumed. "I have to practically stick your nose in it before you even realize a crime's been committed and this is the thanks I get!"

"Mr. Bliss, even I would have noticed the blood sooner or later and reached the same sticky spot where we now find ourselves. But again, thanks for your help. You obviously have a keen artist's eye to notice so many details so quickly. Charlie?" He nodded to the young officer still holding Bliss' easel. "Help Mr. Bliss with his things."

Bliss stood rooted in place for a long moment, glaring at Shepard. Then he turned his baleful gaze back to Holly. Holly returned it with a thin smile of satisfaction. Finally Bliss gave a melodramatic shrug, and lumbered off across the green, leaving Charlie to struggle with equipment that two policemen could barely carry before.

Shepard let out a sigh of relief, but it proved premature. He saw Bliss stop directly beside the pin, and gaze down into the cup. The artist looked back over at Shepard and gave an unpleasant laugh.

"I expect you also would have noticed eventually that there's blood on the golf ball."

Shepard, Charlie, and the three golfers all stared at him in stunned silence.

"Wagner must have been quite a golfer," Bliss continued with a look of almost ecstatic pleasure. "Either he calmly bludgeoned someone with his sand wedge before lining up his shot, or he made the shot of his life shortly after his death."

Bliss turned away without waiting for a response, and tromped toward the distant trees. Charlie stumbled behind like an over-burdened caddie.

CHAPTER THREE

Shepard pushed himself as he jogged north on the white-sand curve of Carmel Beach, going over the coming weekend's repertoire in his mind. Singing in a new bar in a new town unnerved him more than he cared to admit. With only seven days to go until his first local appearance, he felt a familiar uncertainty begin to tweeze the lining of his stomach. Up until now he had either performed in the Akron-Canton area where he was born and raised or in the divisional jazz quartet in the army. Both venues guaranteed at least a few friends in the audience for support. The long hours since moving to Carmel left little time for making friends.

Shepard's first investigation upon settling into Carmel-by-the-Sea two months ago had been to track down a piano tuner to help an upright piano, his most treasured possession, recover after its traumatic journey from Ohio. The piano anchored one corner of the living room in the small stucco house, "Pine Haven," he rented on Third Avenue. Most houses in Carmel sported picturesque or whimsical names like "Windrush House" or "Frodo's Folly." There were no street addresses, no mail delivery.

At first the walk to collect mail from his box at the post office irritated Shepard, one of many sacrifices made by residents to maintain the unique character of the village, along with enduring trees sprouting smack in the middle of the streets, and architecture tending toward the gnomish. He had come to realize however that locals treated the daily mail run as a social outing, a chance to gossip over a backyard fence that served the entire five thousand permanent inhabitants of the one square mile known officially as Carmel-by-the-Sea.

The hard-packed sand along the water's edge offered Shepard a perfect running surface, and he moved at a strong pace, muscles absorbing the impact of shoe on sand, then springing him forward. He'd left behind him lingering traces of morning mist lying like gauze between the beach and Point Lobos. Ahead rose the cliffs of the Carmel Bay Country Club. The equally famous Pebble Beach Golf Club curved out to sea beyond. A few high clouds looked stranded in the blue sky above him.

This beach run had become a lunchtime ritual, prior to heading back to his office. There he could shower, put on a fresh uniform, and face the remainder of his calendar with endorphins happily surging through his body.

Unhappily, the reward for anyone pursuing healthy exercise on Carmel's beach still lay ahead: the long walk up the hill into town. This hill could kill you even if you hadn't been running for an hour. It simply spilled people on to the awe-inspiring half-moon of sand, with no thought as to how they ever were going to get back up.

Shepard could have driven, and parked along Scenic Drive, an understated street name if ever there was one, but Carmel's founders had designed the town for walking, not automobiles. It seemed almost a sacrilege to drive the ten blocks back to the police station at Junipero Street and Fourth Avenue.

He saw more than the hill awaited him when he struggled up to the parking lot that marked the foot of Ocean Avenue. The Mayor of Carmel, Yale Gerringer, fidgeted there, dressed in one of his trademark sloppy sweaters, and neatly tailored slacks, and chewing on a piece of straw.

A former CEO for some Silicon Valley software company, Gerringer had retired young, but apparently still hungered for the reins of command. He ran for mayor, on an impulse he said, and won. Now halfway through his second term, he acted as if he'd be happy to run Carmel forever. Shepard had sensed the first time they met that Gerringer's folksy casualness masked a need for power all out of proportion to his job. He even had christened his cottage, a short, level walk from City Hall, "The Power House." Shepard sighed inwardly, endorphins scattering for cover.

"Where do you get all that energy, Dan?" Gerringer asked, flashing a semaphore of a smile.

Shepard caught his breath. "Have to stay in shape, if I expect to collar any crooks. Crooks run very fast."

"If I were Chief of Police, I'd let my men do the running." Gerringer gave Shepard another peek at a smile.

Shepard grinned. "Now there's an idea. I'll have to try it."

"Mind if I walk with you aways?"

"Be my guest."

The two men started up the long hill beneath a scattering of gray-green cypress and live oaks.

"It's been five days," Gerringer began, glancing around like a British Lord surveying his private estate. "I thought we should talk. Bring me up to speed."

Five days, Shepard reflected. Five days since Alex Wagner had hopped an express train to the heart of nowhere. Five days of much frustration and few leads.

Gerringer munched on his hunk of straw. "I didn't care for that editorial comment in the *Pine Cone*. As if this weird disappearance was just Carmel's way of making its new chief welcome. It must be a joke of some kind though, don't you think?"

"I wish Wagner would show up to explain the punch line," Shepard replied.

A man and woman sat on one of the benches placed at strategic locations along the steep sidewalk, rotating a map. They wore standard tourist uniform: matching t-shirts with the Carmel Mission looking more like a Disneyland attraction than a house of worship, cameras around the necks, baggy shorts over legs the color of a dead fish's eye.

Shepard saw Gerringer take in their perplexed expressions in a practiced glance, and beam at them.

"Welcome to Carmel, folks! Can I help you find something?"

The woman gave Gerringer a bewildered smile. "Yes! thank you! Can you show us the way to Clint Eastwood's house?"

Gerringer chuckled. "Well, ma'am, we really should respect Mr. Eastwood's privacy, shouldn't we?"

"Privacy?" The man chirped up. "He's the mayor. A public official. We have…we have public business to discuss with him."

They nodded in unison, not noticing the flush spreading up from Gerringer's collar.

"He's no longer the mayor," the mayor said. "Have a nice day." He nodded and trudged on up the hill. Shepard followed, seeing the man and woman give each other incredulous looks.

The man shrugged. "Must not be from around here."

"What have you found out?" Gerringer inquired when Shepard pulled even with him again.

Shepard took a deep breath. "Wagner's an attorney with his own practice, and an office down near the wharf. He specializes in real estate law."

"Yes, of course." The mayor cut in with an impatient wave of his hand. "He's one of the most respected attorneys on the peninsula."

"Last year Wagner divorced a Genevra Carroll of Santa Cruz."

"Fine lady, Genevra," Gerringer remarked, but offered no elaboration. "Did you check Wagner's home?"

Shepard nodded. Wagner lived alone, south of Ocean, in a two-bedroom cottage called "Sea Garden" that would probably fetch six hundred thousand dollars in a down market. A wide variety of flowers in precise patterns filled the postage-stamp lot from edge to edge. A small work area in the garage contained potting soils, fertilizers, pots, various gardening and watering utensils, suggesting Wagner saw to the maintenance of the garden himself. Shepard suspected he must have devoted most of every weekend to keep things looking as nice as they did.

Food in the kitchen cupboards and refrigerator gave no indication that Wagner planned on going anywhere, and a check at the post office revealed an overflowing mailbox.

Shepard went on to explain that he assigned two of his officers to sift through the great mass of files and documents from Wagner's office. Many of the papers and blueprints pertained to a new hotel complex under construction on Cannery Row in Monterey.

Loren Holly had confirmed Wagner did much of his work for the developer, and headed the legal team involved in the project. Shepard had an appointment to see Holly first thing after lunch. On the phone Holly seemed to have forgotten his earlier animosity toward the lawyer, and insisted Wagner's absence had hurt the project. Shepard asked Gerringer about it.

Gerringer's ears perked up. "Animosity? Wagner has worked closely with the Holly Corporation for many years. I've never heard of any animosity."

"Holly called him a liar, a cheat and a fraud," Shepard told him. "That doesn't say to me they were best buddies."

Gerringer tossed the straw aside, his brow wrinkled, signaling, Shepard knew, that the conversation needed to grow more serious. "Chick Beal's been on the horn to me just about every day. He says your men have been disrupting play again on the course."

"Yale, I have an investigation to conduct."

"The Ridgeway Pro-Am starts this week. We don't want a thing like this hanging over the tournament."

"I know." Shepard sighed. Beal, the manager of Carmel Bay, had been on the phone daily to him, too, complaining.

"Have you considered the possibility Wagner may be buried under the sand?"

Shepard nodded. "Two of my deputies dug down to the soil beneath the trap. No body. No indication any digging had ever gone on there since the course was originally built."

"Then I'll be honest with you, Dan," Gerringer went on. "I'm not totally convinced someone's committed a crime."

"The blood on the sand wedge and golf ball was human," Shepard pointed out.

"Was it Wagner's blood?"

Shepard gave a frustrated shrug. "It was O positive. Not much help since so is most of the population, and we can't find a local doctor who could give us Wagner's blood type."

Gerringer stopped at Monte Verde Avenue, the beginning of the commercial district with its hundreds of tiny shops and restaurants. Two blocks to the south stood the City Hall. Shepard knew the mayor would not climb one more inch of the hill than was absolutely necessary. They stood watching the endless parade of visitors.

"When do you think you'll have some answers?" Gerringer persisted. "I'd like to be able to tell Chick something."

"I've never run across a situation like this before," Shepard admitted. "If a crime's been committed, is it really murder? Wagner wasn't in that bunker for more than five minutes. How many people were down in there with him? Where did they go?"

"Herman Bliss causing you any trouble?" The mayor's non-sequiter startled Shepard. "Interesting man," Gerringer added when Shepard didn't reply immediately.

Interesting? Shepard stared at the mayor. Re-reading Bliss' file the day before, its strangeness again had struck him. What drove the man to get into so much trouble, and by what epidemic of Christian charity had he been spared prosecution all these years? Nobody seemed to like him. Mention Bliss' name at the station and everyone acted like Transylvanian rustics asked by an innocent wayfarer the way to Dracula's castle. Yet every time Bliss took it upon himself to flout the law, somebody let him off the hook.

"Anything you want to tell me about Bliss, Yale?" Shepard asked with an encouraging smile.

"No, not really," the mayor answered, a shade too quickly. "We need some answers, Dan. PDQ. Your first big case. The citizens want to know our choice was a good one."

Gerringer said this in the mildest of voices, but Shepard knew pressure when he felt it, however skillfully applied.

"We'll get the answers, Yale," he replied.

"Fine. I know you will. I'm looking forward to hearing you sing this weekend."

For some reason that sounded to Shepard more like an outright threat.

The mayor nodded pleasantly to a sleekly groomed female shop owner arranging antiques in a window. "I'd better be getting back. Planning Commission meeting this afternoon. We're looking at designs and paint samples for that new sign the Guardian Inn wants to put up."

He carefully scanned the traffic, found a gap, and headed off across the street. Shepard didn't envy the man his job. Debates over paint samples could last for hours in Carmel.

Shepard walked on, weaving his way through the early afternoon crowds, trying to recover the equilibrium he'd enjoyed before his encounter with the mayor. He hummed the tune he'd started playing with the morning Alex Wagner disappeared. Something about the melody continued to elude him, but he promised himself he wouldn't give up.

Tourists flocked to Carmel. Even though it wouldn't be peak season for another couple of months, they still blanketed the streets. Window-shopping, slurping ice cream cones, ignoring the heavy traffic as they stepped from curbs to examine the quaint architecture or the exuberant foliage. A beautiful little town, Shepard acknowledged, but sometimes hard to see through all the people.

He made it a few more blocks to San Carlos Avenue, and the promise of a slight lessening in the hill's grade before he noticed something off kilter. Farther up Ocean Avenue people suddenly swerved away from one of the stores, some going so far as to step into the gutter to avoid a particular stretch of sidewalk. A leashed dog walking its owner stopped at about the same spot. Shepard crossed the street, hearing the animal's guttural growl. Then he saw the reason for the commotion.

Bliss stood by the window of a store, his nose squashed up against the glass. The window belonged to The Cypress Gallery, one of Carmel's dozens of galleries, and one of the most prestigious. Shepard strolled casually to the shade of a tree to watch.

The dog's owner jerked on his end of the leash, and the creature moved reluctantly on. Tourists continued to give Bliss a wide berth. Easy to see why. The artist didn't appear to have removed his clothes since Shepard had seen him on the golf course five days before. Under one arm Bliss clutched a small canvas, maybe fourteen inches by twenty in size.

From his vantage point Shepard could see into the interior of the store past two oil portraits in gaudy gilt frames. A couple of customers browsed along one wall. A stunningly attractive blonde woman in her early fifties, wearing a blue designer pantsuit, stood by a small desk, talking on the telephone. Bliss watched her with steadfast concentration.

The woman turned her back to consult something on her desk. Almost before she had fully turned, Bliss sprang into action. He glided to the right, and through the open doorway of the gallery. Shepard saw Bliss creep with a surprising feline grace to a room partition where several paintings hung. Did Bliss plan to steal a painting? With the Chief of

Police as an eye witness Bliss would have difficulty weaseling out of this one.

Shepard saw Bliss begin to lift a painting from the wall and headed for the gallery, but he stopped so suddenly several tourists barely missed running into him. Inside, Bliss carefully slid the painting behind a potted agapanthus. Then, with expert swiftness he put his own canvas on the partition in its place.

Despite the speed and smoothness with which Bliss made the switch, he was not quite fast enough. The two browsers, a man and woman in their sixties, spotted Bliss and stared openly. The blonde woman hung up the phone, and turned in time to see Bliss' back disappearing out the door.

"Stop!" she commanded, her voice audible even on the busy sidewalk. "I'll burn it!"

This froze Bliss in his tracks. He turned in the doorway, a puzzled frown on his face.

Shepard casually crossed to the doorway to listen.

"Were you addressing me?" Bliss asked with an unconcerned air.

The blonde woman paused directly in front of the painting Bliss had hung on the partition. She pointed at it.

"Get it out of here. Right now! Or I will burn it!"

Bliss now looked shocked. "You would destroy a work of art? What kind of monster are you?"

"I would never destroy a work of art," she retorted. "But I would gladly put that thing out of its misery!"

Bliss moved back into the gallery.

"Maggie," Bliss said in a cajoling voice. "It shows wonderfully there. Passers-by will casually glance in the door, see my Madonna and Child, and be compelled to enter."

Here Bliss turned an attempt at a benign smile on the elderly couple. They glanced from the smile to the painting and appeared to find one more horrible than the other. Without a word they hurried out past Shepard.

The blonde woman now risked another glance at the painting. "Madonna and Child? It looks more like Freddy Kreuger and Child! Remove it from my wall, and remove yourself from my gallery!"

She stopped, seeing Shepard standing in the doorway. The angry jut of her chin softened into a smile of welcome.

"May I help you?"

Bliss turned to look. Shepard saw him try to pull himself into an erect, blameless posture, but he managed only to look guiltier.

"Ah, Chief Shepard…I'd like to introduce one of my oldest friends and patrons, Maggie Dennis. Maggie, have you met our new police chief?"

Torn between denying the relationship Bliss had imposed on her and acknowledging the introduction, she chose the latter, holding out her hand for Shepard to take.

"Margaret Dennis. Chief Shepard, this is a pleasure."

"How do you do, Ms. Dennis? You have a lovely gallery here."

"Thank you."

"Is there anything I can help sort out?" Shepard asked with a smile.

"No," Bliss replied quickly.

"Yes," Maggie responded in the next breath. "This man has been served with a restraining order. He is not allowed to enter these premises."

Bliss sighed. "Art is not selling as well as it might these days. I try to help by giving Maggie something that would catch the public eye, and she treats me as if I were trespassing."

"You are trespassing!" Maggie thundered back at him.

She removed Bliss' painting from the wall. Shepard could see how it could catch the public eye. There were indeed two figures in the painting, but they certainly resembled no Madonna and Child that he had ever seen. The mother-figure looked like a cross between a Barbie doll and a deranged penguin. The child reminded him of a Transformer robot. Shepard blinked; surprised that he could pick out that much detail from the colliding swirls of color.

"Mr. Bliss, if Ms. Dennis here has a restraining order against you, she could press charges."

Bliss directed a crinkled smile in the gallery owner's direction. Surprisingly, she looked very uncomfortable.

"Really, Chief Shepard, it hardly seems worth it to waste your time. If Mr. Bliss will just take his Madonna and…and Thing and go, that will be sufficient."

Shepard looked at her, then at Bliss, then back at her, and ran his fingers over his close-cropped hair. He was witnessing the Bliss brand of divine intervention at work. Shepard couldn't for the life of him see what hold the man had over her, yet obviously he had something. What could be powerful enough to keep her from pressing charges, yet not strong enough to force her to hang a single painting on the wall?

Bliss looked at Maggie with compassion. "I'm sorry you can't see your way over to my point of view, Maggie. In time you will."

He held out his hand for the painting, received it, and exited with great dignity.

Maggie smiled at Shepard. "Thank you for your help, Chief."

"I'm not sure I did anything." Shepard nodded to her and went out, looking up and down the street. He saw Bliss strolling on up the hill in the direction of Devendorf Park and hurried after him.

"Mr. Bliss?"

Bliss waited as Shepard drew alongside him.

"You feeling foiled in your pursuit of justice, Chief?"

"Not particularly," Shepard said. "Although I'd love to know how you managed to get out of that."

"Maggie and I go way back," Bliss said, with a dreamy look on his face.

"She doesn't seem to share your fond memories."

"There'll always be a place for me in Maggie's heart. There always is for the first, you know."

"The first?"

"Love."

"Love?"

Bliss scowled at him. "Am I going too fast for the Great Mouse Detective?"

"No," said Shepard, keeping his smile fixed firmly in place. "I'm managing to keep up. It just didn't seem possible."

"Oh." Bliss nodded with apparent understanding. "Maggie was quite attractive in her day."

"She's still quite attractive!" Shepard responded. "That wasn't what I—. Oh, never mind."

"Alex Wagner turn up?" Bliss asked innocently. "Not that it's any of my business, of course."

"No. He hasn't and it isn't."

"Any bodies at all?"

"None that can't be accounted for."

Bliss scratched at something under his flannel shirt. "I once saw a movie—Invaders from Mars—scared the hell out of me when I was younger. The Martians had this ray that could dig through the ground. They used to come up underneath people standing in this old sand pit. The ground would open up, and swallow them, leaving no trace behind."

"We dug, Mr. Bliss. We did not find Alex Wagner, or any Martians."

"I don't suppose a big rubber band could have shot or yanked…" Bliss' voice trailed off when he saw Shepard's expression. "Well, we'll table that thought for now."

"Good plan," Shepard agreed.

Bliss considered. "I wonder how Wagner made that shot."

"Couldn't he have just got lucky?"

"No." Bliss shook his head. "Then we'd have to assume that the murderer got lucky, too. And I don't quite see that happening."

"Why do you keep insisting it's murder?"

"What else could it be?"

"Suppose Wagner was lining his shot up. Somebody came up behind him and got clubbed by the back swing."

"I don't know anything about golf, but that would make the shot even more miraculous, wouldn't it?"

Shepard sighed. "Yeah, and why didn't the other golfers see this second person approach the trap?"

"He crawled on his hands and knees."

Shepard stared at him. "You pointed out it couldn't have been someone on their hands and knees!"

"Nonsense. What I said was: the dew couldn't have been crossed by someone on their hands and knees."

"You think someone crawled across the fairway from the other direction in plain view of those three men, and they forgot to mention it?"

Bliss flashed him a wolfish grin. "They might forget, but I wouldn't. The shortest distance a killer could travel to make his getaway would be to the cliff."

"Sure," Shepard said. "But carrying a body? Tiptoeing on needle-thin stilts so as not to disturb the dew? It would have taken too much time."

"Exactly. Because the only way somebody could cross that stretch of ground without my seeing them would be if they sprinted or flew while I was mixing paints," Bliss insisted.

"Then everyone else would have seen them," Shepard finished in frustration.

Bliss sighed. "Round and round we go. Or rather **you** go. I have some painting to do. When you need my help again, and you will, might I suggest you be more ready to listen?"

He started across the street, then stopped part way and looked back at Shepard. "You don't think you'll need my help, do you?"

"No."

Bliss nodded, satisfied. "No."

He was blocking traffic. Cars were beginning to line up, horns honking.

"Mr. Bliss," Shepard pleaded. "The traffic?"

Bliss ignored the comment and the cars. "If I were you, Chief, I'd concentrate on what those four men had for breakfast."

Shepard gaped at him, speechless.

Having given this Delphic pronouncement, Bliss turned to glare at the honking cars and fists being shaken out the windows at him. He bowed from the waist to the enraged motorists, holding the bow for an excruciating length of time. At last he straightened and sauntered off past the center island smack into the path of traffic from the other direction.

CHAPTER FOUR

Holly Development occupied the top floor of a two-story historical landmark building the company owned on Abrego Street in Monterey. Shepard passed through a black, intricately worked wrought-iron gate, and into a courtyard filled with a dazzling, sweet-scented array of spring flowers. The lushness overwhelmed him. He'd grown from boy to man in a state whose most colorful plant was the tomato.

Two men rose when Shepard entered Loren Holly's office. From behind a desk raised like an altar at the far side of a desert-colored expanse of carpet, the elderly head of the company moved to greet him. In a chair near the desk Leonard Romaine put a sheaf of legal-sized documents on the floor and also came forward with out-stretched hand.

"Any news of Alex?" Holly asked, returning behind his desk and offering a chair in front of it. His voice, while measured, betrayed a genuine concern.

Romaine resumed his seat. He retrieved the documents and began leafing through them again.

"None yet," Shepard replied. "We alerted every law enforcement agency on the Central Coast, and issued an all-points bulletin statewide."

Holly shook his head. "It's incomprehensible to me. What happened to him?"

"The blood on the ball and the sand wedge suggests at least an injury," Shepard said.

"If Wagner was injured—" Romaine looked up from the papers in his lap, "—why didn't he call out? Even if he were attacked, why couldn't we hear anything? Or see some evidence of his attacker?"

Shepard smiled. "If I could answer those questions, we might be farther along in our investigation."

"Of course, of course." Holly expelled the breath from his body and seemed to shrink into his chair. "How can we help you, Chief Shepard?"

"Well, sir, you said you sent for us because you thought something might have happened to him the moment you saw he was gone. You called Mr. Wagner a cheat, a liar, a fraud, and maybe a thief—"

Holly held up a thin hand, its skin stretched taut over reedy bones. "I'm sorry about that outburst. My only excuse is my bewilderment and frustration, and the presence of that…that man…."

"Mr. Bliss?"

"He is a boil," Holly said through gritted teeth. "He should be lanced."

"Are you saying that you don't really believe Wagner was any of those things you called him?" Shepard asked.

Holly grunted. "Oh he was a cheat all right—"

"Loren?" Romaine interjected in a bland tone.

The edge in Holly's voice sharpened. "Whatever happened to him, his last shot was not luck or skill, or sunspots. Somehow he cheated."

Romaine shrugged, but said nothing.

Shepard turned his attention to the stout lawyer. "Mr. Romaine, you are Holly Development's general counsel?"

"Yes," he replied.

"For how long?"

Romaine thought about it. "Year and a half, give or take. I moved up here from L.A. a year ago November, wasn't it, Loren?"

"Yes, somewhere in there," Holly agreed. "We were lucky to lure Leonard from a thriving big city practice to our little corner of the world."

"Why'd you move, Mr. Romaine?" Shepard asked.

"It was time. My wife is gone, my children grown. I'm twice the age of most of the movers and shakers in L.A. real estate." Irony creased the corners of Romaine's eyes. "I yearned for a quieter life."

"You've also taken over the reins of the new hotel complex, is that correct?" Shepard asked.

"Yes," Romaine answered. "We're in the midst of a battle with the Monterey Planning Commission on some minor changes we want to make to the site plan. The Coastal Commission has been breathing down our necks as well. There wasn't time to find someone else, and bring him up to speed."

"Then there are the protesters," Holly growled. "Anti-growth activists who won't be happy until we're all back living in caves."

Romaine shrugged. "Actually they've been pretty easy to handle so far. Ineffectual in fact. Not what we would have expected down south. I keep waiting for the other sandal to drop."

"How long has Mr. Webb been employed at Holly Development?" Shepard asked.

"About the same. Almost two years, I suppose. Why?"

"Sounds like you've recently made some major changes in personnel."

"As Leonard said, it was time." Holly glanced at his watch. "Speaking of the Planning Commission, we're late for our daily joust. Was there anything else, Chief?"

Shepard admired the way they'd shifted the discussion from Holly's comments on the character of the missing man. He decided to let them think that they succeeded and turned to his final bit of business.

"Just one more question, gentlemen, then I'll be out of your way. This is kind of off-the-wall, but the answer may be important. What did you have for breakfast Wednesday morning?"

Holly and Romaine stared at Shepard for a moment, then exchanged a baffled look.

"I'll say that's off-the-wall!" Romaine laughed.

"It could help," Shepard insisted, not having a clue how it could help.

Romaine shrugged, and thought for a moment. "I had coffee and Danish from the club shop. Cherry Danish I think. Loren?"

"I'm at a loss to see how it could possibly matter, but I suppose you know your business better than I do. Ben Webb stopped at my house to pick me up. We had pancakes and sausages, orange juice…coffee… maple syrup.…Is that of any help to you?" A dry chuckle scraped its way up out of his throat.

"It may be," Shepard told him, and stood up. "Thank you for your time, gentlemen."

Another round of cool handshakes and he left.

*   *   *

At around three that afternoon the Cassandra Sue, a fishing boat plying its trade off the Moss Landing shoreline, netted two tons of sea bass, and Alex Wagner. Shepard, and a muscular young officer with tousled California blonde hair named Greg Cowles, arrived at the Moss Landing pier forty minutes later. They found the body on the dock, beneath a tarpaulin and surrounded by a group of fishermen discussing the unusual catch of the day with two deputies from the Monterey County Sheriff's Office. Behind them the massive smoke stacks of the Pacific Gas and Electric power plant stood sentry, visible for miles in any direction.

Shepard shook hands with the deputies. "Dan Shepard, Carmel Police."

The first, a stocky man in his late twenties with jet-black hair and dark tan, grinned. "Yeah, I figured you must be. Jesus Carrera. This is Dave Wingbeck."

"I appreciate you giving us a call," Shepard told them.

"Well, after we phoned in the ID, Sheriff Castle said you'd want to know," said the second deputy, an older, taller man with a deeply lined face. He seemed to be enjoying himself, too. "Looks like you found your vanishing golfer." He handed Shepard a waterlogged wallet.

Shepard pulled the sodden leather billfold open. Even after immersion in seawater, the laminated driver's license was still readable: Alex Wagner, and the post office box number in Carmel. He flipped through credit cards in various shades of precious metals. Adding up the cash proved more difficult. The bills tended to stick together, but he managed to count over four hundred dollars.

Shepard waved the wallet at the tarpaulin. "Mind if I take a look?"

"Help yourself," Carrera replied with a hospitable grin. "The Medical Examiner's wagon should be here any time now."

Shepard realized all the cheerfulness was at his expense. He sent Cowles back down the dock with the fishermen to get statements, then took a deep breath, squatted down on the weathered planks, and pulled back the edge of the tarp.

"I wouldn't want to be the pathologist who has to determine time of death." He grimaced.

The body had been in the water for some time, battered by wave against rock, scored by tide-swept sand and shells. Sea creatures had banqueted long and well on the soft tissues. Little remained of the face.

Remnants of the patriotic clothing Wagner wore when he entered the sand trap still clung to the body: red shirt, blue pants, gray socks that once must have been white. A single blue shoe remained on the right foot.

Cause of death might be easier to establish, Shepard hoped. A series of blows had dented the back of the skull. Shepard counted three distinct depressions, short and narrow, no more than two or three inches in length.

He squinted up at the two deputies. "Interesting wounds."

"Yeah," Carrera replied. "Not often you find the weapon before the victim."

Shepard nodded. The indentations were too regular to have occurred naturally. They looked just about the size one would expect, if the killer used a handy sand wedge.

The right hand lay trapped beneath the corpse. Shepard tugged gently at the waistband of the pants, feeling the body slide about loosely beneath the garments. He raised the hip enough to see a gold ring still encircling a small gobbet of skin and ligament on the little finger of the hand. The setting looked like a two or three carat diamond. Added to the money in the wallet, robbery seemed an unlikely motive for the crime.

"Of course, finding the body doesn't help as much as it could, does it?" observed Deputy Wingbeck. "In fact it adds to your troubles, I'd say."

Shepard got to his feet. "Why?"

"Well, not only is it a mystery how he disappeared from that sand trap, but how did he manage to get all the way from a Carmel golf course around the tip of the peninsula to Monterey Bay?"

"Tidal action? If he was dumped in the sea below the seventh green?" Shepard proposed.

"Where you from, Chief?" Carrera inquired. "Some place inland, I'll bet."

"Akron, Ohio. Not tidal action, huh?"

Carrera shook his head. "Not hardly likely. Not unless he had a propeller and fins."

"The tide would've pulled him out to sea, then the prevailing current would push him south, not north." Wingbeck explained.

A black van from the County Medical Examiner's Office pulled to a halt in the paved parking lot near the dock. Shepard turned to greet the pathologist, Catherine Gonzales. She walked toward him: compact, black hair tied back in a ponytail, with all sorts of interesting curves, and a hip-sway that could wake the dead, although the image wasn't something Shepard wanted to dwell on, given her profession.

She threw him a large grin, and he smiled in return. Shepard had met her only briefly soon after taking over the reins as police chief.

Catherine Gonzales was, like him, an outsider. They'd taken to each other immediately. A whiz kid by all accounts, she'd been lured out here from her hometown of Bakersfield. The attraction, she admitted to Shepard, was not picking over the residue from assorted matrimonial squabbles and drug deals gone sour. The cool ocean breezes and pine-scented air of the Monterey Peninsula had called her name.

"What's on the menu for today?" she asked when she reached them.

"There's not much left of his features." Shepard replied. "You should be able to get some prints though, and the teeth look like they're intact."

She strolled over to look down at the body, hands in pockets. "Must've been one hell of a water hazard."

The two deputies laughed out loud.

"Look," Shepard said. "I realize this is probably the most hilarious thing that's happened around here in weeks. I have a sort of witness who also seems to think it's the easiest bit of fun he's had in a long time. But it isn't fun for the victim."

Carrera and Wingbeck exchanged a look.

"That witness wouldn't be Mr. Bliss by any chance, would it, Chief?" Carrera asked.

Shepard studied him. "That's a pretty good deduction, Deputy. How exactly did you come by it?"

"His name was in the papers," Carrera shrugged. "And there's nobody I know better at getting under your skin."

"Okay," Shepard held up a hand. "You know him. Everybody seems to know him. I've read his file, but it doesn't make any sense. Why isn't he locked away somewhere dark and damp?" He looked at Catherine Gonzales.

She shrugged. "He must be still alive. I don't know him."

"It's his name, Chief," Wingbeck answered.

"His name?"

"de Portola?" Wingbeck prompted. "Bliss? It's a potent combination around here."

"Wait a minute." Shepard remembered. "He's named after the Spanish guy, right? The one that ferried Father Serra up and down the coast while he established all the missions?"

"He's not just named after de Portola," Wingbeck continued. "Supposedly he's a direct descendant."

"Even though de Portola was a bachelor," Carrera put in.

Wingbeck nodded. "Bliss claims de Portola had his way with a local Indian maiden on one of his stopovers."

Shepard only felt more baffled. "So? Even if it's true, does that make him somehow immune from prosecution?"

"No," Carrera replied. "It's the last name that does that. Martin Bliss ring an antique bell?"

Shepard searched his memory. "Look fellas, I haven't had a lotta time to bone up on local history. Fill me in."

"It was the Bliss family that helped found Carmel. Old Martin was a painter back around the turn of the century. He wanted to make Carmel like a haven for artists and creative types like that. Everybody says he was a terrible painter—"

Must be genetic, thought Shepard.

"—but he bought up so much property he became the wealthiest guy on the peninsula."

Shepard understood. "My Bliss inherited?"

Carrera nodded. "The son-of-a-bitch owns half of Carmel."

The body at their feet distracted Shepard from considering the impli-
cations of this. Something about Wagner tickled the back of his brain.
He rubbed his hand across his head, but the itch remained. He waved to
Cowles. The young officer came loping back out to the end of the dock.

Shepard held out his hands to the deputies. "Of course maybe the
killer didn't dump him into the ocean off the seventh green. Maybe
somehow he lugged him across the golf course to a car, then drove him
over to the marina, rented a boat, transferred him to the boat, took him
out into the bay, and chucked him over the side."

Carrera and Wingbeck exchanged a startled look.

"Why in God's name would he do that?" Wingbeck wondered.

"He wouldn't." Catherine answered for Shepard. "Unless he was a
total loon. I don't think the Chief was serious."

Shepard shook his head. "He was not." He glanced down at the
corpse again. "Cowles, get on the radio. Have Amy read you the exact
description of what Alex Wagner wore when he disappeared."

Cowles nodded, and trotted off. Shepard saw the pathologist staring
at him.

"What he wore?" She studied the body. "Presumably he had on both
shoes."

"Presumably," Shepard agreed. "Did you read the report?"

She frowned. "Yes, but the clothes…Red shirt, blue pants, blue
shoes…Sounds like your average Saturday night cruising uniform in
Bakersfield."

"Tell me about the socks," Shepard prompted.

Catherine knelt beside the feet. "Dirty as all get out." She stared at
them for a long while. Finally she looked exasperated and stood up
again. "Look, I'll be able to give you a list of every single bacterium
that's busily decomposing Mr. Wagner, but clothes aren't exactly my
line."

Shepard saw Cowles approaching from the direction of the police car
and sighed. "I really don't want to hear this."

Cowles began talking when he was still a few yards away. "Blue pants. Red shirt. Blue Shoes. White socks."

Shepard nodded, not at all happy. All eyes turned back to the body. And the socks. The others crowded close while Shepard squatted down. He gingerly pulled back the top of the fully exposed sock on the left foot. Despite the material being soaked through, the inside of the sock wasn't as soiled as the outside.

"Would you call that dirty-white?"

"No." Catherine shook her head. "I'd call that gray."

Behind them the smokestacks of the power plant continued to pump steam into the atmosphere. Across the parking lot the Harbor District office conducted business pretty much as usual. Shepard had a sudden flash of whimsy. Wouldn't it be wonderful, he thought, if he could be magically transformed into a guy with a clipboard checking for power spikes, or the Harbor Master issuing a fishing permit?

He saw realization hit the others gathered round.

Carrera laughed. "Let me get this straight. Not only does the guy vanish from the scene of the crime, and wind up someplace he really can't be. But somewhere along the way he changed his socks?"

CHAPTER FIVE

Santa Cruz sprawled along the top of Monterey Bay. Lovingly rebuilt after a devastating earthquake in 1989, that afternoon the city wore a golden and sun-tanned face. They drove past the gaudy old boardwalk with its massive wooden roller coaster ringing with screams and laughter.

Shepard glanced at the young man driving. Cowles looked right at home. He might have grown up on the crowded beach they passed before turning into the drive of a nicely restored Victorian house of light blue clapboard and white trim.

Genevra Carroll, Alex Wagner's ex-wife, met them at the door and ushered them into a spare but comfortable front room whose walls were almost as tall as they were wide. A bow window looked out over a neat expanse of grass to a row of eucalyptus trees and the beach beyond.

She looked younger than Shepard expected, in her early thirties. Shepard approved of the natural cut of the brown hair and limited makeup, but there was a wide-eyed, almost haunted look to her face that distracted from its regular features. She moved in short, jittery bursts like a humming bird flitting from flower to flower.

"The Santa Cruz police were here last week, Chief Shepard." Her voice caught as if her throat were unwilling to release the words. "I really had nothing to tell them about Alex's disappearance. I wish I did."

"I'm afraid it's no longer a disappearance, Ms. Carroll."

She stared at him for a long moment. "He's dead?"

"I'm afraid so."

"Murdered?"

"It looks that way."

Shaking her head slowly, she sank on to a wicker chair. "It doesn't make any sense." She shook her head again.

"I understand how you feel," Shepard tried.

She jerked her head up, eyes wide, tearing. "Do you? He shouldn't be dead. That's what I feel. It wasn't part of Alex's plan ever to be dead." Her lower jaw quivered. Her eyes darted this way and that, unable to light on a single object for more than a second.

"I'm sorry," Shepard said. He noticed Cowles trying to disappear into his chair. Her reaction struck Shepard as very strange: her grief felt real enough, but somehow unfocused.

She looked at the delicate white-on-blue pattern of the room's wallpaper, then back at Shepard. "Why are you here?"

Shepard gave her a sympathetic smile. "For more details about his life. I realize this has been a shock, but we do need help."

"I haven't seen him in a year."

"Anything you could tell us of your life with him might be helpful," Shepard explained. "He seems to have been a very private man."

The hint of a smile brushed her full lips. "You could say that."

"How long were you married?"

"Five years."

"Mind telling me how you met?"

For a minute it looked as if she wouldn't be able to, but she finally said, "We met at a social function in Carmel. A mutual friend introduced us. Alex was very charming, removed from all the hubbub. He became ill. The crab dip or something. I went home with him that night and looked after him. He got better. I stayed."

She darted a glance at Shepard, as if expecting him to pounce on the speed at which the relationship developed. When he didn't, her eyes began to wander again.

"Where was he living then?" Shepard asked.

"A condominium in Pebble Beach. Up on the hill. We lived there for all five years of our marriage."

Shepard thought about this. "Then he sold that and bought the house in Carmel?"

"Yes. Alex always wanted a real house, he said. He was much keener on housework than I was. And yard work."

Shepard glanced around the impeccably clean room.

She saw the look, and responded with an apologetic, almost pleading tone. "I have someone in to do for me…" Her voice trailed off.

Shepard studied her. Her thin hands wrestled in her lap, wrinkling her skirt. He'd seen the same sad, rabbity behavior in battered children.

Shepard kept his voice low and gentle. "Did he speak much about his work while you were married?"

Shepard noticed the breath of a pause before she answered him. "Alex loved to talk. About his work, his ambitions, everything. At least most of the time, but he had his moods like everybody. Then he changed. Almost overnight."

"When was that?"

"Eighteen months ago. He became…quieter…not secretive exactly. It wasn't as if he was hiding anything. More like he'd lost interest in his work." Another pause. "And me."

"Did you ask him about it?" Shepard probed.

"Of course! It only made him withdraw more. From me, I mean. But even though he was quieter…his emotions…underneath…" She struggled with the words. "He seemed filled with a steadily building agitation of some sort. Every week it grew and possessed more of him. Like a smoker trying to kick the habit, or a heavy drinker trying to cut back, but he didn't smoke and drank only socially."

It was a long speech for her and the effort appeared to tire her. The nervous movements slowed.

"Do you know if he took any drugs?"

She gave him a sudden, frightened look. "I'm not sure of my legal position here."

Shepard held out his hands. "I'm looking for a murderer, Ms. Carroll. Nothing else."

Her eyes scoured his face for the truth. Finally she said in a small, helpless voice, "We…experimented a little…cocaine…But Alex didn't take to it. He was too fastidious I think."

"And you?"

"I stopped when he stopped." She met Shepard's eyes, a note of assurance somehow finding its way into her voice. "It was a long time ago. We'd only been married about a year. Whatever flame started to consume my husband, its origin wasn't chemical."

Shepard thought about it. "His becoming less talkative and this increasing agitation happened six months before you were divorced?"

"Yes. It finally got more than I could bear."

"You left him?" Shepard asked.

"Actually no," she replied, tears again filling her eyes. "He divorced me. Out of the blue."

"Was there another woman, do you think?"

She almost gasped. "I don't know. I moved out immediately, came up here. It was all as civilized as possible. I didn't ask for much of a settlement. I own my own real estate company. We have offices in both Monterey and Santa Cruz counties. I was self-sufficient before I met Alex. I'm self-sufficient now. He was just an interlude I thought I'd put behind me."

Shepard heard the plea in her voice: acknowledge that I am self-sufficient. Acknowledge I have worth.

He gave her an impressed smile. "Tough business. You've done well for yourself."

"Yes." She nodded. "Yes, I have…"

"We're having trouble locating any next of kin," Shepard continued. "Alex wasn't from around here, was he?"

"No." She shook her head. "He was from Seattle. Born there at least. He has a brother still living up there someplace. I never met him. I don't have an address."

"You remember his brother's name?"

"Bruce."

"Any other family?"

"No. His parents are both dead." She looked at Shepard expectantly.

"You were playing golf last Wednesday morning?" Shepard asked.

"Yes," she answered promptly. "With two women from our office here in Santa Cruz and the manager of our Monterey office."

"But not at Carmel Bay."

"No. A local course here in Santa Cruz."

"Kind of a coincidence you playing golf up here at the same time your ex-husband played down in Carmel," Shepard observed.

"Not coincidental at all. We both love golf. It was one of the few things we could still enjoy together in the end. We played Cypress the day our divorce became final. He won. I think he cheated on the scoring, but there didn't seem to be much point in arguing. That was the last time I saw him."

She turned again to trace the pattern of delicate paper on the wall with her eyes. Shepard stood. Cowles, who'd appeared almost comatose through the interview, lunged to his feet. Shepard looked at him.

"Greg? Anything you'd like to ask?"

Genevra, brow furrowed, looked over at Cowles.

Cowles seemed embarrassed by her concentration. "Uh, no, not me, Chief. I'm cool."

"Thank you for your time, Ms. Carroll." Shepard headed for the door.

"If you think of anything I can do, please…please give me call," she beseeched them both.

"I'll do that," Shepard answered. "Oh, there was one other thing. We'd like to talk to some of his friends. People who knew him, but were unconnected to his work."

The brow tightened again, shading the haunted eyes. "Friends? Unconnected to work? That animal has been extinct for a long time, Chief Shepard."

"What about this party where you met? You mentioned a mutual friend."

"Oh, that. I wouldn't call Yale Gerringer a friend really. Alex and I both supported him, that's all. It was to celebrate his election to his first term as Carmel's mayor."

They were well on their way south again along Highway One, the sun easing lazily into the sea on their right, before Cowles worked up the courage to speak. "She didn't kill him, right?"

"Hard to see how she could have," Shepard responded. "She might have hired somebody, I suppose, but I don't see her having the connections or the nerve to track down a reliable hit man."

"What's wrong with her, Chief?"

"She's been hurt, Greg. Badly. A pattern of hurt, not a one time thing."

"That shouldn't happen to people." His jaw worked.

Shepard agreed.

✶   ✶   ✶

In the wee hours of the following morning, Herman de Portola Bliss, half-owner of Carmel, kneaded clay between his fingers, shaping it with the loving care of the sculptor. Clay was not Bliss' medium of choice, but under these special circumstances, he knew of no better. At last satisfied with the phallic-shaped blob he massaged, he mashed it ever so gently against the small pane of glass in the side door of Alex Wagner's garage. He fumbled in his pocket for a moment until he found a small glasscutter. Pressing it to the pane, Bliss began to draw it across the smooth surface.

Chapter Six

Overhead a nearly full moon watched Bliss' artistry, its illumination more than enough for him to mark his progress. An occasional late traveler drove past beyond the gate at the front of Wagner's house, but otherwise Bliss remained undisturbed.

When he heard on the local evening news that fishermen hauled a body believed to be Alex Wagner out of Monterey Bay that afternoon, Bliss knew the time had come to act.

Dressed in burglar's basic black, the few odd tools he'd need quickly assembled, Bliss set out from his own home a few blocks to the southeast shortly after midnight, confident of his ability to pass along the streets unnoticed. Streetlights, too, were victims of the Carmel mystique, as few and far between as parking spaces. The fog leeching through the live oaks and pines subdued the illumination from the few you could find. The insistent thump of the surf helped muffle sound as well.

Soon after reaching "Sea Garden," Bliss chose the entry most protected from observation: the door along the side of the garage. He set to work. To tell the truth, this was not the first time Bliss had broken and entered, but he only resorted to such gray tactics in pursuit of a greater good.

Now, the circle completed, Bliss used the glasscutter to tap just inside its perimeter. In his other hand he held the lump of clay adhering to the center. With what he considered a diamond cutter's precision, he tapped his way around the circle.

To his dismay, a slightly over-enthusiastic knock shattered the window. Glass tinkled to the concrete floor inside. Bliss froze, eyes and ears alert. No porch lights suddenly flicked on. No petulant inquiries cut through the damp night air. He finally assured himself no one could hear the noise over the hollow drum of the distant surf.

When the sharp barks began directly behind him, Bliss shot upright so fast his spine cracked. The cutting tool clattered to the gravel. The section of glass with its clay handle slipped through the hole to crash on the concrete inside. Worse, when Bliss jerked around, his arm upraised to fend off whatever Hound of the Baskervilles was leaping for his throat, his elbow smashed into a second pane. It splintered with a crack that resonated even above the relentless barking.

He realized at once the six-foot high wooden fence that separated Wagner's narrow lot from the house next door shielded him from the dog on the other side. His heart leap-frogging around his chest cavity, Bliss took a couple of deep breaths to relax himself. He listened for sounds that the dog's barking had awakened its owner or other neighbors.

Sure enough, a door creaked and a woman's tired voice came from the adjacent house. "Muffin! Get in here right now! You silly little dog! Muffin!"

Bliss pictured the animal, its size shrinking rapidly in his imagination, as it turned with reluctance from its unseen quarry. It would now be trotting into its master's home, tail pumping, the picture of doggie obedience. Dogs were the slavering sycophants of the animal kingdom, sheep in wolves' clothing. Bliss had no use for them.

The voice of Muffin's owner added "Naughty dog!" The door closed with another creak and a clunk.

Bliss hoped there would be a sound whipping awaiting the little beast, but he doubted it. He knew from experience that the owners of noisy little dogs deserved whipping just as much as their pets, but received them just as infrequently.

He reached inside the first hole he'd made and flipped the deadbolt open. Once inside the garage, Bliss closed the door. The moonlight pooled on the concrete floor near the broken window, glinting on bits of shattered glass. The rest of the garage lay in darkness, but he had brought along a flashlight the size of a cigar. He switched it on, then played the thin bright beam around the one-car garage. Glass crunching underfoot, he moved deeper into the gloom.

A car under a brown cover filled most of the space. He lifted the front edge of the canvas. His light reflected off a silver Porsche with an ugly rubber bra protecting its grillwork. It reminded Bliss of people who bought beautiful furniture, then wrapped it in plastic. A painting occurred to Bliss. He envisioned a work of exquisite loveliness more representational than his usual style, but covered with a thick black mask of paint that totally obscured the beauty of the work.

He looked around the garage some more. Besides the normal complement of household tools, a great stock of gardening implements met his eye: rakes, trowels, and a full line of dangerous-looking claws in various sizes. He looked over bags of mulch, potting soil, a cornucopia of fertilizers and plant foods. On one wall hung pesticide and plant food sprayers in capacities ranging from a couple of pints to several gallons. A menu of lethal entrees for bugs, slugs, snails, and weeds of every persuasion lined the shelves above them.

Bliss reflected that if someone had wanted to kill Alex Wagner, they needn't have strayed far from Wagner's own garage, and its Murderer's K-Mart of poisons and weapons both blunt and razor-edged. He even spotted a roll of plastic leaning in the corner, perfect for smothering, or gift-wrapping the consequent corpse.

Certainly the killer could have chosen better than a golf club. The use of the sand wedge suggested immediately an un-premeditated act, but everything else about the crime shouted careful, if eccentric, planning.

Bliss suspected an important insight lay huddled at the heart of that paradox.

He shone his light at the tip of his shoe. Stains of various colors, splatters of paint in a mix some might call incoherent, but which pleased Bliss' eye, covered it. He couldn't detect any of the milky goop he'd stepped in on the seventh green.

At the time he'd assumed the culprit to be the seagulls, or a diarrhetic wild goose without the continence to produce golden eggs, but soon after he wondered. The only such dropping in sight, he remembered its odd consistency, almost crystalline. Given the care with which he felt sure this crime had been planned, he couldn't dismiss any oddity, including ones organic.

He asked Chief Shepard to find out what the golfers had to eat for breakfast the morning Wagner disappeared, but regretted he missed his chance at the golf course. If he'd been more alert, he could have requested that Shepard and his men shoot down as many of the gulls as possible to study their stomach contents. Maybe they could have bagged a few golfers and dissected them as well.

He moved to the wall beyond the Porsche. Beneath an extension ladder of considerable length hung two golf bags filled with clubs. Bliss couldn't tell if any were missing. There appeared to be a number of irons resembling the one found in the trap. He assumed the police had the clubs Wagner used on that last morning. Three sets of clubs seemed excessive to Bliss, who owned two pairs of shoes.

The door connecting the garage to the house was unlocked. Bliss opened it and slipped inside.

He stood in a kitchen. All of the appliances looked computerized and expensive, but unwashed dishes in the sink and a nearly full trashcan marred the otherwise spotless room. The odor caused the hairs inside his sensitive nose to recoil, but he steeled himself, and carefully examined the plates. On top of the stack he found a dish with the congealed remains of what looked like processed turkey, thin gravy and dehydrated mash potatoes. A quick glance at the trashcan revealed a low cholesterol frozen dinner box featuring this appetizing gourmet treat on its cover.

The next plate down held bits of scrambled eggs turned to stone and a darkened sliver of bacon glued to them by grease. The last breakfast eaten by the condemned man? Bliss could see no signs Wagner had carefully packed a lunch box of white goo to snack on while he played.

A sortie inside the refrigerator revealed additional foodstuffs: milk; cream; vegetables; eggs and meat, beginning to spoil. The freezer compartment held a selection of low fat, low cholesterol frozen dinners, arranged, Bliss realized, in alphabetical order. He wondered if Wagner ate them that way, starting each month with aspic, and ending with zucchini.

There were also some trays that froze ice cubes into novel shapes: spherical; triangular; hearts; flowers; even some representing female breasts with erect nipples. An ice cube for every occasion. The collection failed to impress Bliss, who was not a big party-giver.

Through an archway directly opposite the door he'd entered the kitchen, Bliss found an oak dining table with five chairs and a wet bar. Wagner imaginatively stocked the bar with glasses in all kinds of shapes and sizes, and a supply of napkins to match the various themes already introduced in ice.

Moving farther into the darkened living room, Bliss's feet crackled beneath him. He looked down. Trails of plastic, obviously from the roll in the garage, protected the thick off-white carpeting. They marked the main trade routes from the front door to his left, the kitchen behind him, and a short hallway to the right running toward the back of the house. He swung his flashlight across expensive-looking furniture also encased in plastic like lumpish condoms.

A quick visit to the two bedrooms and baths confirmed a growing suspicion. You could bounce a five-dollar bill on the taut bedspreads. The bathroom tiles made the mirror redundant. All toiletries were discreetly tucked away. He couldn't find a single article of dirty clothing. A meticulous rainbow of shirts hung next to trousers mated with custom-tailored sport coats and blazers. Suits had a wing of the walk-in closet all to themselves. Shoes ringed the floor of the closet in a neat row like polished stones bordering a garden path.

Bliss wondered if in Wagner's last moments, he remembered the slight mess he'd left behind in his kitchen and wished he'd been granted time to tidy up. Bliss painted a picture in his mind's eye of someone so disgustingly neat and organized, Bliss might have had to kill the man himself.

When Bliss returned to the living room, he walked to a desk in its windowed alcove on the far side. Here he found books on real estate law, site plans, blueprints, and pages of reports. The sixth chair from the dining table sat in front of the desk. One leg had at some time made a slight tear in the unprotected carpet.

Bliss plucked a stapled report of several pages from the desk and swept his light over it. It concerned a proposed hotel and retail complex in construction along Cannery Row. Bliss growled, recognizing the project as another of Loren Holly's attempts to inter the vulnerable past beneath an ugly and unnecessary monument to his own greed.

Bliss hoped with all his heart Holly murdered Alex Wagner. If the old man found a way through teleportation or astral projection or something to enter that sand trap and club Alex Wagner to death, Bliss planned to be in court to hear the death sentence read aloud.

He opened a drawer and took out a framed picture. When Bliss turned the flashlight on it he became very still. He held a glamour photograph of a particularly beautiful woman taken maybe thirty years earlier. Bliss recognized the face. He'd seen it, hard and full of indignation, less than twelve hours before. He ran a finger along the mouth that threatened to burn his Madonna and Child, the mouth that not many years before the photograph had been taken, kissed his and made promises its owner never meant to keep, the mouth of Maggie Dennis.

Suddenly the glare of a flashlight reflecting off the alcove window directly into his eyes derailed his train of reverie. The scuff of a foot on the plastic covering the carpet behind him reached his ears. The overhead light snapped on, and he heard the unmistakable double-click of the hammer on a revolver being cocked back.

CHAPTER SEVEN

At eight-fifteen Tuesday morning, Shepard walked the two blocks from "Pine Haven" to the Carmel Police Department. When he came through the rear door he knew something was up. Amy Ryerson, the chunky desk officer at that hour, could barely suppress a look of glee. Her eyes shone behind her round glasses and her cheeks flushed. Cowles and Charlie Revere, the young officer who had escorted Bliss from the golf course on the day Alex Wagner died, appeared from the back. They both could not keep from grinning at Shepard the moment they saw him. Everybody stayed like that for an excruciatingly long time.

Shepard looked down at his pants to check his zipper, then he craned around to study his reflection in the glass partition separating the front desk from the small waiting area. He saw no blobs of white shaving cream decorating his dark complexion. Giving it up, he scowled at his officers.

"Would someone like to let me in on it?" His eyes came to rest on Amy.

"It was Charlie's collar, Chief." She burst into a set of giggles that rolled on and on like waves slapping the beach.

Shepard, still maintaining his cool, turned a look of expectant interest on Charlie Revere.

Charlie wrestled with his grin, fought it into momentary submission, and glanced at a typed report in his hand before beginning. "It's like this, Chief. I was making my rounds last night—early this morning I mean—just before one—and when I passed Alex Wagner's house, I slowed down because…well, you know…"

Shepard nodded. "It's the only house whose owner was murdered this week?"

"Yeah. Anyway," Charlie went on, his voice growing hushed. "I spotted a flashlight inside, moving around."

Shepard waited while Charlie and Cowles exchanged a conspiratorial glance. "What happened? You caught the murderer, he confessed, you're a hero, and the mayor wants to make you Chief of Police?"

"No, I didn't catch the murderer—least I don't think so—I caught—"

A noise rose from down the hall. It reminded Shepard of the raccoons that sometimes fought over his garbage cans in the middle of the night. The screeching resolved itself almost immediately into a chorus of several male voices raised in something trying desperately to be song.

"You've nabbed the barber shop quartet who placed last in the county fair competition?"

Without waiting for a reply, Shepard grabbed the report from Charlie and strode off down the hall toward the holding cell.

For safekeeping the Carmel police, like other local law enforcement agencies, shuttled its prisoners to the Monterey County Correction Bureau, a division of the Sheriff's Office in Salinas. The small building at Fourth and Junipero that housed the Carmel Police Department featured only a single room set aside as a holding cell for the short-term incarceration of prisoners. Stuck at the end of a long hall of offices, it contained two bunks, linoleum floor, a couple of chairs and a single window with heavy mesh protecting it.

Shepard managed finally to translate the cacophony into an attempt at a Bob Marley hit from the seventies: "I shot the sheriff…but I did not shoot the deputy…"

Halfway down the hall, he recognized one of the voices: a loud, mawkish baritone that swarmed around the notes like a gnat circling a light bulb, coming close, but never landing. Shepard stopped outside, and peered through the small window of reinforced glass in the door.

Rail-thin Jimmy O'Conner, a sixty-five-year-old busboy who changed restaurants more often than his underwear, sat on a top bunk, leaning against the wall, with his eyes closed, and singing in a shrill tenor. Shepard knew Jimmy lasted just long enough at each place of employment to discover where they kept the key to the wine cellar. Then, after a midnight-to-dawn private tasting of the most prized occupants of that cellar, Jimmy could be found passed out, usually near the public rest rooms in Devendorf Park.

Sprawled on the bunk beneath Jimmy, bearded, longhaired Merle Graff anchored the bass line of the tune. Police caught Merle, a transient fisherman who lived in the hills in upper Carmel Valley, snagging steelhead trout in the river. Locals considered this a miracle of a crime, since after years of drought very few steelhead managed to find, much less swim up, the Carmel River.

Shepard knew the owner of the baritone voice only too well. Herman de Portola Bliss. While he sang, Bliss used a spoon to carve something into the pale green paint on the wall: a single stroke to indicate the extreme length of his imprisonment.

Shepard unlocked the door and opened it. The singing trailed off.

"You're not supposed to count a day until a full twenty-four hours have passed, Mr. Bliss. I understand you've been our guest less than eight."

Bliss shrugged. "Eight hours can be a lifetime to a condemned man, Chief."

"We don't execute people for breaking and entering in this state, Mr. Bliss."

"No," Bliss agreed. "You feed them breakfast. Substantially the same thing."

"Would you mind coming with me?"

"As you like."

Bliss paused long enough to give Jimmy and Merle a raised-fist power salute. Then he followed Shepard out. In the hall Shepard locked the door and showed Bliss into his office.

Shepard saw Bliss running his artist's eye over the room, probably to check out any alterations that had been made since his last arrest. He smirked at the bland green paint covering the walls, the utilitarian furnishings including a steel desk, a few stiff-backed chairs, a couple of filing cabinets. Bliss eyed the single bookcase Shepard had stuffed with his books on criminal law and a biography of Billie Holiday, then turned the lamp of his interest on the desk.

"Nice desk," Bliss said. "Not a pencil or paper out of place. Do you do any actual work here or is this just for the layout in Better Jails and Prisons?"

Shepard crossed behind his desk. "I don't believe in going through life disorganized."

"I can see that," Bliss remarked. "You have something in common with Alex Wagner."

Shepard saw Bliss studying the framed diplomas and citations on one wall. "Please sit down, Mr. Bliss."

Bliss ignored him, muttering instead. "Masters degree in Criminal Justice…Citation for Valor, Akron, Ohio Police…Lots of other awards and commendations."

"Sit down."

Bliss collapsed into the chair opposite the desk with a sigh. "I supported the mayor when he decided to look outside Carmel for the new Chief."

"Good for you," Shepard said.

"I read your application. He was kind enough to let me have a look at it."

"Let's cut the crap, Mr. Bliss. I've been informed of your family's standing in the community."

Bliss attempted to brush this aside with a wave of his hand. Shepard expected him to be pleased by this acknowledgment of his status, but for some reason Bliss appeared genuinely irritated.

Shepard pressed on. "Your connections may have helped you avoid court in the various civil suits that have been filed against you. They may have been enough to get the long line of petty misdemeanors you've been charged with dropped, but breaking and entering is a felony."

Bliss leaned forward. "Has the body been positively identified as Wagner?"

"Mr. Bliss, I'm conducting this interrogation. Not you. Were you informed of your rights when you were arrested?"

"Yes."

"You declined to make a statement. You also declined the services of an attorney."

"Yes."

"Why?"

Bliss at least had the decency to look uncomfortable. "Because I wanted to explain this misunderstanding to you personally, Chief."

"Misunderstanding?"

"Surely you don't think I was burglarizing the place?" Bliss asked in a wheedling tone that set Shepard's teeth on edge.

Shepard looked over Bliss' black outfit. "Now what would give me that idea?"

"I was helping you."

"Did I ask for your help?"

"No," Bliss answered with a prim expression. "That's how I knew you needed it."

"Mr. Bliss, you're not going to jive your way out of this one." Shepard held up the report. "You were caught by one of my officers going through Alex Wagner's desk."

"I didn't steal anything."

Shepard looked over the report. "When Officer Revere turned on the light, he saw you trying to shove a framed photograph inside your coat."

"It was mine."

"You brought the photograph with you?"

"Yes."

"To keep you company while you broke into Alex Wagner's house?"

"I keep it with me always."

"Oh, come on, Mr. Bliss! You don't expect people to take most of the things you say seriously, do you?"

The lines and furrows of Bliss' face scrunched up like a basset hound's. Shepard realized he was trying to look innocent. "You don't believe me?"

"No."

"Why not?"

Shepard shook his head, picked a second file folder from a neat pile and opened it. "One advantage to being organized is being able to find what you need when you need it."

"Put it on a doily," Bliss rumbled.

Shepard ignored him. "My men went over Wagner's desk when Wagner first disappeared. Included in their list of the contents is a framed photograph of an attractive woman, apparently taken some time ago. Isn't that the photograph you had in your possession?"

Bliss squirmed in the chair. "You haven't seen it yet, have you?"

"No."

"It was a picture of Maggie Dennis. I explained to you what we were to each other. Seeing her yesterday brought it all back to me—"

"Mr. Bliss—"

"I found the picture locked away in a trunk in my attic—"

"Mr. Bliss—!"

"I wanted to keep it close to me to try and understand what our time together so long ago really meant—"

"Mr. Bliss!!! I haven't known you long, but long enough to know you pretty well. That's the biggest bunch of romantic hooey I've ever heard. It isn't you. And I don't believe it for a second!"

Bliss looked disgruntled. "I thought it sounded good."

"No. It didn't. You found the photograph there, and when Charlie caught you, you tried to hide it to shield a woman who may have once meant something to you from being implicated in Wagner's death! Maybe that's romantic. I don't know. All I know is it proves I don't need you to help solve this crime."

Bliss blinked. "It does?"

"Yes. Because simply finding that photograph there wouldn't implicate Ms. Dennis in anything more than a relationship with Wagner. He was divorced last year—"

"How old was he?"

"Forty-four," Shepard answered.

Bliss sighed. "Maggie, the dear, will never see fifty again."

"You ever hear of May-December romances? That one would barely qualify as May-August. Besides, if anyone managed to haul Wagner out of that sand trap without being spotted, it certainly wasn't a woman. Did you see Margaret Dennis anywhere near the seventh green?"

"No, of course not!"

"Then you are a worse detective than you think, Mr. Bliss. As far as I can see Ms. Dennis had no means, motive or opportunity, yet there you were, trying to spirit her photograph away."

Bliss spoke in an aggrieved tone. "I never claimed to be a detective. I do have certain powers of observation—"

"What did you observe in Alex Wagner's house?"

"Several interesting things."

Shepard sat forward. "Name one."

"He had scrambled eggs for breakfast. And I expect they were far superior to the ones served here."

Shepard shook his head in frustration. "We're back on breakfasts?"

"Did you find out what the others had that morning?"

"Why would I bother?"

"There was a curious little blob of white goop in the center of the green." Bliss told him.

"White goop."

Bliss nodded. Shepard realized that in spite of himself, he'd let Bliss take the conversational bit in his teeth again.

"About ten yards from the hole. At first I thought it was seagull droppings."

"Then you decided it was golfer droppings?"

Bliss scowled, but went on. "It was crunchy, granulated or crystallized. I thought one of the golfers might have brought along some oatmeal or something." He leaned forward, a pleading look in his eyes. "Did any of them have oatmeal for breakfast? Or one of those thick chemical shakes yuppies sometimes lap up in the mornings?"

Bliss looked so forlorn, Shepard gave in. "No. I don't remember all the details, but none of them had anything like that, and nobody took any food out on the course."

Bliss absorbed this in silence for a moment, then said, "So Wagner must've been responsible for the goop. I wish I'd thought to taste it."

Shepard, convinced it was bird droppings, privately wished the same. "Let's put the goop aside for a moment."

"I don't think we should."

Shepard attempted to regain control of the questioning. "Do you know if Margaret Dennis had a relationship with Wagner?"

"I brought the photograph to the house."

"I will be asking her, too."

Bliss looked trapped, but made an embarrassing attempt at a cheerful smile.

"Okay, copper. Ya got me. I paid that visit to Alex Wagner's house to steal that priceless photograph."

"No, I think you broke in there to nose around in the mistaken belief that I was going to let Wagner's killer walk. You saw the photograph, were discovered, and panicked."

Shepard could tell by the wounded look Bliss cast at the wall, that he'd guessed correctly. "Whatever your motive was, it's time to bring you down to earth, Mr. Bliss. You are going to be charged. Being the pillar of the community you are—" Here again Shepard saw Bliss look pained. "—you'll make bail, but I promise you that you'll come to trial, and you'll be convicted. First offense, you may get off with only a year or less. I hope whatever time you spend behind bars will finally convince you that no man is above the law."

Bliss stared at Shepard in silence, apparently gauging his sincerity. When he spoke, Shepard strained to hear the words.

"I won't post bail."

"Why not?"

"I'm guilty. I'll take my punishment."

"You can still have a few more months of freedom."

"No."

"To paint?"

Bliss looked almost wistful. "They'll allow me a few small hunks of charcoal and a scrap of paper or two in prison, won't they?"

In spite of himself, Shepard felt a sudden surge of pity for the man. Hadn't he realized sooner or later it would all catch up to him?

"Surely you can afford the bail."

"It's the principle of the thing."

"What principle?" Shepard asked, puzzled.

Instead of answering, Bliss again switched the subject.

"You could let me go."

"No."

"Oh, I don't mean drop the charges. You must do your duty as you see it. But you can ask the judge to release me on my own recognizance, can't you? Or into your custody, or something?"

Shepard shook his head. "Mr. Bliss, I would rather ask the judge to release Jack the Ripper on his own recognizance. If you want to stay in jail, stay with my blessing. I'm sure hundreds of Monterey County residents will sleep more soundly at night."

He didn't like the shrewd look Bliss threw at him, and he liked Bliss' next words even less.

"It looks like I'll have to make you want to release me."

"No way."

"Let's try this then: how about if I show you a way Alex Wagner could have been killed, and removed from that sand trap, without anyone catching a glimpse of the murderer."

"Mr. Bliss, as a citizen, it's your duty to cooperate with the police—"

Bliss looked disappointed. "Now who isn't expecting to be taken seriously, Chief?"

"Tell me."

"I can't. I have to show you. And I have to be out of jail to do that, don't I?"

Shepard shook his head.

"I'm sorry, Mr. Bliss, but that won't be possible." He stood up. "I'll return you to the holding cell. In a little while one of my officers will drive you over to the courthouse for formal arraignment. I strongly urge you to get an attorney or the court will appoint you one."

The irritating man still crouched in his chair, the grin widening like an awful parody of the Cheshire Cat, as if some jackal with a talent for mimicry had decided to try it on for size. The grin grew and grew, stretching Bliss' face more than a human face should be stretched.

Bliss spoke with the sweet, innocent voice of a young child. "Chief, did your men find a ladder near the seventh green?"

CHAPTER EIGHT

Bliss shouted all the way from the holding cell to the parking lot. He shouted as Officers Revere and Cowles guided him into the back of the patrol car. He shouted when the car pulled out of the lot and disappeared up Fourth Avenue headed for the county courthouse on Aguajito Street in Monterey. Shepard imagined he still could hear Bliss even now, incredulous that his proposal had failed to win Shepard over, enraged he helped choose the new Chief of Police and insistent he would do better choosing the next one.

Shepard asked Amy for the property room key. His men had crawled up and down the thirty-foot face of the cliff below the sand trap for days. Divers caused some excitement when they came up with an extension ladder, almost covered with sand, only a few yards offshore.

He stared at the ladder, then moved to the shelves lining one wall of the room to study the morass of flotsam and jetsam collected in the search. The first plastic evidence bag contained the miracle ball itself, a Spaulding Six, dusted for fingerprints, and blood-typed. Forensics found one partial print, a possible match to Wagner's right thumb. The sand wedge lay in Catherine Gonzales' capable hands in the Medical Examiner's lab where she tried to match its blade to the wounds on the back of Wagner's head.

Replacing the first bag, Shepard picked up one containing seven golf balls in various stages of decomposition gathered from below the cliff.

There were two Spaulding's, no Sixes. Even if they found a mate, he couldn't see any significance in it.

He turned his attention to a rusted nine iron possibly flung over the cliff by the frustrated owner of some of the golf balls. It didn't belong to the set Wagner had been playing with. He picked up a battered thermos. The stopper and cap were missing, the metal outer skin dented, but the plastic lining appeared to be intact. None of the foursome brought food or drink with them when they played. He set it back on the shelf.

A water-logged paperback book with only a partial title remaining, "Love's Lonely..." Losers? Lunch?, seemed irrelevant, too, its pages fused together now that they had dried. Most likely the surf stole it from a careless sunbather on a nearby beach.

A single dead seagull, never a popular clue, ended up in the station's trash. If it held the key to the murder, or Bliss' blob of goo, it took its secret to a lonely grave at the county landfill.

He spent the most time with two square yards of fishing net, not torn loose from a larger net, but deliberately cut. Had an accomplice trawler somehow netted Wagner, and hauled him out to sea? Would that explain how his body managed to travel around a headland and several miles north? Shepard shook his head, frustrated. The net came apart easily in his hands. A fisherman had probably snipped it out and replaced it with a sturdier patch.

He put the net down and turned back to the extension ladder. It looked almost new. It certainly hadn't been in the water very long. How did Bliss guess they'd found a ladder? The department didn't release information on any of the items discovered at the scene.

He stared at the ladder, searching for the significance Bliss claimed to have found. He rubbed his hand over his hair. When he did, a tiny cloud lifted from his brain. His jaw dropped. His mind worked. He began to see what Bliss must have seen, and he considered the possibility.

*   *   *

Bliss shouted at Cowles. "He's not a police chief! He's the town's chief nitwit! Fear! That's what it is! Stark, blubbering fear in the face of a greater intellect! I can understand that," Bliss added with a gracious nod of his head. "I thought he'd have the sense to at least acknowledge the fact! But no! What do I get! I get blind, mule-headed stubbornness! I get long speeches about law and order and the public welfare!"

"Police chiefs usually have those things on their minds, sir," Cowles interjected with a smirk at Bliss in the rearview mirror.

"Don't get smart with me, twig," Bliss said, eyes narrowing. "You don't have the wit to carry it off."

Cowles shrugged his shoulders. "You can yell all you want to, Mr. Bliss. Fact is there are quite a few peace officers in this county who're circling today on their calendars."

"Oh? Why?" Bliss illustrated his lack of interest by studying his manacled hands.

"The day Herman Bliss finally got nailed. A lotta people are saying Chief Shepard's a hero."

"A lot of people watch television."

"So? I do."

"Exactly my point."

Bliss could see Cowles casting a confused look at him in the mirror. He leaned forward in his seat, his fingers curling around the wire mesh separating them.

"What is it? Pesticides in the vegetables? Steroids in the beef? How is it we're managing to father these new generations whose neck sizes exceed their IQ's?"

A dispatcher's voice booming over the radio intruded.

"All units in the vicinity of Cannery Row. Officer needs assistance." A car responded, asking for more particulars. The dispatcher rattled off some numbers. Cowles was nearing the streetlight at Aguajito.

"Those numbers," Bliss said. "What do they mean?"

Cowles answered, "It's a civil disturbance of some kind. A protest. At the new hotel."

Bliss hiccupped with excitement. "Civil disturbance?" At a new hotel on Cannery Row?" If he had been a bull spotting a herd of attractive cows grazing on the other side of a gate, he couldn't be more eager. He saw that they were in the right hand lane, preparing to turn toward the courthouse.

"Listen to me very carefully, Officer Cowles. A protest march can turn ugly fast."

"I guess you'd know," Cowles agreed. "How many times have you been arrested—"

Bliss bulled ahead. "How are you going to feel if you abandon your fellow peace officers to face an angry mob? How are you going to look yourself in the mirror to shave tomorrow morning, if you shave, knowing those poor, hospitalized wretches could have been saved by your timely intervention?"

Bliss saw Cowles throw a worried expression in the general direction of Cannery Row. They came to a stop at the light. It was red. Cars in the intersection prevented an immediate turn.

Bliss went for the jugular. "Chief Shepard doesn't need to be today's only hero, does he?"

Cowles looked back over his shoulder, checking the two lanes next to him. Bliss could feel the gate opening, green pastures beyond. He held his breath. The light changed.

"I guess it won't hurt to have a look," Cowles told him. "Hold on, sir."

He flipped switches on the dash. The siren began to wail. Cowles brought the police car around in a sweeping turn, weaving through the traffic, then picking up speed, heading west. Red and blue lights from the bar on the roof reflected off automobiles swerving out of their way.

Siren whooping, the police car sped toward the waterfront, soon only seconds from Cannery Row. The sound filled Bliss with exhilaration. The springs creaked beneath him as the car hit a bump.

A few of the original buildings still remained from the Cannery Row of Steinbeck's day, or at least the shells of them, now stuffed with shops and restaurants instead of salmon and crab. From a long stretch leveled by bulldozers on the seaward side of the Row rose the steel skeleton of a new hotel complex.

"Tell me, Officer Cowles." Bliss worked up an expression of casual interest. "Isn't that the Cannery Plaza? Loren Holly's project?"

"Say, that's right," Cowles answered. "The old gentleman who was playing golf with Wagner!"

"We may be able to pick up some clues," Bliss continued with an air of only moderate attention.

Cowles shook his head as he turned off the lights and siren, easing up on the accelerator. "Sir, if it's necessary for me to leave the vehicle, you'll be remaining inside."

"But young man—"

"I'm the policeman, Mr. Bliss. You're the prisoner."

Which summed up a lot that was wrong with the Monterey Peninsula these days, Bliss reflected sourly.

They pulled to the curb just north of the construction site. Bliss leaned forward. Through the front windshield he could see maybe two-dozen people stretched in the familiar picket line that always reminded Bliss of the mechanized clothing track at a dry cleaners, trundling its garments in an endless parade. Instead of sporting clothing tags, the chanting protesters carried the obligatory hand lettered signs.

Bliss could easily make out a couple: STOP EXPANSIONISM! Now that sounded like a nice generalized motto for our times, useful over and over to the canny rebel. Another said: SAVE THE WATER FOR OUR CHILDREN, NOT THE TOURISTS! More to the point, but Bliss liked the next one he saw better: LOREN HOLLY IS DESTROYING THE PENINSULA! That slogan Bliss could get behind.

Cowles jumped out to confer with two Monterey police officers near the curb. Suddenly someone yelled and the crowd surged toward the

Carmel police car. Bliss twisted around to see the new focus of their attention.

A Mercedes rolled to a stop behind Bliss. Ben Webb climbed out of the driver's seat. Leonard Romaine followed from the passenger side. Webb climbed up on a convenient cement block, Romaine remaining at ground level. Cowles and the two Monterey officers moved to confer with Romaine. Whatever they suggested, Romaine vetoed with a marginal shake of his head.

The protesters jockeyed for position between Bliss and the new arrivals. Bliss strained forward to keep Webb in sight between bobbing heads and placards. Webb held up his hands, calling for quiet. Slowly the shouting began to subside.

"Folks, I'm Benjamin Webb, Vice President of the Holly Corporation!" he began.

Greeted by a few shouted demands for "the old bastard himself," Webb only smiled.

"I'm sorry, but Mr. Holly is in Planning Commission meetings all day. I'm sure you folks can understand how aggravating bureaucracy can be!"

"No, you tell us, asshole," a young woman with curly blonde hair called out.

Webb maintained his composure. "Mr. Romaine, chief attorney for this project, and I have just come from the meeting to find out what the problem is."

Another arrival interrupted Webb's speech. A van from the local CBS affiliate rumbled to a halt. A well-groomed reporter that Bliss recognized, with some generic reporter-type name he couldn't recall, climbed out, followed by a scruffy-looking cameraman, and a young woman with sound equipment.

"We demand action!" a voice shouted from the crowd. "Your company is once again tearing down the history of this peninsula in the name of profit!"

Bliss scowled. He recognized the voice even before he saw the tall young man, black hair tied back in a ponytail, pushing to the front of the assembly. Bliss studied the lean face with its classic features that looked almost sculpted. Those who knew where to look could find Jason Kiley tending some of the most prominent landscaping in the area. More often he was spotted in his natural habitat: heading marches; chairing committees; or passing out leaflets printed on recycled paper. Trust Jason to wait for the press before launching his attack. He'd probably called them himself.

Before Webb had time to respond, Jason launched into a prepared speech. "We, the citizens of the Monterey Peninsula, demand that the Holly Corporation abandon the destruction of this historical landmark and their long-term plans to turn the beauty of the land into a Xanadu of corporate greed!"

Xanadu, oh right, sighed Bliss. It annoyed him that he didn't like the young man more. Jason possessed all the ecologically correct credentials. He served time in both Greenpeace seal boats and Brazilian rain forests, but there remained something about him that disturbed Bliss. Maybe it was the man's consuming pursuit of publicity that sometimes seemed to overshadow his need for change.

"We warn the Holly Corporation and its executives that if they ignore our demands, we will bring them down. Already one of their creatures has fallen. More may follow!"

Bliss realized with a start that Jason must be referring to Alex Wagner. Could the fool be suggesting his group had something to do with Wagner's death? Bliss reached over and rolled down the window nearest the crowd. Designed to keep prisoners in, it only moved a few inches, but that was enough.

Waiting for a lull, Bliss slid down in the seat and shouted, "Who's this out-of-town attorney Romaine? Let's do him next!"

Bliss peered through the window and could see several people in the crowd swiveling around, trying to locate the source of the voice. Cowles and the two Monterey cops looked in the direction of the street, too.

Ill at ease all of a sudden, Webb raised his voice. "People, please! We can talk out our differences without threats, can't we?"

Bliss waited until the crowd turned back toward Webb, sat up and hollered again. "Maybe Romaine killed Wagner himself 'cause he wanted his job!" Then he ducked down again until he could just see over the lower rim of the window. He watched with glee.

Romaine's usually florid complexion bordered on alizarin crimson. Webb scanned the crowd, searching for the source of the anonymous yells. The police contingent, Cowles included, began to spread out, the same objective written on their tense faces. Even Jason looked annoyed as the news reporter shifted his deeply tanned attention from him to his unseen comrade.

Still Bliss appeared to be safe. No one looked directly at the police car. Better yet, the reporter decided to follow up.

"How about that, Mr. Romaine? Care to comment?"

Romaine gave an angry shake of his head.

Webb spoke directly to the reporter. "The accusation is absurd."

"He does have Mr. Wagner's job, doesn't he?" The reporter persisted.

"Mr. Wagner was going to step down as legal counsel for the Holly Corporation—" Webb went on, not seeing Romaine's shaking head redirected to him, "—some time ago."

"Isn't it true you were considering legal action against the deceased?"

Bliss flushed with satisfaction. Things could not go much better. Webb wriggled like a hooked fish, but obviously could not think of a way to extricate himself.

Romaine stepped forward. "We're here today to meet with citizens of the community concerned with the Cannery Plaza development to reassure them that their fears are unjustified. The Cannery Plaza Hotel will be a proud addition to the peninsula. It's been painstakingly designed to co-exist in harmony with its historic surroundings—"

Romaine impressed Bliss. The lawyer deflected the dangerous line of questioning with all the skill of a major league hitter fighting off a difficult pitch.

The reporter knew his job, too. "Is that why it's taken over two years to get this project off the ground?"

Bliss sat up to hear Romaine's response, but a tapping on the opposite window rattled his teeth. Fearing the long nose of the law, he turned.

A small old man with a pale, lined face and wearing a raincoat, bent over and smiled in at him. He rotated his hand to indicate he wanted Bliss to roll down the street-side window. Bliss slid across the seat to comply.

The little man nodded pleasantly. "Mr. Bliss, isn't it?"

"Who are you?"

The man in the raincoat stepped aside, and Bliss could see a limousine pulled up across the street, its occupants hidden behind tinted glass.

"Mr. Bliss, Mr. Cosentino would like a word with you."

Bliss froze. He hoped his face hid his reaction to the news, but could tell by the little man's alert expression that he failed. Bliss held up his cuffed hands with an apologetic shrug.

"Please tell Mr. Cosentino that I'm afraid my schedule is going to be pretty full the next few days."

The little man chuckled at the handcuffs and shook his head. "Don't worry, Mr. Bliss. I'm sure we'll be able to arrange something."

With that he gave a polite nod and scampered across the street with a spring to his step that belied his years. Bliss sank back in his seat with a strangled gasp. It looked as if he wouldn't be spending much time in jail after all. Armando Cosentino, the number one organized crime figure on the peninsula, could unlock a lot of doors.

CHAPTER NINE

Shepard stood on the hill overlooking the seventh fairway at the Carmel Bay Country Club, a pair of binoculars around his neck and a walkie-talkie in his right hand. He watched the golfers below, parading from hole to hole like faithful disciples following the Stations of the Cross. The early morning fog had burned off to reveal an eggshell blue dome of cloudless sky, and the sun, just past its apex, heated the air enough to make it shimmer in the near distance.

Each foursome passing behind the curtain of heat resembled Bliss' abstract painting of the scene: small vivid blobs of color over-lapping and blending in sometimes excruciating combinations. Some sly devil in his mind whispered that maybe Bliss did know something about art. Shepard shook his head to dislodge the thought.

Next to him stood MacGregor, the head of Carmel Bay's private army. The golf club employed more security men than Carmel had police officers. Their budget made the city's outlay for law enforcement look puny by comparison. At the moment MacGregor did not look happy.

"Chief, The Ridgeway Tire Pro-Am starts in two days," MacGregor clenched his teeth. "It brings in millions of dollars to the peninsula every spring. It will be internationally televised. Golfers and celebrities are already beginning to arrive. We can't have policemen tramping all over the place, disrupting play."

"Who knows, Mr. MacGregor? We may have the case solved by then."

MacGregor snorted. "If you were close to solving it, we wouldn't be standing here on this hill."

Shepard squinted at the scene before him. The bowl-shaped depression in the fairway where the other three members of Wagner's foursome had been standing; the entire surface of the seventh green; and the fold of ground that marked the near edge of the sand trap; all wavered in the heat. He raised the binoculars to his eyes and adjusted the focus.

The magnification increased the heat distortion, but Shepard could make out one of his officers crawling along an extension ladder stretched from the sand trap to the cliff's edge. He muttered under his breath.

"Bliss, you son-of-a-bitch."

"What was that, Chief?" MacGregor asked.

"You can see the edge of the cliff beyond the sand trap: just a thin line with a few of those rocks sticking up."

"Is that important?"

"We've got a killer and a victim who both vanished from that sand trap. The killer didn't take an invisibility pill. He didn't tunnel. He would've been seen by the three men if he'd tried to cross the fairway."

"He didn't crawl to the cliff. We can see your officer plain as day."

"Yeah, even if Bliss looked down for a minute or two to mix a new color, it still takes too long to crawl all that way." Shepard said.

"Then the killer must've crawled in the other direction. Away from the men, across the green, and down the other side to the path."

Shepard shook his head. "That route would have forced him to crawl for almost forty yards in plain sight of this hill. Bliss would have seen him then, too! But that's not the craziest, most aggravating part of this case."

"What is?"

Shepard exploded with exasperation. "Why would anybody plot to kill somebody with witnesses only a few yards away and escape routes that can only be crawled over? Why, if the murder was premeditated, wasn't it premeditated better?"

"Maybe it wasn't premeditated."

Shepard laughed. "A chance encounter? Two mortal enemies happened to run into each other in that sand trap? 'Hello there, Wagner. What a coincidence meeting you here. Say, that's a nice sand wedge. Mind if I take a look at it? Oh, could you turn your back for a second? Thanks.' Whap. Whap. Whap?"

MacGregor now looked angrier than ever. "And you expect to have this solved by next week? Let's get your experiment cleaned up. There's golf waiting to be played!" He started down the hill.

By the time they reached the green, Charlie Revere and an older officer stood talking beside the aluminum extension ladder. It had been extended to reach from the rocks near the cliff to the sand trap. In the center it sagged even without a man's weight to mat the grass underneath.

Carl Lorch, the older of the two policemen, nearing retirement age, had a broken-veined nose and hammocks under his eyes. A candidate for the job Shepard now held, Shepard soon discovered why the mayor passed him over. Lorch's imagination could handle what brand of whiskey to drink at lunch. Beyond that it floundered.

Charlie fidgeted, clearly disappointed. "It took almost fifteen minutes, and I made a mess of the grass. The ladder scarred the rocks here by the edge, too." He walked over to the cliff to point out the damage inflicted on the rocks, then stopped dead, staring over the edge. "Uh, Chief...?"

He stepped aside. Dislodged pebbles rattled. A great huffing and panting rose from below. Bliss' shaggy head appeared over the rim. He glared up at Charlie.

"Don't just stand there! Give me a hand!"

Charlie looked to Shepard for instructions. Shepard considered whether he should tell him to help the artist or to give him a good kick under the point of the jaw. Reason asserted itself. Shepard closed his eyes and nodded.

Charlie hauled Bliss up the final few feet. Not bothering to dust himself off, Bliss looked around with the frisky interest of a gecko. Shepard stalked over to him.

"Mr. Bliss."

"Chief!" Bliss nodded with a crooked smile. "I'm pleased to see you decided to test my theory!"

"Mr. Bliss, why aren't you in jail?"

Bliss waved the question aside. "Oh, Officer Cowles can explain all that." He glanced at MacGregor. "Those lifts you're wearing in your shoes don't really help much, do they?"

MacGregor glared at him. "Kill any deer lately?"

Shepard made a "T" with his hands. "Time-out. Mr. Bliss, don't keep me in suspense. Why don't you explain how you got out?"

Bliss shrugged. "When we reached the courthouse, a lawyer awaited me. He posted my bond."

"Would you like to tell me how that could be? You refused to consider the possibility when we last talked. You didn't make any phone calls while you were at the station."

"It's a mystery, isn't it?" Bliss' grin widened.

Shepard tried to remain calm. "What was the lawyer's name?"

"Brown, I believe."

"Lester Brown?" Shepard asked, failing to keep the anger from his voice.

"You know him?"

"We've never met, but I've been briefed. Lester Brown has only one client, and it isn't you."

Bliss turned away without replying.

Shepard opened his mouth to pursue the matter, then decided against it. Discovering why the personal attorney to the area's Mafia kingpin bailed Bliss out could wait.

"All right, Mr. Bliss. You understand, if I find out you haven't been released on bail, but actually escaped, I'll be forced to shoot you."

Bliss chuckled. "I like you, Chief. I don't like you stealing my idea, but I do admire the audacity it takes to consider killing me to cover your tracks." He studied the ladder at his feet. "It doesn't work though, does it?"

Shepard shook his head. "Not even close. Even if Charlie rehearsed it a dozen times, he would've left traces in the morning dew. And it took almost fifteen minutes for him to crawl along the ladder. Webb testified the other three arrived at the bunker in less than five."

Shepard saw Lorch smirk out of the corner of his eye, then turned to Bliss. "How did you know we'd found a ladder?"

"I didn't, but it seemed like something too big to carry away. Where was it?"

"In the water. A few yards offshore," Shepard answered him. "But we've just proved the ladder wasn't used to commit the crime."

Bliss nodded. "Beyond a shadow of a doubt. I couldn't miss someone creeping along a ladder or any other makeshift bridge."

"Good," Shepard said. "Then the ladder has nothing to do with the case."

Bliss looked startled. "Did I say that? Surely you don't think its being there is coincidence? Clues like that don't turn up lying around a murder scene like red herrings from an old mystery story and smelling just as bad." He turned, and headed for the cliff.

"Bliss! Where are you going?" Shepard demanded.

"Home." Bliss indicated the sweep of Carmel Bay to the south. "It's shorter this way."

Shepard watched Bliss climb down until he disappeared from sight, then turned to his officers. "Charlie, take the ladder back to the property room. And locate Cowles. Last time I looked Bliss was in his custody."

Suddenly Bliss' head popped into view above the edge of the cliff. "Was Wagner's foursome the first to tee off every Wednesday morning?"

"Why?" MacGregor snapped at him.

"I remember Webb saying they always teed off at six, but I don't recall if they were the first."

"Were they?" Shepard echoed, interested in spite of himself.

"Yes," MacGregor replied through clenched teeth.

"Had to be, didn't they? The ladder could have been put there earlier. That would cut the time down some."

"Not enough," Shepard snapped.

"No," Bliss agreed. "And if it had been there, I would have painted it."

"So the ladder wasn't used to cross the grass," Shepard persisted.

"I know, Chief." Bliss vanished from view again.

"Revere—" Shepard began. He got no further.

Bliss' head sprang back up again. "Who takes care of the equipment on the course?" he asked. "The ball washers, and flags, and those round things that mark the tees."

"The groundskeepers," MacGregor answered, barely able to get the words out.

"The same ones who cut the grass?" Bliss went on, apparently oblivious to MacGregor's growing rage.

"Of course!" MacGregor yelled.

Bliss nodded, as if this confirmed yet another opinion, and dropped from sight. Shepard waited this time. Sure enough Bliss' head emerged once more.

"I must have seen something, you know," he remarked, his brow wrinkling. "Up there on that hill."

"It would sure help if you could remember what it was," Shepard pointed out.

Bliss shook his head. "Doesn't matter. My painting will remember for me."

Shepard watched the man scuttle bug-like down the rocks, then turn to look back up at him.

"You're right, Chief. Armando Cosentino did post my bail."

"Why would he want to do that, Mr. Bliss?"

"He asked me to find out who killed Alex Wagner."

Shepard watched Bliss climb all the way to the gravel beach below, hoping he would fall. But he didn't.

CHAPTER TEN

The unseasonably hot weather pasted Shepard's uniform to his skin. The air conditioner in the department's Ford Tempo had decided to take a vacation, and even at four o'clock in the afternoon he felt like a grilled trout.

He left the brown, anonymous sedan in front of a small red building on North Main Street in Salinas, tugging the sticky cloth from his thighs, and noticed a green van parked directly across the street. On its side were the words: SEA ORCHARD FISH COMPANY. Sun glancing off the van's tinted windshield made it impossible to see the occupant or occupants, if there were any.

He walked through the low gate, crossed a neatly trimmed yard, and entered the bright red building, its cheery cherry color courtesy of the place's former identity. It once housed a pre-school. When two years before the county finally approved sufficient money to staff a Medical Examiner's office, they neglected to provide enough for a building to house it.

Then the pre-school went under, and the elderly woman who owned the land, died. In a fit of civic philanthropy she willed the place to the county. So the building, with its walls painted in eye-popping primary colors, and its doors bedecked with decals of furry animals and dinosaurs, became the next-to-last resting place for victims of violent and suspicious death. Traces of stegosaurus still remained behind

Catherine Gonzales' name on her office door. Shepard knocked and went inside.

He found Catherine at her desk, entering something in a desktop computer; her black hair pulled back, its ponytail bobbing slightly while she touch-typed. She wore a summery beige cotton dress that made her look cool and relaxed. Shepard became more aware of the wrinkles and patches of perspiration on his usually spotless uniform. She hit the enter key and looked up, surprise crossing her features.

"Chief Shepard?"

"I got a message you'd called," Shepard said. "I was out at the golf course."

"Well, yes, I did," she acknowledged, giving him a puzzled frown.

"Sorry I don't have much time. I'm on the way to the airport to meet Wagner's brother."

"Have a seat. I didn't know he had any family."

"His ex-wife gave us the name." He eased into a comfortable chair in front of the desk. "I had somebody run through Wagner's address book, and we came up with a Bruce Wagner in Seattle. He's flying in to take care of the funeral arrangements and so on. What did you find?"

She gave him another look he couldn't interpret, as if she didn't expect him to ask the question and dragged a file towards her. While she hunted for the report, Shepard looked around the room. Decals of fluffy animals trooped across the window in the wall directly behind her desk

"Didn't the county have enough money to re-decorate this place?"

She laughed. "Are you kidding? We're lucky we're not sitting in toddler-sized chairs and dissecting on a foot high table. Here we go. What do you want to know first?"

He caught another perplexed look cast in his direction and tried to figure out what bothered her. "Time of death?"

She consulted her notes. "Your report said he entered the sand trap around six-fifty? That's square in the center of the ballpark. Not enough remained of the stomach or its contents for analysis."

"Damn." Shepard shook his head.

"There are some other indicators that help us," she assured him.

"It's not that. There was some white stuff on the seventh green Bliss couldn't identify. He thought it might have been food brought there by one of the golfers. A dirty plate in his house had remains of scrambled eggs on it, but confirmation would have helped."

"Un-cooked egg whites?" Catherine wondered aloud.

He shrugged. "I'm not even sure it's important, but Bliss seemed to think it was."

She looked startled. "Are you and the peninsula's most notorious artist working together on the case?"

"No, of course not! I'm just considering every possibility."

"I'd love to see this guy in action. His advance press is fascinating." She smiled.

"Believe me, Bliss in the flesh is not an experience I'd wish on anyone lightly. It's something you need to work up to over time."

He tried to move the conversation beyond Bliss. "Okay, the stomach's out. What else do you have?"

Again Catherine checked her notes. "Here's the rundown: Dead male Caucasian. Blue eyes, brown hair. Five feet ten inches tall, hundred and sixty pounds. Forty-four years of age. General health good, although he wouldn't win any physical fitness awards. Dead before he entered the water. Rigor hadn't passed off entirely. Lividity patterns were well established."

"Is it Wagner?"

"I'd say yes. Besides the physical description we got O positive blood. Fingerprints match those your team took from the house. Fillings don't quite line up. Two pre-molars on the right side aren't in the x-rays his dentist sent over. But they were new. Maybe he got them someplace else."

"Time of death. You said six-fifty's in the ballpark. How big is the ballpark?"

"On a witness stand I'd have to hedge three or four hours either way."

"That's a lot." Shepard attempted to pinch the crease back into the right leg of his trousers.

"Is it a problem?"

"It's not the biggest one."

"Yeah," she nodded sympathetically. "The vanishing act. Any ideas?"

"None that don't sound like science fiction. Anything else?"

"Plenty. We're up to our eyeballs in physical evidence, but nothing indicates he'd recently been aboard a flying saucer."

Shepard managed a rueful smile. "Somebody actually wrote a letter to the *Pine Cone* editor suggesting something like that. Sea monsters in Carmel Bay was another thought."

"Well, no giant teeth marks turned up, but we found quite a lot of sand in the clothing," she told him. "I've asked for samples from the trap, the beach beneath the cliff, the nearby sea bottom, and the bottom off Moss Landing where the body was discovered. We're also checking for fibers that don't belong and so on. Nothing yet."

"I'm not surprised, considering the beating the body took."

"Pooling of blood indicates he'd lain on his right side for some time after he died. Here's one I can't track: both of his legs were broken post mortem."

Shepard considered the possibilities. "So maybe he was murdered, then his body was somehow thrown from the cliff?"

Catherine shook her head. "Bodies don't usually fall feet first, Chief. The weight distribution's all wrong."

"It would be," Shepard sighed, rubbing his hand over his close-cut hair. "Why should any of the answers be easy?"

She hesitated, her round cheeks dimpling unhappily. "I'm afraid it gets worse."

"I can't wait to hear this," Shepard said.

She took a deep breath, and plunged in. "There's something wrong with the murder weapon."

Shepard stared at her, unable to keep the dismay from his face.

She nodded. "It matches the wounds. The blood type is identical, but…Oh, you're going to say I'm imagining things!"

"Go on," he replied.

"The wounds were too clean."

"He'd been submerged—"

"I know all that," she answered with an impatient nod. "But the report says he made this miracle chip shot from the sand trap or something, right? There was sand on the club! If somebody borrowed it from him right after he made the shot, then clobbered him with it, granules of sand would have been driven deep into the brain tissue. I don't care what happened to him after he hit the water, some sand would have remained embedded!"

Shepard thought for a long while before replying. "There was blood on the ball."

"I know!" Catherine agreed, her expression miserable. "So what did the killer do? Bean Wagner, then make his shot for him?!"

"Why not?" Shepard groaned. "Nothing else the killer did makes sense. Why not that, too?"

"Chief—"

"Dan, please. If you're going to torture me like this, we should be on a first name basis, don't you think?"

Her expression brightened for a moment. "Fair enough, Dan." Then the puzzled look stole over her face once more. "Can I ask a question?"

He nodded. "I owe you at least one."

"Why did you put yourself through this? Why didn't you just wait for your detective's report?"

Shepard frowned in bewilderment. "My detective?"

"The one you sent over half an hour ago? Detective Lautrec? I told him everything I just told you."

Shepard jumped to his feet, almost knocking over the chair.

"Detective Lautrec!" he exclaimed.

"Guess he's not one of your more popular officers."

"He's not one of my officers at all!" A horrible suspicion grew within him like a tumor. Anger followed swiftly behind. "Did you check his I.D.?"

"He knew you. He knew the case," she replied.

"He would," Shepard said.

Catherine turned to look at him. "Who would?"

"Toulouse-Lautrec? Famous short person?"

She blinked. "But he's an artist—" She stopped dead as the truth hit her. "Oh you don't mean…Bliss? Impersonating a police officer?!"

"Impersonating a human being," Shepard amended. "What's one more crime to a man whose file's long enough for its own cabinet? Toulouse-Lautrec!" he raged. "When I get my hands on him, he'll have to stand on tiptoes to reach the john!"

Catherine rose, grim determination hardening her usually cheerful features. She only stood five feet two, but at that moment she looked as if she could wrestle any dinosaur in the place into submission. "That could be easier than you think. He asked to examine the body. Maybe he's still back there!"

She swept out of the room, jaw set in determination, Shepard on her heels. They headed down a short bright yellow corridor that smelled vaguely of chemicals to a door at the far end. Catherine slammed it open hard enough to bang it against the wall. Shepard followed her through, matching her stride for stride.

They marched into a comfortable viewing area in subdued grays and blacks, a striking contrast to the pre-school jollity in the offices. The room allowed the relations of victims to see the remains of their loved ones on a closed circuit TV. It added an often-necessary distance to the grisly procedure.

Stretched out on a sofa, Bliss stared at the acoustic tiled ceiling, as if he were counting the holes. The suit he wore looked at least thirty years out of date, the tie black and narrow and stained with something yellow. He'd made a futile effort to comb his hair, but the attempt failed so utterly the comb might still be stuck in there somewhere and nobody would ever know.

"On your feet, Mr. Bliss. You're under arrest. Again. You have the right to remain silent. I really wish you'd exercise that right." As he continued reciting the Miranda warning, Shepard glanced at his watch. Wagner's brother would be landing in less than half an hour.

Bliss folded himself forward, pivoted, planted his large shoes solidly on the carpeting, and pushed himself to his feet with a grunt.

Catherine strode over until she stood face to chest with him, and glared into his eyes. "How dare you?!"

"It was easy!" he growled back down at her. "I'll be out on bail before sunset."

Catherine glanced at Shepard. He gave her a frustrated nod. "Mr. Bliss has friends in low places."

Bliss turned on Shepard, a savage look in his eyes.

"Cosentino is not my friend. If the ground opened up and swallowed him, I'd sow the earth with salt. But he is useful. I will use him."

Shepard took Bliss' arm. "Great. You do that. In the meantime you're coming with me. The Carmel Jail Choir needs its conductor." He glanced at Catherine. "Did he live up to his advance press?"

"He's worse." She glowered at Bliss, her hands planted on her hips. "I'll keep working on the weapon."

"Thanks." He gave her a grateful smile.

"Yeah." Bliss nodded. "Those wounds should not have been clean."

Shepard guided Bliss firmly out the door.

*   *   *

Shepard steered his car on to Highway Sixty-eight, heading west back towards the peninsula. He glanced casually in the rearview mirror, then looked again. Was that the same green van he'd seen parked outside the M.E.'s office, now a couple of cars back?

Bliss sat on the seat next to Shepard, twisting his wrists inside his manacles. Even with the windows open both men were working up a sweat.

"No air conditioning?" Bliss whined.

"Not today."

"Carmel can't afford a car for their Chief of Police that works?" he went on.

Shepard sighed. "The siren works."

"You didn't have to handcuff me," the artist grumbled.

"I wish I was allowed to gag you," Shepard answered, clutching the steering wheel, his eyes returning to the road ahead. They passed Laguna Seca, a huge raceway hidden on the other side of sprawling brown hills, host to prestigious Formula One and motorcycle events.

"I meant what I said," Bliss went on. "About Cosentino. He's a necessary evil."

"I agree he's evil. Necessary, no. One of my main priorities will be to squash his sleazy little operation once and for all."

Bliss snorted. "Sleazy? You'll get no argument from me there. But little? The man has his tentacles into the fishing industry, food services, land, tourism, not to mention the old standbys like drugs and prostitution."

"What's his interest in Alex Wagner's murder?"

"He didn't say. He just wants it solved as soon as possible."

"He really thinks letting you loose to trample on my investigation is going to do that?" Shepard asked. He turned his head, flashing the artist a look of disbelief.

Bliss squirmed in the seat. "Well, he knows I sometimes helped…in the past…"

"Helped who?"

"People…Burt Grimaldi's son…" He forced the words out. "The Seaside police arrested him for car theft. I proved he was innocent."

Shepard sensed Bliss felt a huge embarrassment admitting this, and this newly revealed side of Bliss' character again baffled him. The man acted arrogant and boastful when discussing his abominable art, but when forced to reveal he'd actually achieved some good, he could barely bring himself to do it.

"Why didn't you tell me that before?"

Bliss shrugged. "It wasn't anything much. One of Bobby's classmates set him up. They were in love with the same girl."

"How did you figure it out?"

"I saw a photograph of the three of them with some of their friends."

"And?"

"And nothing," Bliss concluded. "It was all there in the picture for anyone to see. In the eyes."

"And there were other times you…helped…people?"

"A few," came the grudging reply.

They were nearing the turnoff to the airport. A plane roared past overhead, coming in for a landing. Shepard had a decision to make. What was he going to do with Bliss?

He made it, sighed. "I'm going to hate myself in the morning." He yanked at the wheel. The brown Ford turned left on to Olmstead Road and crested the hill above the airport. A moment later he parked in a No Waiting Zone near a rotund fountain of conglomerate and steel. He removed Bliss' cuffs in the car, and they got out.

"Thank you," Bliss said, rubbing his wrists.

"It'll save explanations," Shepard answered, casually glancing behind them. A green van pulled to a stop in front of the United Airlines section of the terminal. Shepard couldn't see from this angle if the words SEA ORCHARD FISH COMPANY were lettered on the side.

He walked into the terminal, Bliss at his heels.

"Who am I?" Bliss inquired with the air of a Greek philosopher. "Why am I here?"

Shepard scowled. "We'll let Bruce Wagner think you're a detective."

"I love you for that, Chief." Bliss' smile grew soft and puckered like a baby's bottom.

They'd missed the scheduled arrival time of Bruce Wagner's plane by ten minutes. A turbo-prop out on the tarmac disgorged the last of its passengers. Receiving confirmation from a ticket agent that the plane was indeed the connecting flight out of San Francisco, Shepard steered Bliss toward the center of the terminal.

They passed through the automatic glass doors, and out to a baggage area that stood open to the runway beyond a low wall. The newly disembarked passengers descended like flies on dead meat to snatch luggage from the single long, sloping counter. The sound of an airplane revving its engines a few yards away made conversation difficult.

"How will we find him?" Bliss hollered.

"Hopefully," Shepard shouted back, "he'll find us."

The last of the passengers from the flight trickled in, and both men understood simultaneously that recognizing Alex Wagner's brother would not be difficult at all.

A man entered the baggage area, grasping a tennis racket in one hand, a carry-on bag draped over his shoulder. He had blue eyes, and brown hair; stood five feet ten inches tall; weighed about a hundred and sixty pounds. Forty-four years of age. General health good, Shepard guessed, although he might not win any physical fitness awards. They were looking at Alex Wagner's face on Alex Wagner's body. The brothers were twins.

CHAPTER ELEVEN

"So where can I get a good game of tennis around here?" Bruce Wagner asked, gazing out the Tempo's window.

Shepard glanced at the man sitting beside him. The heat of the car did not seem to affect Wagner. In the back seat sweat streamed down Bliss' face. At that moment Shepard felt a kinship with the painter that surprised him.

For the second time that afternoon the unmarked car headed west on Highway Sixty-Eight. Now the sun sank directly in front of them, its glare turning the dirt and the corpses of bugs smeared by windshield wipers into a splotchy curtain almost impossible to see through.

After picking Wagner up at the airport, they had returned to the Medical Examiner's office to view his brother's body. So little remained of the features Wagner couldn't make a positive identification, but he remarked offhandedly that the remnants of clothes reflected his brother's garish tastes in golfing attire.

Now here they were, moments after seeing the mutilated cadaver of his only living relative, and Wagner's biggest concern seemed to be tennis. Shepard reflected you'd have to dive deep into the marine canyon that lay at the mouth of Monterey Bay to find a colder fish than this. He looked in the rearview mirror, and saw Bliss eyeing the back of Wagner's neck the way somebody might regard a patch of fungus he'd just discovered between his toes.

"There are plenty of public courts around," Shepard began.

Wagner shook his head. "I want players, not a bunch of retirees who can barely swing a racket."

"Since Mr. Wagner's period of mourning appears to have come to an end, maybe he'd be kind enough to tell us something about his brother," Bliss snarled from the back seat.

Wagner swiveled around to glare at Bliss. "Who did you say you were?"

"The name's Lautrec," Bliss answered in a passable imitation of Jack Webb. "Detective Lautrec. Homicide."

Shepard winced. Bliss had leaped into the role of police officer with both of his convincingly large, flat feet. Shepard still had no idea how he would face Catherine the next time he saw her. She'd met them on their return with a look of anger and incomprehension.

Shepard realized he'd come to some kind of turning point in his relationship with Herman de Portola Bliss. The man was an atrocious painter, and by most accounts a not much better human being; an unrepentant felon. Yet despite all that, he knew they were somehow no longer adversaries.

How could Shepard explain to Catherine that he felt he had come to understand Bliss a little better, at least enough to suspect the man might be a genuine asset to the investigation? He couldn't. So he didn't.

Now the hole Shepard had dug for himself yawned open like the pit of hell. Detective Lautrec had taken it upon himself to grill the witness.

"I gather you weren't close."

"So?"

Bliss yawned. "I thought most twins enjoyed an especially close relationship."

"Not us. It's no secret we never had much use for one another in recent years."

"Who was born first?" Bliss inquired. "You or Alexander?"

"Alex," Wagner replied. "By about twenty minutes. That's why his name begins with an A, and mine a B. Our parents were very methodical."

"You have a younger sister named Clarabelle, maybe?" Bliss snorted.

Shepard felt Wagner tense next to him.

"There were only the two of us."

"Your brother arranged the food in his freezer in alphabetical order," Bliss observed. "Guess he was sort of methodical, too."

Wagner gave a humorless laugh. "Yeah, Alex led a very orderly life. He would not have approved of his death."

"Nothing wrong with order," Shepard put in, with a look at Bliss in the back seat. The painter stuck his tongue out at him. Shepard hadn't caught the alphabetical food, but he had noticed the closets with their clothes organized in precise rainbows.

"Did you and your brother see much of each other?" Shepard asked, going with the thread Bliss had started tugging.

"No, we had very little contact. Last time was our mother's funeral."

"Got in a couple sets of doubles after the internment though, I'll bet," Bliss remarked.

Wagner turned on Shepard. "Where did you find this guy?"

"He found me," Shepard answered. "When did your mother die?"

"Six years ago."

"In Seattle?"

Wagner nodded. "Our family's originally from the Pacific Northwest. Our father died when we were young."

"What is it you do for a living, Mr. Wagner?" Shepard asked.

"I'm a doctor."

"Veterinarian?" Bliss inquired with exaggerated interest.

"OB-GYN."

In the mirror Shepard saw Bliss recoil and could understand why. He sympathized with the women who looked down and found Bruce Wagner between their legs.

"Dr. Wagner, there were some anomalies in your brother's dental records." Shepard told him.

Wagner smirked. "His teeth weren't in alphabetical order?"

"There were two fillings his regular dentist knew nothing about."

"I'm not sure what you're asking me." Wagner's smirk turned down at the edges. "Are you suggesting Alex had his teeth filled illegally?"

"As a physician you might be aware dental records are one of the primary means we have of determining identity when other physical characteristics have been…damaged…"

Wagner gave an elaborate shrug. "I don't know anything about Alex's teeth. I told you I haven't seen him in six years."

"You wouldn't mind giving me the name of your dentist, would you, Dr. Wagner?"

Shepard could feel Wagner's eyes boring into the side of his face and caught a crooked smile of approval from Bliss in the mirror.

"I don't allow my teeth to be x-rayed," Wagner replied. "Somehow the thought of a cavity going un-noticed is nowhere near as frightening to me as gum cancer from being over-radiated."

Shepard persisted. "Your dentist will have charts."

"You think I might be Alex in disguise? Having murdered my poor unsuspecting brother I now return to take his place as the rightful heir to the family fortune?" Wagner asked.

"What fortune?" Bliss responded.

"There isn't any." The chill in Wagner's voice lowered the temperature of the car's stifling interior by several degrees.

"The name of your dentist, Dr. Wagner? Is there any reason not to tell me?"

"Larrimer. Doctor Donald Larrimer was the last dentist who treated me, but it's been a couple of years."

"For methodical men, you and your brother sure didn't care much about the health of your mouths," Bliss remarked.

"I gave you his name," Wagner growled over his shoulder at Bliss. "If I hesitated, it's only because I don't like my private life pried into. Now about that tennis game. I don't suppose either of you belong to a racquet club?"

"Sorry," Shepard said. Something in the mirror distracted him.

"I might be able to fix you up with a game," Bliss replied. "I know a couple pros at local clubs."

Shepard only half-heard the brief discussion that followed: Wagner asking questions; Bliss all at once replying with the equanimity of a travel agent dealing with a preferred client. Shepard's eyes strayed again to the mirror, past Bliss and out the rear window.

The green van kept pace with the car about fifty yards back, never closing, never falling farther behind. Shepard couldn't be sure it was the same one he thought he'd been seeing all afternoon. He couldn't be sure the vague tickling he felt at the top of his spine wasn't simply paranoia, but his cop's instinct told him the same van followed him, and its presence back there was no coincidence.

They dropped Wagner at the Seawind, a sprawling convention hotel near the wharf in Monterey. Shepard paid little attention while Bliss made some final promises about a tennis match now scheduled for the next morning. Instead, he covertly scanned the open area in front of the hotel. If the green van lurked out there in the traffic along Del Monte Avenue, or in the darkness of the nearby parking structure, he didn't see it. He couldn't tell if its absence made him feel relieved or uneasier.

The green van was nowhere in sight when the Ford at last turned on to Carpenter Avenue and headed for the Carmel police station. Bliss refused a ride to his home, preferring, he said, to walk.

As they pulled down into the small parking area behind the station, Shepard told Bliss he'd like to have another look at the seascape the painter had been working on Wednesday. Bliss' entire body swelled at the interest in his work and suggested late the next morning. He couldn't make it earlier because he had a tennis match with Bruce Wagner.

Shepard stared at him. "*You* are going to play him?"

Bliss shrugged. "Golf is not my game. I never said I couldn't play tennis. You can tell a lot about a man when you face him across a net. If he can't work himself up over the death of his brother, maybe a few lobs and drop shots will get through to him."

Shepard closed his eyes. It was one thing to discuss the peculiarities of the case with the painter, but the thought of him out there again, investigating on his own, made a muscle over Shepard's right eye begin to spasm rhythmically.

"Where do you plan to play?" he asked, trying to think of some way to prevent the match.

"Carmel Rancho Racquet Club. Out in the valley."

"But you can't go out there as Detective Lautrec!" Shepard insisted.

Bliss thought about it. "Deputize me, or something."

"No! We've already booked you for breaking and entering! Today you impersonated a police officer!"

Now Bliss flashed him a big, toothy smile. "But you aided and abetted, didn't you?"

"I never told Wagner you were Detective Lautrec!"

"You never told him I wasn't!" Bliss climbed from the Tempo. "I won't mention names. We'll play on a back court. No one will see us."

Shepard slid out on his side and faced the artist across the roof of the car. "Look, Bliss, I gave you a little leeway. Don't make me regret it."

"Why did you?" Bliss leaned forward across the roof.

Shepard took a deep breath. "Because you do seem to have a talent...for observation...and frankly because every time I learn something new about this case, it only grows more baffling, but you...you keep acting like it all makes some kind of sense!"

"Ah!" Bliss said, soaking in the words like a contented sponge.

Shepard wanted to yell at him right then, but knew he wouldn't. The realization confounded him. He wondered if he somehow were becoming used to Bliss. Could such a thing be possible?

"You've been honest with me, Chief," Bliss replied after a moment's thought. "I'll be honest with you. There are one or two aspects of the problem that suggest certain possibilities to me, nothing more."

"Oh, don't start in like Sherlock Holmes humoring Watson!" Shepard groaned. "If you have something, tell me!"

"But I don't!" Bliss insisted. "A few vague ideas as to how it was done, but not why, or by whom…"

Bliss straightened, brushing grime from the car's roof off his hands and turned away. He only took two steps before he pivoted. "What if Bruce Wagner ended up floating in the bay instead of Alex?"

"We won't let the possibility slide. With fingerprinting and DNA sampling we'll know for sure. Even with twins."

Bliss nodded, started off again, but Shepard didn't move. Sure enough, Bliss stopped and turned again. "Did Officer Cowles mention the name Jason Kiley to you?"

"Kiley…" Shepard searched his memory. "Some guy at the demonstration down at Holly's project?"

Bliss nodded. "He's a part-time gardener, full-time activist. He bragged his group had something to do with Wagner's death."

"What *is* his group exactly?"

"Its concerns are environmental."

"You seem to have similar concerns," Shepard pointed out.

"Of course, but there's something about Kiley I don't like. He's too smooth…something…" Bliss gave his head an irritated shake.

"He claimed they should kill people to save the earth?"

"He didn't go that far, but the threat was implicit," Bliss asserted.

"Jason Kiley. Okay, I'll check him out." Shepard nodded.

"Then there's Wagner's ex-wife, what was her name? Minerva?"

"Genevra. Carroll."

"Have you spoken with her?" Bliss asked.

"Yes. She hasn't seen Wagner since their divorce became final last year."

"I assume she has an alibi," Bliss mused.

"Yes. We've confirmed Wednesday morning she was on a Santa Cruz golf course from six AM until after nine with three other women. Golf appears to be the only thing she and her husband had in common."

"No wonder they got divorced." The artist started up toward the street. Still Shepard didn't move. At the top of the small incline leading from the street down into the parking lot, Bliss turned yet again and looked back down at Shepard.

"Hasn't it occurred to you that everyone connected with Alex Wagner appears to have an alibi? Holly, Romaine and Webb were in plain view of each other and me, although they didn't know that. His brother was way off in Seattle. His ex-wife played golf. I wouldn't be a bit surprised if anybody else your investigation turns up also has a water-tight alibi."

"Like Margaret Dennis?" Shepard interjected.

Pain flashed in Bliss' eyes for a brief moment, then vanished as fast as it had appeared. He scuffed his feet on the blacktop like a shy little boy. "Maggie didn't kill him. Did you talk to her?"

"She's next on my list."

Bliss nodded. "Give her my best."

He trudged up to the street without another word, and turned the corner of the building.

Shepard rubbed his hand over his short hair, feeling the bristles tickle his palm, suddenly conscious of the fact that in his sweaty, rumpled uniform he even began to look like Bliss. Just as he turned to enter the station he caught a flash of green out of the corner of his eye. He whirled, trotted up the short drive to the sidewalk in time to see the Sea Orchard Fish Company van turn on to Junipero.

Out on the street he spotted Bliss lumbering south along the opposite sidewalk, already most of the way down the block. The van headed in the same direction, un-hurried. The deep-throated rumble of its engine spoke of power held tightly in check. Shepard remembered it had been already waiting when he first arrived at the M.E.'s office that afternoon. Shepard realized that he didn't interest the Sea Orchard Fish Company. They were trolling for Bliss.

CHAPTER TWELVE

Shepard snared Charlie Revere inside the station and set him to running down what he could find on the Sea Orchard Fish Company, then detailed two other officers to keep an eye on Bliss throughout the night. If the van loitered, they were to notify Shepard immediately.

He walked home. After a microwaved frozen pizza and a can of diet Pepsi, he showered and changed into civilian clothes: a gray sport coat, slacks, and a pale blue shirt.

The lingering sun still brushed the tops of the tallest pines with gold, but the air cooled rapidly, washed by a persistent breeze off the Pacific. The tireless surf clapped against the beach. Wood smoke scented the air.

It was the time of day Shepard liked best in Carmel. The last of the afternoon shoppers had fled up Ocean Avenue, and the dinner and drinks crowd were still in their nests, preening. The town lay quiet around him, almost dozing, as he strolled southwest toward the final blue-green streaks of the sunset.

Shepard found Maggie Dennis' house on Scenic Avenue between Eleventh and Twelfth. It rested on some of the most expensive real estate in the world, proof that some gallery owners did quite well in Carmel. Only a few feet of road and a crushed-granite walking path separated it from the beach.

Shepard saw a couple of fires in pits out on the sand, shadows of people moving about them, silhouetted against the sea. The water glowed with an icy blue iridescence now that the sun had slipped all the way down. Laughter drifted up to him, and with it the tinny throb of an old Motown favorite he used to dance and court to back in Ohio a lifetime ago.

"Stop! In the name of love! Before you break my heart…Think it O-Over…Think it O-Over…"

Shepard stopped outside the gate of a white picket fence. White shingles covered the exterior walls of the cottage set with windows trimmed in a dark color that looked navy blue or black in the failing light. Two bedrooms, Shepard guessed. Probably would fetch close to a million and a half.

Maggie Dennis, her hair pulled back in a scarf, wore jeans and a plaid flannel shirt similar to the ones Bliss favored. She knelt on a stone path leading to the front door where simple black letters on a white sign announced the small house's name: "Earthly Delight."

Her garden filled nearly every corner of the tiny lot, as had Wagner's, but there the similarity ended. Whereas the attorney had laid his out in precise groupings, each flower distinctly demarcated from the next like one of those colorful children's maps of the world, Maggie's garden erupted in an orgy of color: a luxuriant, lustily intertwined mass of roses, camellias, carnations, bougainvillea; the list went on and on. Near where she knelt, the stone path diverged, a short arm extended to a small open space where a narrow white table and two thin chairs sat on a small, circular island of stone, surrounded by the sea of color.

Shepard watched her dig into the dark earth with gloved hands, slaughtering weeds with practiced yanks, her concentration intense. Perspiration beaded on her forehead despite the evening chill.

"Ms. Dennis?" Shepard said.

She looked up at him, squinting at his silhouette.

"Dan Shepard," he told her.

She stood in one long graceful motion and wiped at her brow, leaving a faint smear of dirt behind. The difference between this woman and the one he'd met in her gallery only the day before staggered him. It was as if the cold chrysalis of Margaret had broken open to reveal the sleek, winged form of Maggie within. Bliss' Maggie, Shepard had no doubt.

"Chief Shepard." She acknowledged him with a slight nod, stripping off her gloves. "Taking a walk?"

"Actually, I came by to see you."

"Really? Then come in, by all means."

"I'm afraid this is sort of official," he warned as he passed through the gate.

"Dear me," she said, without a trace of concern. She gestured at the table and chairs. "Shall we sit out here?"

"If you won't feel cold," he said.

"I'll be fine."

They sat in the chairs, facing west. Shepard saw her give a quick glance at her watch and frown.

"How can I help you?" she asked him.

"I'm investigating the death of Alex Wagner. Did you know him?"

She gave a long, drawn out sigh. "In time everyone comes to know everyone else in this town."

"How well did you know him?"

She flashed him an amused smile. "I expect you found my photograph at his house, so there's no sense in being coy."

"You were involved."

"Involved…" She chuckled. "Hardly that. Alex was like a nasturtium. Do you know the flower?"

"Not intimately."

"Very nice to look at, but with a weak root system. Could be blown away with the slightest breeze. I don't usually spend much time on nasturtiums."

"Were you still seeing each other when he died?" Shepard asked.

"How tactfully you insist on putting things, Chief. We were lovers about a year ago. For a few short, boring weeks."

"I'm afraid this question won't be quite as tactful. Was this around the time of his divorce?"

Maggie laughed out loud this time. Shepard realized that she was becoming more relaxed as the questions got more intimate.

"Yes, I'm afraid it was. We began it shortly before the divorce and ended it shortly after. I suspect the clandestine nature of our first intertwinings was what attracted me. His compulsiveness drove me up the wall. Then there were the mood swings. Something as disorderly as adultery must have been hard on such an orderly man, don't you think?"

"I guess. Tell me about the mood swings."

"Oh, one night he'd be terribly passionate, trying to rip my expensive lingerie to shreds. The next time we got together, he made love as if he were entering my figure in a calculator. I can't see how Genevra stood it as long as she did. They were married for almost six years for God's sake!"

"You knew his wife?" Shepard asked.

"I told you, Chief. Everyone knows everyone. We worked on committees together, charities, and so on."

"You have any idea why somebody might want to murder him?"

"Alex was a hustler, always working on some scheme or other. The law was just a tool to him, like a crowbar to pry money loose so he could get his hands on it. He used people the same way. He used my connections in the art world to meet potential investors. He used my body for the obligatory once a week hump and pump Genevra no longer provided him."

In spite of himself Shepard felt shocked by the woman's bluntness.

"Find his murderer, and you'll find someone he used. There was no room for love in the man, no room for warmth of any kind. He was encased as surely as the furniture in his house, protected from being used himself."

She stopped, the energy leaving her body in a rush. However much she wouldn't admit it to Shepard, he guessed Wagner had touched her more deeply than she would have liked. She couldn't forget it, or forgive it. Shepard wondered if she could kill a man as easily as she could threaten to burn Bliss' art, for he now had no doubt she would have done just that.

"How long have you known Herman Bliss?" he asked.

She groaned. "Oh, God. I knew sooner or later we'd get around to him. Is it important?"

"He does seem to be tangled up in the case," Shepard admitted.

"I'm not surprised. If Alex was a nasturtium, Herman Bliss is a vine. Major root system, back to the dawn of California, if he's to be believed. He clings. He slowly prods and pushes his way into the cracks of your life until there's no dislodging him. Did you know he's my landlord? At the gallery?"

"I knew he owns a lot of Carmel property."

"Oh, yes. At least the trust does."

"Trust?"

"The Bliss family estate. Don't ask me the ins and outs of it. The whole thing's a nightmare to try and unravel."

Shepard remained puzzled. "If he's your landlord, how can you refuse to show his pictures?"

"His paintings are awful! Anti-art! Anti-matter for all I know. If I hung one on my wall it would probably suck all the real art into it like a black hole."

"But can't he boot you out?"

She shook her head. "The bank administers the trust, sees to the leases and so on. As long as I pay my rent, and don't object to the exorbitant increases every two years, he can't do a thing about it." She cocked her head to one side, considering. "Although I don't think he'd kick me out, even if he could."

"Why?"

"His pride wouldn't allow it. He'd rather try to win me and the other galleries over with his art. I don't know how much of the Bliss fortune he can actually get his hands on, but he has never to my knowledge used it to leverage one of his atrocities on to the wall of a local gallery."

Shepard thought about that. Maybe the family had set up some sort of trust to keep Bliss from getting his hands on the money. That might explain why he wouldn't make bail. He couldn't. He might actually have very little personal income from the trust.

"Does anyone buy his work?" he asked her.

She shook her head again. "Not that I know of. You heard his great-grandfather was an artist? Never sold anything either that I'm aware of, but he did have enough cash to buy up the land around here. Herman's grandfather and father were hardheaded businessmen, much more interested in development and expanding the family's holdings than art on any level. Nobody thought Herman had artistic inclinations either. In high school he was more concerned with cars and tennis, and—"

"Tennis?" Shepard asked.

"—girls…" She finished, frowning at a memory. "Tennis? Best player Carmel High's ever produced. But after high school he got stranger and stranger. Disappeared for awhile, then turned up in Paris."

"As an artist?"

"No," she said, her eyes wide with a sort of wonder in them. "An art critic, and he was good! I've read some of his stuff! He had the eye. The gift. Not much diplomacy…I remember death threats…"

"Bliss can get on people's nerves alright," Shepard said with feeling.

She shook her head. "You misunderstand. It was Bliss who made the threats. In the critiques themselves. He threatened to kill a couple of the artists unless they stopped painting. He may have had a point, but the job didn't last long."

"What happened then?"

"The family intruded, tried to shoehorn him into the business. He was surpassingly odd by that point anyway, but…still somehow…interesting…"

She looked embarrassed, and Shepard realized she must be remembering those days when she posed for the photograph. Days of Bliss?

"After he'd been home awhile he went off to live in Big Sur with two Chinese girls. I'm not a racist, Chief, but they weren't Chinese-American. Or Taiwanese. They were from Mainland China. Red China! And this was the early sixties! McCarthy was hardly lukewarm in his grave. Bliss called them his models, but no one ever saw a painting of them, or if they did, nobody recognized the fact."

Night had descended while they sat there talking. Bird song quieted. By contrast the waves seemed all the louder.

Maggie was rising to her feet, gazing out at the road. He followed her eyes. A van pulled into one of the parking spaces by the walking path. The color was dark, but Shepard couldn't detect a Sea Orchard Fish Company sign on its side.

Its engine switched off, and then its lights. The driver's door opened. A tall man climbed out, dimly seen beneath one of the few streetlights. He crossed the road toward them, boots scraping on the road. Shepard judged him to be in his mid-twenties, handsome, his dark hair tied back in a ponytail longer than Catherine Gonzales'.

The young man hesitated outside the gate; looking from Maggie to Shepard, then back again. She waved him in with a tired-looking lift of her hand.

"Chief Shepard." Her voice sounded strained. "This is Jason Kiley. My gardener."

CHAPTER THIRTEEN

Wednesday morning the Carmel Valley hills were blue and green, already heated by an advancing sun. Shepard tried to concentrate on the phantom melody that refused to become a song while he drove out the valley road toward the Carmel Rancho Racquet Club. Working on his songs introduced a comforting level of order into his day. They existed in a world where rules of composition of tempo and meter were absolute. Directions were clear and everybody carried a road map. The unruliness of the Wagner case, how it shot off in new directions just when he thought he had it in his sights, drove him crazy.

He glanced at the Tempo's dashboard clock. Bliss' match with Bruce Wagner would be well under way by now. The melody lingered on the tip of his mind, taunting him, still untamed. Thoughts of the case kept intruding.

Before he headed out to the tennis club, Shepard had tracked down Charlie Revere in the tiny lounge at the back of the station. Crammed with vending machines, a couple formica-topped tables, and a clump of molded plastic chairs, the lounge also served as ready room, and general gathering place for on-duty officers.

"Any luck with the Sea Orchard Fish Company?" he asked the young, red-headed man.

Charlie nodded eagerly, fishing for his notepad. "Enough to know they've got something to hide." He found the place he wanted. "They've had offices out on the commercial wharf in Monterey since I was a kid. But the company was bought by something called Mutual Holdings two years ago."

"Who are they?"

"Mutual Holdings is a paper company. Right now I'm having a hard time attaching any human beings to it at all."

"So," Shepard nodded, "if you're having a hard time, somebody must not want to be attached."

"That's how I figure it!" Charlie grinned. "But I'm following the paper at the courthouse. This really nice clerk is helping me."

Shepard caught the glow in Charlie's eyes. The clerk sounded nice and female.

"Hopefully, by this afternoon I'll at least have a lead on the front man. She's gonna call me."

"Good work, Charlie." Shepard smiled. "Keep me informed."

"You bet!"

With that Shepard headed off to the tennis match. Now, turning the Ford into the narrow, winding road that led to the Carmel Rancho Racquet Club, he thought again of Maggie Dennis and her visitor, Jason Kiley, sometime gardener, full time opponent of the Cannery Row hotel project. Shepard maintained no illusions that Kiley showed up to help Maggie with her garden. You don't carefully clip your fingernails or apply a full ounce of Eau de Masculine to weed and prune. On the other hand, he observed wryly, plowing and the planting of seed could require such preparations.

Gardens. Shepard thought about the many gardens that blossomed in the case. First he had the garden-like formality of the Carmel Bay Country Club's landscaping. Where did they find the grass that felt as if you were walking on a thickly padded rug, springing back into place after you passed? Then he thought of the courtyard at Holly Development, like a painting by Rousseau, but with the bananas the right way up. Finally he compared Maggie's riot of blooms to Wagner's rigidly arranged garden. Shepard's sense of order *should* have drawn him closer to Wagner's compulsive design, but instead he found he liked Maggie's vision more.

Gardens…Orchards…Sea Orchard…His mind continued to free associate as he pulled into the parking lot of the racquet club. He got out and scanned the lot, but didn't spot the Sea Orchard van. He did find Greg Cowles parked in an unmarked car nearby. Shepard walked over to him.

Cowles glanced up, saw Shepard, and lowered the Sports Illustrated he'd been reading. "Hi, Chief," he said with a guilty smile. "What're you doing here?"

"I thought I'd come watch some tennis."

"No sign of the van," Cowles volunteered.

"Where are they?"

"Court seventeen." He gestured up the canyon. "You want me up there with them?"

"No, it's all right," Shepard decided. "Just keep your eyes open and out of the magazine."

"Right, Chief!" Cowles tossed the magazine aside. "No problem!"

Shepard headed in the direction the young officer indicated, following a dirt service road. Eighteen tennis courts and two swimming pools covered several acres tucked in the mouth of a wooded canyon. A lone hawk hunted overhead. A seasonal stream wound its way through the property, chuckling to itself. The regular thwock…thwock…of tennis balls ricocheting off racquets and courts and occasionally kneecaps filled the air.

Shepard found the gladiators sweating on a back court that butted up against a steep grassy hillside, out of view of the clubhouse. He stood in the shadows of the trees to watch. Wagner dressed like a pro on the circuit, his shirt in particular splashed with a fruit bowl of color in an incomprehensible design that Bliss might have been proud to paint. The cut of the clothes went a long way to disguise the not fully toned muscles and a small, but developing paunch. The racquet he used looked large-headed, unusually thick, and glinted like a weapon in the sunlight.

Bliss, on the other hand, might have stepped from the pages of a fifties' tennis magazine. Except his white shorts were a little too baggy, and the white shirt and sweater vest far too tight around a waist spreading like a chestnut tree to shade the ground beneath. If Bliss had first impressed Shepard as a middle-aged Pigpen, he now resembled one of Dr. Seuss' impossibly thin-legged, wild-haired, floppy-nosed creatures. To complete the picture of a tennis player from another era, Bliss carried a wooden racquet, minuscule in comparison to Wagner's high tech model.

It didn't take Shepard long, however, to realize that Bliss was winning. He lumbered and stumbled around the court like a man walking on stilts, but when he reached the ball, and somehow much of the time he did, he swung through it with authority. He didn't hit the ball hard. On the contrary every shot seemed playable. Yet the ball traveled according to its own physical laws, swooping suddenly, bouncing crazily to one side or the other. In the few moments Shepard watched, Bliss hit a series of demoralizing, improbable winners.

Shepard heard the sharp snap of a branch high up on the hillside past the court. At first he could see nothing but grass and brush, but then a flicker of movement near the top caught his eye. A dark shape huddled there…The sudden glint of sunlight on glass…

Shepard opened his mouth to shout a warning, but he was too late.

The first bullet struck Bliss somewhere in the left side, and spun him around. He staggered, dropped to his knees, then fell over on his face.

CHAPTER FOURTEEN

A second bullet smacked into the other side of the court. The two sharp cracks sent the hawk spiraling out of the canyon.

Shepard unsnapped his holster and yanked the six-inch Smith and Wesson .357 magnum from the leather. Shading his eyes with his other hand, he caught a blur of motion near the top of the ridge, heading toward the mouth of the canyon. He sprinted to the narrow path between the courts, then turned to glance at where the two men had been playing.

Wagner had hit the ground when the first shot struck Bliss. Now he eeled his way to the net, forced one side of it up, and dragged himself underneath. He reached Bliss in a couple of squirms and felt for a pulse.

"How is he?" Shepard yelled to the doctor.

"Breathing," came the terse reply. "I'll look after him."

Shepard took off again, legs pumping, heading for the hill. He didn't try to scale the rock and scrub, but ran along another path at its bottom, paralleling the assailant's probable direction.

The land began to flatten, densely packed with trees and bushes. Above him on the ridge Shepard heard a shout, a shot, then two more shots. He picked up his pace, looking for a break in the foliage that would allow him easier access to the hillside.

Ahead on his left a finger of land covered with brown scrub stuck out from the ridge. The path wound around it, disappearing on the other side. As he circled the obstruction he heard an engine crank over and roar into guttural life. Gears whined, and gravel pelted something hollow and metallic.

On the far side of the hill he found another dirt service road, ending at a maintenance shed of rusting corrugated metal. A cloud of dust blossomed up from the rutted road. The back of a van thudded over a tree limb and careened around a patch of live oaks. Shepard ran after it, feeling his ankles slip and twist in the ruts and potholes.

On the other side of the trees a wooden gate blocked the service road from the parking lot. Shepard arrived just in time to see Greg Cowles leap to one side as the van smashed through the gate, teetering dangerously on two wheels as it tried to make a sharp left turn. It righted itself with a shuddering jolt, and shot off along the road leading away from the club.

Cowles scrambled to his feet, waving his gun wildly. Shepard ran up to him, took hold of his officer's weapon and firmly lowered it.

"Get on the radio to Amy!" he barked at the young man. "Did you recognize the van?"

Cowles nodded, trying to catch his breath. "Sea Orchard…"

"Have her call County and the Highway Patrol! If they can get cars to the mouth of the valley, and the Laureles Grade we can bottle him in!"

Cowles nodded, started to run back to his car. Shepard grabbed his arm, swinging him around.

"And get an ambulance out here!"

Cowles moved off once more, Shepard right behind him. Shepard flung open the Ford's door, leaped inside, and thrust the key into the ignition. Slapping a bubble light on the roof, he switched on the light and the siren. Moments later the car blasted out of the parking lot past a growing crowd of baffled tennis players. The brown car slammed over a speed bump, rattling Shepard's teeth. On the radio he heard Amy relaying his instructions to set up roadblocks.

Carmel Valley Road wound along the Carmel River for miles in either direction. Its only exits lay at the mouth to the west where it connected with Highway One, up a wide, steep pass called the Laureles Grade that headed north over the mountains to Highway Sixty-Eight, or a tortuous route south and east that went on for miles and miles of gullies and switch backs. If you wanted to commit a crime, and needed a quick getaway, Carmel Valley was not the place to do it.

When he finally reached Carmel Valley Road, Shepard instantly assessed the situation. If the driver of the Sea Orchard van was local, he'd know the fastest way out lay west to Highway One. He would have a wider, straighter stretch of pavement for the entire run. If he cut down to Rio Road, and made it safely across the highway, he could choose from several routes north past the Mission and across Carmel. Shepard's men couldn't block them all. Shepard floored the accelerator and shot west on to the valley road.

The siren screamed. The bubble light flashed. Shepard picked up his radio microphone.

"Amy, this is Dan."

"Chief!" Amy's voice couldn't hide her excitement. "Two CHIP's were having lunch at Baker's Square! They'll set up a roadblock by the Union station!"

The restaurant and the Union Seventy-Six gas station were only seconds apart. The station stood at the first traffic signal out of the valley and the California Highway Patrol officers would beat the van there. Plenty of streets wound up into various canyons along the way, but they all dead-ended. If the van tried to make it all the way out, they had him.

The needle on his speedometer scratched past eighty. Traffic obediently hugged the shoulders of the road. Shepard's car rocketed past.

He almost missed it: a white Toyota Corolla a little way up a small road on the right leading north into one of the sub-divisions tucked into the hills between Monterey and Carmel Valley. The white car balanced on the edge of a drainage ditch, canted at a thirty-degree angle.

An elderly man and woman stood alongside, stooping over to examine it.

Shepard kicked at the brake pedal, pumping it, turning in the direction of the inevitable skid that occurs when an automobile, executing a high-speed turn, flaunts centrifugal force. The police car's speed dropped to forty by the time he took the corner, still more than fast enough to land him in the drainage ditch, but he tugged on the wheel, keeping the car in the center of the road. The Ford shimmied, fishtailed, and rattled to a halt a few yards past the wide-eyed couple.

Shepard switched off the light and siren. "Green van?" he asked, indicating the Toyota.

"You better believe it!" the old man shouted. "Ran us right off the road! Who needs fresh fish that bad?!"

"I'll call a tow!" Shepard yelled back, putting the Ford in gear again. He drove north into the hills. On the radio again he informed Amy of the van's new route.

"The Vista Colorado sub-division is shaped like a three-pronged fork, Chief," she reported. "Center prong's the longest, that's Steamboat Springs Road. Vail Way cuts off north about a mile in, and Aspen Way winds south not too far after that."

Shepard slowed as he neared the first intersection. "Amy, if he takes off on foot, which one gets him closest to Aguajito, or whatever road's on the other side of the hills?"

"Well, Steamboat Springs goes the farthest in, but it starts to curve south, too. I think Vail Way.

"Chief Shepard," a male voice cut in. "This is Lew Toback, California Highway Patrol. I'm with these folks and their Toyota at the bottom of Vista Colorado. Over."

"Thanks, Officer Toback. Hang tight in case he slips past me. Over."

"I'll send backup along as soon as they arrive. Ten-Four."

"Roger that," Shepard replied, and put the microphone on the seat beside him. As he did so, his hand found the .357 magnum. He tucked it slightly under his thigh, and took the left hand turn into Vail Way.

The houses looked twenty or thirty years old, surrounded by carefully tended landscaping and mature plantings. On the left side of the road, the land fell away sharply. On the right it rose, the road twining deeper and higher into the canyon. Unless the suspect found entry to one of the garages, there was no place for the green van to hide.

It wasn't hiding. Around a bend to the right, the road ended at a circle of pavement ringed by three homes hanging on the edge of the cliff. A fire road behind a steel gate meandered off into the brush and the beginnings of the Monterey pine forest. The green van, the words Sea Orchard Fish Company on its side, stood near the gate.

Shepard parked, and again lifted the microphone. "It's at the end of Vail Way."

"You want me up there, Chief? Over?" came the CHP officer's voice.

"Yeah," Shepard responded. "Thanks."

He switched off his engine, and sat there, staring at the van. Nothing moved. He looked around at the cluster of homes. No cars in the drives. There was no compelling need for the driver of the van to try and enter one of the houses, unless he lived there, which Shepard seriously doubted. They would have to be checked anyway.

A black-and-white purred to a stop behind him. Shepard bounded from his car, never taking his eyes from the van. He flicked off his magnum's safety, cocked back the hammer and kept its muzzle pointing straight up.

Toback came up alongside him, his weapon also out, and ready. The CHP officer stood shorter than Shepard, lean and wiry, his uniform crisp, shoes gleaming. Shepard approved. "Let's have a look."

The two men split up, approaching the back of the van from either side. Crickets chattered. From somewhere down the canyon a woman's laughter tinkled. They reached the van. Toback stationed himself beside the rear door.

Shepard slid along the dusty flank of the vehicle until he could look into the front. The inside was a mess, piled with fast food debris, but the bucket seats were empty, and what he could see of the rear looked unoccupied, too. He pulled open the driver's door, and the odor of ripe fish assaulted him. Leaning forward, he surveyed the interior. The rear of the van held a single wooden crate, shaped disturbingly like a small coffin two feet by two feet by four. The lid lay to one side. Shepard strained over the top of the driver's seat. The box was empty and smelled of fish.

He turned to look down at the detritus littering the front seats. Amidst smeared candy wrappers, greasy boxes containing Kentucky chicken bones, and paper cups of all sizes, were piles of used Kleenex tissues. There were two boxes of tissues on the floor of the passenger side, one of them still unopened. Next to that lay a small plastic bottle of cold capsules, and a nasal spray.

Shepard started to move back out, then stopped, and instead slid behind the wheel, noticing how his knees knocked up against the steering column. Finally he squirmed out again and stepped away from the van.

He eyed the fire road for a long moment. A gray cat strutted into view, tail high, master of all it surveyed. If someone crouched around the corner of the hill, it would have not walked past with such confidence. It traveled that stretch of the fire road alone.

He released the hammer, slipped the safety back on, and holstered his weapon. Toback joined him, doing the same.

"We're going to need help from Monterey," the CHP officer observed. "We'll get air support up here, but there's a lot of ground to cover."

"Too much," Shepard agreed.

"He knew the land, didn't he?" Toback went on. "He found himself a back door."

        *   *   *

Shepard parked in the lot outside the Monterey Peninsula Community Hospital. The modern, white building sat on a forested hillside high above the city, designed by its architect as a series of terraces, one jutting out from the next, conforming to the lay of the land.

The main reception area contained a pond filled with brightly colored carp and a fountain in its center. Various specialized wards sprouted in all directions from this central hub. Near a tiny snack bar an eager candy striper directed him toward the Emergency wing. There Shepard found Charlie Revere wearing a hole in the linoleum.

"What's the word, Charlie?" he asked.

"Doctor says the wound isn't serious. The bullet caught him high in the left shoulder, nicked the bone, then passed out laterally, gouging out a small chunk of his arm."

"Where's Wagner?"

Charlie indicated the corridor leading back toward the center of the building. "I didn't think it was such a good idea, letting him hang too close to Mr. Bliss, him being a suspect."

"Good move. How'd he take it?"

"He objected a little," Charlie replied. "Then went off to get coffee. The doctor told me he did a good job stopping the bleeding, and bandaging before the paramedics got there."

Shepard looked back down the corridor. "I just came from there. I didn't see Wagner. Round him up."

An attractive blonde woman in a white coat approached. Charlie suddenly went all shy, obviously taken with her. She shook hands with Shepard.

"Liz Robinson, Chief Shepard. We gave Mr. Bliss a shot. He'll sleep for awhile."

"Thanks, doctor."

She hesitated. "That is *the* Herman Bliss, isn't it?"

"I'm afraid so," Shepard said.

"It's a wonder someone hasn't shot him before this." She gave a mystified shake of her head and moved off.

"Chief—" Charlie began.

"Where's Bliss?"

"Down there. Second on the left." Charlie nodded past the desk. "Chief, the paper trail I was following…Mutual Holdings?"

"Let me check on Bliss first, Charlie, before he nods off. All right?"

"Okay." He headed off down the corridor. Shepard nodded to the nurse at the emergency desk, got a smile in return, and passed through a set of swinging doors.

In the second of a series of curtained cubicles Shepard found Bliss stretched out on a gurney. The painter looked gray, dark hollows under his eyes; his usually animated face relaxed into a pale mask of its former self. Shepard watched him for a moment, then noticed a flutter of the eyelids. He moved closer to the gurney.

Bliss opened his eyes a little, looked up at Shepard, and tried to move. He didn't get very far, wincing as his injury punished him for the attempt. He tried to speak. Nothing came out. He tried again.

"Was it my line calls?" he asked.

Shepard gave a laugh, triggered by relief as much as humor. "I thought he hooked you more than the other way around."

"You play tennis?" Bliss inquired.

"Enough to know you were winning, and it wasn't because of bad line calls."

Bliss' face scrunched up in one of his crooked smiles. "Haven't played in thirty years. Enjoyed it. Always fun to beat somebody who cares more about the game than you do."

"I'll bet."

Bliss tilted his head to examine the bandages on his left shoulder, a look of concern crossing his features. "How bad am I hurt?"

"I think you'll live to paint again," Shepard told him.

He'd meant it lightly, but he saw Bliss took the answer seriously, folds of worried flesh above his brows smoothing out.

"Who shot me?"

"Since yesterday, maybe before, a van from the Sea Orchard Fish Company's been following you around. Ever heard of them?" Bliss shook his head. "We watched your house last night. And one of my men was at the tennis club, but I guess it wasn't good enough. I should have done more. I'm sorry."

Bliss studied him a long time without speaking, his face revealing nothing.

"So what is it, Mr. Bliss?" Shepard asked him. "What do you know that's dangerous enough to get you killed?"

The artist snorted. "Most information is dangerous to somebody or other. I've lived long enough to accumulate quite a bit." Shepard could see Bliss consider the idea, then shake his head. "I'm no threat."

"Maybe your picture is," Shepard suggested.

"My picture?"

"The seventh hole at Carmel Bay Country Club."

Bliss seemed to take to this idea, but his short nod went on a couple of times of its own volition. Whatever sedative Dr. Robinson pumped into him started to assert its hold.

"You rest," Shepard commanded.

"The painting…" Bliss mumbled through lips that looked as if they weren't working quite right.

"I'll collect it," Shepard promised him.

Bliss started to say something else, but the drug gathered him gently into its arms and didn't let go.

Shepard frowned. When he'd tried to reassure the artist that he'd look after the painting, it sounded as if Bliss had said "Nooo…" Shepard found Bliss' house keys on the table nearby.

Shepard found a perplexed Charlie Revere waiting for him by the emergency desk. "No sign of Wagner," Charlie told him. "I searched everyplace. He sure didn't go near the snack bar."

"Great." Shepard checked his watch. "At three this afternoon I want everybody working on the case at the station. We've got to sort out a few things."

"Okay. And Chief? About what I found out?"

"Yes?"

"Sea Orchard Fish owns a green van like the one you described."

"Just one?"

"The company's office is an empty, broken-down shack on the commercial wharf. They used to buy and sell fish, but the Harbor Master says there hasn't been anybody around the place for a couple years now."

"Then where was the van?" Shepard asked.

"It used to be parked in the security lot there. Two weeks ago the only human being I can so far connect to Mutual Holdings showed up and drove it away."

"Who?"

"Our victim. Alex Wagner."

CHAPTER FIFTEEN

Shepard's team packed the small coffee lounge at the back of the Carmel police station. Squeezed between the vending machines and the bulletin board were the five officers at the center of the investigation into Alex Wagner's death. Shepard reflected, picking his way between the molded plastic chairs to stand in front of the bulletin board, that in a room larger than a broom closet their numbers would be unimpressive. He turned to face the rest of his team.

Charlie Revere sat up front, an eager expression on his face. Stan Durbin, next to him, sipping coffee from a cardboard cup, low key as always. Carl Lorch seemed fascinated by the view out the window, as if there were a dozen other places he'd rather be. Shepard suspected most of them featured tall stools and all the pretzels you could eat.

Greg Cowles crouched on the edge of a chair near the door, his thick leg muscles tensed for a rabbit-like bolt for cover if Shepard started shooting at him. Amy Ryerson entered, then settled herself in a chair by a wall phone, notepad and pencil in hand.

"Chief?" She spoke up before Shepard had a chance to begin. "The mayor would like you to call him."

A snort escaped from Carl Lorch like a bubble of gas rising to the surface of a swamp. When Shepard glanced in his direction, Lorch closed his eyes, and yawned.

"Thank you, Amy. First, I want reports," Shepard began. "Greg, you start."

"There were two people up on that ridge!" Cowles blurted.

Shepard nodded. "I heard a yell, another shot, then two more. The last two sounded like a heavier weapon than the rifle that was fired at Bliss."

Cowles looked at the floor again.

"Go on," Shepard prompted.

"Well, yeah." Cowles raised his head, but didn't meet Shepard's eyes. "We found two shell casings in some brush on the hillside above the court. Twenty-two longs. A third twenty-two long was in a bare patch on the ridge a few yards from the first two. We also found the bullet that hit Bliss on the tennis court. Also a twenty-two, but up behind the crest of the ridge we found two casings from a forty-five."

Shepard considered. "So we have a perp armed with a twenty-two rifle and a forty-five automatic; or we have two different armed individuals on that ridge at the same time." He gave Cowles a piercing look.

"Chief, I—," Cowles started, then floundered, casting a glance out the doorway at uncertain freedom.

Shepard cut in. "We'll talk about it later. Anything else?"

"We also found a used Kleenex by the forty-fives."

The laughter that followed this revelation died quickly when Shepard's eyes flicked around the room. He nodded. "The driver of the Sea Orchard van apparently had a bad cold or allergy."

The phone on the wall rang. Amy moved to answer it, then she pushed a button to put the caller on hold. "It's the mayor again."

"Tell the mayor I confessed to Alex Wagner's murder, and have just hung myself in my office." Shepard turned to Lorch. "What have you discovered, Sergeant?"

"That sifting through a stack of papers isn't gonna solve anything," came the reply.

"What would you suggest then?"

"You're letting Bliss lead you in circles. Get him to tell what he really saw out at the golf course, and we can all go home early today."

"Maybe you're right." Shepard allowed himself a feeling of satisfaction at the surprised look his admission painted on Lorch's face. "We have another problem, too. The Ridgeway Pro-Am descends on us tomorrow. It produces a lot of dollars for the entire peninsula, and unfortunately this investigation is distracting us from preparations for the event."

A pleased smile flirted with the edges of Lorch's lips. "Yeah, I guess bein' police chief even in a small town isn't the cinch some people think it is," he observed.

Shepard smiled. "You're right again, Carl. Other than grilling Bliss, you have any more suggestions regarding the Pro-Am?"

Out of the corner of his eye he caught Amy giving him a puzzled look. Lorch seemed to swell under the attention. "Sure," he began. "Lots."

"For instance," Shepard went on. "How do we route the traffic in and out of the town more effectively? Reports say last year was pretty much a gridlock."

Lorch agreed. "The traditional route down Ocean Avenue gums everything up. We gotta use Carpenter and Junipero, too. So we route 'em south outta their way a bit, then bring 'em back in by Rio Road. The club has three ways in. We should have three ways to get people there."

"Carl," Shepard began, glancing at the ceiling, as if the thought had just dropped on him from above. "There's a final security coordination meeting tonight. I need to concentrate on Bliss. Why don't I appoint you Carmel Police liaison in my place? Think you could handle it?"

Lorch sat up more alertly than Shepard had ever seen him. "With my eyes closed."

The beefy officer handled most things with his eyes closed, Shepard thought to himself. The man took the bait without a whimper. Shepard almost felt sorry for him; the subterfuge had been far too easy. Lorch obviously felt he should have been given Shepard's job, but a man with so little on the uptake would never be chief of anything. Shepard saw that Amy now regarded him with amused comprehension.

"You're it, then," Shepard concluded. "I know you'll do a good job. Amy, why don't you scare up a copy of the file for Carl to study before the meeting tonight?"

Amy's eyes twinkled. "Maybe I should include some of the past years, too, Chief. So Carl can check all the different ways people have tried to solve the traffic and security problems."

"Good thought," Shepard agreed soberly. "Let me know if I can help you, Carl."

Lorch pulled himself to his feet, and smirked. "I won't need any help." He clumped out after Amy.

Shepard turned to Durbin. "Stan, Alex Wagner's main client was the Holly Corporation, right?"

"Yeah, Holly was pretty much his only client."

"Charlie tells me Wagner also fronted for a company called Mutual Holdings," Shepard informed him. "They own the Sea Orchard Fish Company. See if you can link Mutual Holdings or Sea Orchard to Loren Holly."

"I'll get right on it," he assured Shepard.

Amy returned at that moment, and with a straight face told them that Lorch had so much background information to go through, he might not be able to return to the meeting.

"Then we'll have to muddle through somehow without him," Shepard replied. "Amy, did you get in touch with Bruce Wagner's dentist?"

"Yes, sir," she answered promptly. "His records should be here by tomorrow. Federal Express. The Seattle police are also tracking his movements for the day his brother was killed."

"Good job."

Amy smiled, obviously pleased. Most of the drudgework at the station fell to her. She put in long hours, despite being a single mom with a nine-year-old boy, and rarely got much recognition for her mostly menial efforts. Shepard knew she felt good playing an active part in the investigation.

Shepard looked around the room, his eyes again coming to rest on Greg Cowles. He wanted to give the young man another chance. Sending him off as he had Lorch wouldn't solve anything, but he also didn't feel confident enough in Cowles' abilities to allow him to pursue one of the major lines of the investigation. Shepard picked up a piece of chalk from the blackboard, tossed it idly in the air. "Greg, I have to go round to Bliss' house, and pick up a painting. The killer may try to get to that painting, too. I want you as backup."

The request seemed to pull the young man upright, like a string attached to his spine. "You can count on me," he promised.

Shepard considered, then replaced the chalk on the blackboard rack. "Charlie, did Wagner return to the Seascape?"

Charlie shook his head. "No sign of him."

"Find him," Shepard ordered. He started for the door. The others mobilized. The phone rang again. Amy answered it.

"Carmel Police, Officer Ryerson speaking." Shepard saw her expression go grim. She hung up the phone, and turned to him. "That was the hospital. Bliss is gone."

Shepard stared at her. "Gone? The man was unconscious!"

She shrugged. "When the nurses came to move him to a room, the gurney was empty. His clothes and tennis racquet were gone, too."

Shepard sighed. "Who's still on the duty roster?"

"Just regular patrols," Amy answered.

"Charlie?"

Revere grinned. "Find Wagner. Find Bliss. Got it. Maybe I'll turn up Amelia Earhart along the way, too."

Shepard headed for his office. Inside Yale Gerringer slouched in a chair, his feet up, chewing on a piece of straw. Shepard wondered if the mayor kept a supply of it in a wooden box on his desk the way some men kept cigars.

"This investigation seems to be distracting your department from finalizing the security arrangements for the Pro-Am. Chick Beal thinks we're falling down on the job. He's looking for us to pick up the ball and run with it."

"Confusing his sports a little, isn't he?" Shepard asked innocently.

"Dan, we don't have a problem here. I'm behind you a hundred percent. You know that."

"Listen, I realize how important the Pro-Am is to everyone. We'll do our part."

"Good, good!" Gerringer's voice chimed in heartily. "I'm glad you understand that our law enforcement concerns are rather specialized in Carmel."

"Of course we still investigate murders, and ordinary crimes like that, right?"

"There's no need for sarcasm. I wouldn't want to minimize my deep anxiety over the murder either. It's all very unpleasant, realizing one of your own neighbors is a murderer. I don't suppose there's a chance it was a serial killer or a random, irrational act of violence?"

"Murder is always irrational, but random? No, in this case I don't think it's an under-tipped caddie lurking in sand traps to get his revenge. The killer is probably someone Wagner knew, maybe someone we all know. That will help us catch him."

"Oh…Bliss…" Gerringer sighed.

"I thought that would make you happy."

"I meant Herman Bliss. I hear he's taken on some sort of ad hoc role with your investigative team."

Shepard closed his eyes. "Not really, but I am interested in one of his paintings."

"That must be something of a first."

"Yale, someone shot him this morning."

That brought the mayor's feet crashing to floor.

"Good God…Is he…?"

"It wasn't serious. He's apparently already discharged himself from the hospital."

"I'm mighty glad to hear that. Herman Bliss is one of our leading citizens."

Shepard tried, but could detect no hint of irony in the mayor's voice. Gerringer shook his head. "What's happenin' to our peaceful little town, Dan?"

"The shooting wasn't really in my jurisdiction. The Sheriff's Office is handling it."

"Now that's a cop-out answer, if I ever heard one." Gerringer made half of his face screw up in a folksy scowl. "This…incident…connected with the Wagner thing?"

"Yes, I believe it is."

"Damn it, Dan! Who's next? Are you doing your job? Are any of us safe? The city council will be all over me about this Bliss thing!"

"More than about the Wagner thing?"

Gerringer stood up, flicked the straw into the wastepaper basket with un-erring aim. "I have work to do." He stopped in the doorway, and looked back. "I must say I'm becoming increasingly disappointed in your lack of progress, Dan. And I'm not the only one. I have a warm personal regard for you, but your conduct is beginning to cause me to doubt my judgment. For now I'll accept your promise that we'll have someone behind bars soon."

"Wait a minute—" Shepard began. "I didn't—"

"I can't wait until your debut at Ramblin' Rick's. Show tunes are my favorites. I hope you sing some show tunes." Hands in pockets, he strolled off down the corridor.

Shepard and Cowles exited the rear door of the station, and headed for the brown Ford. Before they reached the unmarked car Charlie Revere burst out the door behind them.

"Chief!"

Shepard grinned at him. "You found Amelia Earhart? That was fast."

"Aw, give me time," Charlie laughed. "I just got off the phone with that nice clerk down at the courthouse who's been helping me track Mutual Holdings?"

"What's her name?"

"Milly Sweetwater. Is that something, or what?"

"What color are her eyes?"

"Green. Maybe hazel." Charlie answered automatically, then his brow squeezed together. "What's that got to do with anything?"

"Just testing the observation skills of one of my officers," Shepard told him. "I gather she had something for you besides a smile?"

Charlie gave him a suspicious look, but nodded. "Yeah, I'll say. You wanted a connection between Mutual Holdings and Holly Development?"

"Give."

"It's not what you think. Holly doesn't own Mutual Holdings."

"I'd be disappointed," Shepard replied, "if you weren't dying to tell me something more."

Charlie's face widened into another grin. "He may not own Mutual Holdings, but he's sure in business with them."

"How?"

Charlie had been bursting at the seams when he exited the station. Now the seams ripped open. "They own four acres of land down on Cannery Row!"

Shepard stared at him. "The new hotel complex?"

"Yep, and Holly didn't even buy the land outright. It's some kind of complicated lease/option. Holly had to make all sorts of guarantees about completion dates and occupancy levels just to get that."

Shepard put it together. "So Alex Wagner, the attorney supposedly handling Holly Development's interests in the project, was also the front man for this mysterious holding company that can hang Holly and his hotel out to dry?"

"That's about the size of it," Charlie agreed.

"Damn," Shepard said. "If Holly found out, he might be inclined to call Wagner a cheat, a liar, a fraud and a thief."

Cowles bobbed his head in agreement. "I'd be surprised if that's all he called him."

"He also might be inclined to brain Wagner with a sand wedge," Shepard concluded. "Gentlemen, we have our first real motive."

CHAPTER SIXTEEN

Bliss' house, nameless, sat back from Junipero near the Carmel Mission, on several acres forested with pines and live oaks, and surrounded by a crumbling stucco wall. The Tempo pulled up to the entrance, and Cowles clambered out to open a sagging iron gate. It screeched in protest when he dragged it open. He hopped back into the car and they drove up the narrow, twisting drive.

The huge house sprawled across the landscape like the bleached remains of a dinosaur that had fallen there when the world was young. Ivy blanketed it. Tree limbs shoved their way into softened stucco, or plowed up whole stretches of Spanish tile on the roof. The stucco, formerly white, had been weathered to an unhealthy gray and yellow, streaked and damp stained. The once red tiles were green with moss. Small plants sprouted between them, adding to the chaos.

They stopped near the front entrance, and climbed out. Slabs of age-darkened wood bound with once decorative iron, now rusting, formed the tall, bullet-shaped door.

"You ever read any Poe, Officer Cowles?" Shepard stared up at a disintegrating chimney.

"The House of Usher," Cowles answered.

Shepard nodded. He fished out Bliss' key ring, selected the only key not dwarfed by the ancient lock set below a thick iron rung. It fit, but although Shepard strained mightily, the tumblers wouldn't turn.

Cowles stepped forward. "Want me to give it a try, Chief?"

Shepard moved aside without a word. Cowles took a deep breath, and applied himself to the key like an Olympic weight lifter going for the gold. The bolt shrieked. The young man expelled the breath, and tried the iron rung. The door grated open.

They entered a long hallway with stained plaster walls, its shadowy ceiling supported by beams of black wood. On the walls Shepard saw light oblong patches, ghosts of paintings removed long ago. A squat table and two chairs looked carved by hand from the peninsula's redwoods. Dust covered everything.

Cowles looked around, and gave a nervous chuckle. "If Mrs. Haversham comes through one of those archways, and invites us to a wedding party, I'm outta here."

Shepard glanced at him in surprise. "You must do a lot of reading."

Cowles looked embarrassed. "Oh, I listen to those books on tape when I work out. I know they're condensed and everything, but they help pass the time."

"Let's see if we can find his nest," Shepard decided. He started off down the hall, Cowles at his heels.

A dark figure lurched out of an archway into their path.

"Oh…." Bliss scowled at them. "Since you are here, I guess…well…" His voice trailed off as he shuffled back into the gloom.

Shepard waited until his heart slid back down out of his throat, then pried Cowles' fingers from where they had ploughed furrows in his shoulder. He hurried to catch up with Bliss.

Bliss had changed back into work clothes: flannel shirt, paint-spattered corduroy paints. A sling ripped from what looked like a faded blue satin dressing gown cradled his left arm. Apparently Bliss had seen to his own medical needs.

"You're supposed to be in the hospital," Shepard told Bliss. He received no reply. They trailed the painter through a series of rooms protected from the light by heavy curtains falling so far from the tops of enormous windows they looked like brocaded waterfalls. A few vague shapes of furniture huddled beneath dusty sheets and blankets here and there.

Finally they arrived at double oak doors set in a naked, wainscoted wall. Bliss yanked one open. The gates of Heaven could not have swung open with more brilliant light. Squinting against the glare, Shepard moved forward into what might have once been a huge solarium, forty feet to a side. Glass, scrubbed until it glittered, rose to the treetops all around, beyond it the jungle of the grounds. Even the late afternoon sun filled the space with an awe-inspiring radiance.

A second door, cut in the glass, led outside, presumably Bliss' usual form of entry. A large bed occupied one corner of the room. Next to it a single wardrobe and dresser, handmade like the furniture Shepard had seen in the entry. In another corner a makeshift kitchenette hid behind a tattered folding screen. A table. A single chair. And in the space directly in front of the astounding wall of glass: an easel; paints; and a stool.

"I'm fine," Bliss said at last. "There was no need for me to stay at the hospital."

"Don't you think the doctors should decide that?"

"No," Bliss answered. "You came to see the painting. I'll get it."

He left them there, exiting through the door they had just walked through, his steps fading into silence.

"Wow," Cowles murmured.

Soon they heard the shuffling footsteps returning. Bliss entered, canvas under his arm, and handed it to Shepard.

Shepard forced himself to study the picture. Once again the clash of colors assaulted his eyes. The green looked like a bleeding pancake stabbed by the pin. The ocean beyond rose up in a molten curtain. Kaleidoscopic smears on the fairway could be the golfers, but any violence in the scene remained the artist's alone. Shepard tried to focus on the kidney-shaped splotch near the cliff's edge. It still looked more like the front end of a dead fish than a sand trap.

Bliss spoke, as if reading his mind. "The colors are meant to suggest the pollution caused by avarice of course."

"Ah," Shepard responded.

"You think the image is too blatant?"

"I think it fits in with the overall theme quite well," Shepard answered. "I don't quite get the tiny American flag though. That is a flag, right?"

He pointed. Bliss squinted as if seeing the flag for the first time, then shrugged. "The Japanese own Pebble Beach, not Carmel, at least not yet. You have to understand that many of the symbols spring directly from my unconscious, unedited. My talent simply opens the floodgates. I can't restrain what pours out."

"No," Shepard agreed. "You don't do that." He forced his eyes back down to the canvas. Try as he could, he saw nothing that resembled a clue. "Can we keep this at the station?" he asked. "It would be safer there."

Bliss nodded in agreement. "I suppose in the interests of justice, we can withhold it from the world a little while."

Shepard saw him swell with pleasure, eyes gleaming at what the man perceived as approval of his art. Shepard realized that compliments on Bliss' work must be few and far between. "Have you sold anything lately?" he asked.

Bliss looked affronted. "Of course. I'm a professional artist, not some weekend dabbler! I sold one of my sculptures to a wealthy landowner in Salinas. It was commissioned actually. I don't accept many commissions, but occasionally I can be persuaded."

Shepard thought for a moment, then turned to Cowles. "Greg, you go on back to the car."

Cowles glanced at the darkness beyond the double doors.

Bliss snickered. "It's safe enough. All my homicidal aunts and uncles are safely locked away in their attic rooms. Or the cellar."

Cowles took a deep breath and marched out. Shepard could hear his echoing footsteps picking up speed, then fading in the distance.

"Look," Shepard began. "I'm sorry we came out here without your permission."

Bliss held up his good paw. "My keys."

Shepard handed them over.

"I like the way I live," the artist told him. "But some people might not understand, or think I should be the object of their pity. People need to pity others, Chief Shepard. It disguises the pitifulness of their own lives."

Shepard said, "You own some of the most expensive real estate in the world—"

Bliss interrupted him. "Tell me about the case."

When Shepard hesitated, Bliss scowled. "You wanted my help. Has that changed?"

"No," sighed Shepard. "I can use all the help I can get, but I'm used to rules and regulations. I grew up to respect them. With you in the last week, it seems like I've broken more than in my entire life."

"It's high time you loosened up a little."

"I'm an officer of the law, Mr. Bliss," Shepard responded, standing erect, jaw tightening.

"At ease, Chief. Be an officer of justice. More difficult, I know, but far more rewarding."

Shepard scraped a hand across his hair. "You almost got killed because of this case, you deserve to know."

Bliss gave a crooked grin. "I'll accept that rationalization."

Shepard glared at him, hemmed and hawed, but in the end found himself bringing Bliss up to date about everything he knew, from Jason Kiley showing up at Maggie Dennis' house to Alex Wagner playing both ends against the middle in the Cannery Row hotel complex. He could see the news about Maggie and Jason disturbed the painter most.

Bliss listened, pacing back and forth in front of the glass. The sun lowered and the room grew darker. Finally Shepard stopped.

"We should take a look at Wagner's house again," Bliss told him. "Without delay. Do you have a key?"

"I can get one at the station. What's the hurry?"

"As long as Bruce Wagner is unaccounted for, anything can happen," Bliss responded.

At that moment it did. A dark silhouette appeared as if by magic on the other side of the expanse of glass, directly behind Bliss.

Shepard lunged for the painter, and bullied him behind the screen that hid the kitchen from the rest of the room. Snapping open his holster, Shepard removed the magnum and flicked off the safety with a practiced thumb. He looked around the screen.

The figure stood there unmoving, too small and thin to be Greg Cowles. It raised a hand, and its knuckles rapped on the glass of the outside door.

Bliss shook off Shepard's hand and stalked across the studio. Shepard followed, still alert for danger.

Bliss stopped at the door, unlocked it, and the figure entered with a bouncing step: a small, wiry man, well into his sixties, but with energy to spare.

"Didn't mean to startle you, Mr. Bliss!" the man exclaimed with a big smile.

"You didn't startle me. You startled our Chief of Police."

The white-haired man stepped forward and stuck out his hand. "Carmel's new police chief! Good to make your acquaintance! I'm Victor Dewalt."

"Nice to meet you, Mr. Dewalt." Shepard holstered his gun and took the man's hand, trying to remember where he had heard the name.

"Victor works for Armando Cosentino," Bliss explained with a casual air. "A prominent local businessman."

Shepard's smile slipped. This made Dewalt's smile grow larger.

"When Cosentino wanted me to look into Alex Wagner's death, he sent Victor here to collect me," Bliss explained.

"That's why I'm here now, Mr. Bliss," Victor offered. "Mr. Cosentino would like another word with you."

"Actually," Bliss told him. "The Chief and I were about to go follow up a lead. Maybe I could call Mr. Cosentino in the morning."

"That might not be convenient." Dewalt thought about it and obviously decided it wouldn't be convenient at all. "He is very eager to talk to you."

"How about an hour?" Shepard suggested. "I'd like a word with Mr. Cosentino myself."

"Ah, well…As to the time, I suppose an hour would not be too bad, but Chief, no offense intended, Mr. Cosentino is an extremely busy man, and I'm afraid he really has time only for Mr. Bliss this evening. If you'd like to make an appointment."

"I'm investigating a murder," Shepard told him. "Doesn't Cosentino want that investigation completed successfully?"

Dewalt nodded vigorously. "More than anything he has on his plate right now."

"Then why don't you tell Mr. Cosentino we'll be by in about an hour?"

Dewalt, unfazed by his insistence, just smiled, and nodded. "He lives on Jack's Peak. Mr. Bliss has the address. Gentlemen."

He bowed very formally to both of then, then went out the way he came, melting into the darkness of the surrounding trees.

*   *   *

The Tempo slid to the side of the street a short distance from Wagner's house. Shepard and Bliss got out. Shepard noticed that Bliss eased his door closed with a barely audible click. Shepard did the same, then leaned forward.

"Greg, keep your eyes open."

"No problem, Chief." Cowles answered.

Shepard scowled. No problem? A notorious suspected killer waltzed right past him only minutes before. Cowles still didn't know Dewalt had been there.

Shepard and Bliss approached the house on foot, keeping to the shadows of the overhanging oak trees that lined the street. Nearing the gate, they stopped simultaneously. From inside the house came a flicker of light. A flashlight beam swept across a front window, then disappeared. Shepard looked at Bliss, then slid his gun from his holster.

Bliss tried to look innocent. "It isn't me this time, Chief. I swear."

Shepard motioned the painter to stay back, unlatched the front gate, then moved along the stone path to the front door, Bliss at his heels. Shepard tried the knob. It turned. The door opened. He tensed.

Inside, a dark shape huddled over the bookcase next to Wagner's desk. Shepard felt for a light switch, found it, and flipped it up.

CHAPTER SEVENTEEN

Light flooded the living room. The figure whirled. Bruce Wagner glared at them, a small sheaf of papers clutched in his hand.

Shepard half-expected to find Wagner here after Bliss' earlier warning. What the man had been doing at the bookcase interested him more. A section three feet off the floor had swung open. Behind it a tiny wall safe stood ajar.

"Dr. Wagner," Shepard began. "We thought we'd lost you."

Wagner stared at the .357 in Shepard's hand. "There's no need for that."

Shepard engaged the safety and re-holstered the gun. He could see Wagner forcing himself to relax.

"Nice to see you up and about, Detective Lautrec. Or should I say Mr. Bliss? According to the news reports you seem to be quite a local celebrity." The doctor's lips flattened out into a professional bedside smile.

"Thanks," Bliss answered. "Sorry I couldn't finish the last game."

"I doubt it would've been the last game," Wagner countered.

Bliss looked at Shepard and elevated his shoulders. "Six-four. Five-three. And I was about to serve."

Wagner's thin smile contracted. "I'll look forward to a rematch."

"Mind telling us what you're doing here?" Shepard asked him.

"Trying to make sense out of my brother's affairs."

"In the dark?" Bliss snickered. "Must be interesting affairs."

Wagner stepped forward, his shoes squeaking on the plastic covering the floor. He faced Bliss across the sofa the way he'd faced him across the net earlier that day.

"However interesting they might be, they're certainly none of your business." Wagner thrust his body forward, as if delivering one of his hard groundstrokes at Bliss' toes.

Shepard interjected. "Why the flashlight?"

Wagner's gaze reluctantly left Bliss to focus on Shepard. "My brother murdered. Mr. Bliss wounded. I thought it prudent to maintain a low profile."

Bliss nodded, as if understanding, then scooped up the conversational ball and lobbed it deftly back. "That must be why you left the front door unlocked. To confuse an attacker."

"Did I leave it unlocked?" Wagner retreated and tried to look concerned. "That was stupid of me."

"Where'd you get a key to unlock it in the first place?" Bliss responded.

Shepard could almost see the drop shot just clearing the net.

"Alex left it with me. In case of emergencies," Wagner sputtered, barely able to reach the ball.

Bliss looked up, as if contemplating a short lob, then drilled his overhead home. "I thought you hadn't seen him in six years. Your brother moved into this house last year after his divorce."

Wagner glanced from Bliss to Shepard. "I don't know what Mr. Bliss is insinuating. I have every right to be here. My brother's will clearly names me his executor.

"How did you get the key, Dr. Wagner?" Shepard asked.

"Alex must've mailed it to me."

"With instructions on where he hid the safe?" Bliss interjected.

"Yes." Wagner's body relaxed to indicate that should be an end of it.

"What have you got there?" Bliss stared at the few items Wagner carried, eyeing what looked like bank statements with unnatural glee.

"Private papers." Wagner's anger rose. "Just what am I suspected of here?" he demanded. "I was a thousand miles away when Alex was murdered!"

"People have been known to hire people to kill people," Shepard answered.

"That's ridiculous!" Wagner thundered. "If your investigation is going so poorly that you need to suspect me, the killer will probably never be caught!"

Shepard saw Wagner edging back toward the bookcase. The safe had a combination lock. If Wagner managed to replace the papers in the safe, it could require a court order and a stick of dynamite to get it re-opened. He swung around the sofa.

Wagner lunged toward the safe. He would have made it, but the leather of his shoes slipped on the plastic. Shepard reached him in two long strides, his left hand clamping down on the wrist that gripped the papers.

Wagner's face contorted in rage. "Let go of me, you black bastard!" he screeched.

Shepard had a built-in safety valve when confronted by such a burst of overt racism like that. He grew more calm and polite, letting the words wash over him and dissipate.

"You wouldn't want to obstruct the investigation, would you, sir?" Shepard asked with a carefully measured smile. He squeezed with his left hand, and removed the papers with his right. "Thank you." He released the wrist, and looked down at the papers with interest.

"Look, I…" Shepard could hear Wagner's attempt at a placating tone of voice. "I'm sorry I said that."

Shepard nodded, acknowledging the apology, but he had no intention of accepting it. "These bank statements are from half a dozen different banks. Five up in San Jose. The one local bank is First Federal. I thought all of your brother's accounts were at Pacific."

The energy had drained from Wagner's body. "I told you I'd just begun to go over his things."

"Considering he trusted you with a key to his house, and the combination to his safe, it's strange he neglected to mention that these accounts had grown to over three million dollars in less than a year." Shepard looked up at Wagner then, his eyes steady, unblinking. Wagner said nothing.

"Ah," Bliss murmured, "the heir apparent stumbles across the family fortune after all."

"It also says here," Shepard continued, "that your brother made a series of large, regular cash withdrawals from the local account over the past year."

"How large? How regular?" Bliss wanted to know.

Shepard's eyes never left Wagner. "Ten thousand dollars on the first day of every month since last March. Dr. Wagner? You know anything about it?"

"Nothing," Wagner insisted, but his eyes drifted away from Shepard's, and didn't return.

Shepard put the statements aside. The last few items were newspaper clippings. A browning residue across each corner suggested someone had taped the corners to a wall, or in an album. They were each crisply folded to fit inside a business-sized envelope. Shepard looked at each one in turn. "They're all about a ferry accident. A passenger and automobile ferry sank between Seattle and Port Washington the night of February fifteenth, six years ago." He looked at Wagner.

Wagner sighed and nodded. "It was a disaster, a horrendous tragedy. Over thirty people died."

"What did it have to do with your brother?"

"Nothing. At least not directly. But I was aboard that night."

Shepard studied another clipping. "It mentions you here. The only doctor on board. It says you valiantly tried to save many lives."

"Not…enough…" Wagner's face had gone pale. He lowered himself into a chair. "Thirty-four died."

"Your brother must've thought you did quite a lot," Bliss observed. "For him to keep those clippings."

"He didn't," Wagner blurted, then shook his head. "I don't know. I don't know what he thought."

Shepard could see Bliss trying hard to fit Bruce Wagner, OB-GYN, into the role of hero, and not succeeding very well. Shepard had trouble with it, too. Why would a man unmoved by the death of his own brother risk his life to save complete strangers? He checked the date again. Six years ago.

"Didn't you also lose your mother right around then?" Shepard inquired.

"Yes," Wagner nodded his head, all the combativeness, every ounce of energy, drained from him. "She died about a month later. She wasn't on the ferry that night. She'd been very ill for some time. There's no connection."

Shepard found it odd Wagner needed to answer a question that no one asked. How could there be a connection?

"And her funeral was the last time you saw your brother alive, too?" Bliss added.

Wagner glared up at him. "Yes. I told you!"

Shepard recalled something else. "Your brother married Genevra Carroll that same year."

Wagner's head jerked around so fast Shepard thought he'd snap his spinal column. "What does that have to do with anything?"

"She told me she met Alex Wagner at Yale Gerringer's election night bash. Carmel votes for its mayors the first week of June. That would be three months after your mother died. Four months after the accident."

"So?!" Wagner's voice thundered. He seemed far more disturbed by the direction the questioning now took than the discussion about the three million dollars.

"You're holding out on us," Bliss remarked, putting voice to Shepard's own thoughts.

"You're crazy," Wagner shot back. He looked at Shepard. "I'd like to go now."

"Hell no," Bliss began. "You're under ar—"

Shepard interrupted. "As executor of his brother's estate, Dr. Wagner has every right to be here."

"He broke into the safe!"

"He had the combination."

"He's lying!"

"If we threw everybody who lied in jail, there wouldn't be much room for thieves and murderers, would there...Detective *Lautrec*?"

Shepard excused Wagner, after obtaining a promise that the man would stay in town for a few more days. He still had his brother's funeral arrangements to attend to, and the little matter of an estate that had swelled to over three million dollars.

Shepard watched Wagner get into a rental car and drive off. He trotted over to where Cowles sat in the unmarked car.

"Greg, that's Bruce Wagner. Keep on his ass."

Cowles turned the key in the ignition. "What about you?"

"We'll walk to the station and get another car."

Shepard waited until Cowles moved off before walking back through the lovingly groomed garden and into the house. Bliss had vanished. He tried the kitchen and on an impulse popped open the freezer. Sure enough, he found the frozen dinners arranged alphabetically. He looked over the novelty ice cube trays, pausing at the cubes shaped like female breasts. What side of Alex Wagner did they appeal to? Did he serve them to his fidgety, haunted ex-wife, or did they give the surprisingly lusty Maggie Dennis a good chuckle in her lemonade?

Shepard found Bliss in the garage, staring at the ladder on the wall. "Two weeks before he died, Alex Wagner borrowed the Sea Orchard Fish Company van. Presumably to transport something."

"Presumably," Shepard agreed.

"You couldn't stick a ladder in that Porsche." He indicated the car beneath the canvas cover.

Shepard noticed something else. "This ladder's the same brand as the one we found in the ocean." He turned on Bliss. "The one you say wasn't used to sneak out of the trap and across the dew!"

"It wasn't. You proved that, but why would he buy two of them?"

"You're leaping to a pretty huge conclusion there, aren't you?" Shepard challenged. "What makes you think Wagner bought both ladders?"

"Look through his receipts," Bliss suggested with a leer. "A compulsive like Wagner will have saved every one."

Shepard's professional cool served him well with Bruce Wagner. How did Bliss manage to puncture it so thoroughly and so often? "The ladder couldn't have been used! It didn't work!"

Bliss turned a mild look on him. "Wagner couldn't know that, could he?"

"Bliss, damn it, if you know how he was killed—!"

"I don't! Not for sure! But if I'm right, look around you! Observe! This house is like one big Clue Museum! Not only is there enough here to get a possible fix on what happened out on that golf course, but thanks to Bruce Wagner's visit, I'm beginning to see how it might shed some light on why his brother was killed, too!"

Shepard stared around him: one sports car; many gardening utensils of every description; fertilizer; seed; pots; watering cans; sprayers; hoses; golf clubs; plastic sheeting and that damned ladder...Shepard stormed back into the living room, Bliss tagging along.

"Three million dollars…Wagner represented both Holly Development and Mutual Holdings." Shepard raked his hand across his head. "A man in that position might find it easy to skim."

"He might indeed." Bliss nodded. "I think it's extremely probable Wagner had his hand in the cookie jar."

"Somebody found out," Shepard went on. "Those payments of ten thousand dollars every month could have been blackmail."

Bliss scratched his nose. "Do blackmailers kill their victims? Isn't it usually the other way around?"

"Usually," Shepard admitted. "But nothing else is usual about this case! Come on, Bliss! Okay! You don't know for sure, but you have theories! Give!"

"All right," Bliss sighed. "But you won't like what I'm thinking."

"Try me."

"I don't think Alexander Wagner planned his own death. No. But I'm pretty sure his killer didn't either."

Chapter Eighteen

Armando Cosentino's house hid in a narrow gap between two ridges extending down toward Monterey from the area's tallest point, Jack's Peak. Named for the man who gave the world Monterey Jack cheese, the mountain's wooded slopes sheltered many of the most wealthy and influential citizens on the peninsula. No whimsical house names up here, only high walls and security systems.

Dewalt opened a solid, windowless front door that creaked like a drawbridge lowering. He turned a pixie smile on Shepard and Bliss. "Gentlemen, welcome!"

He closed the door, and led them across an entry tiled with great blocks of rust-colored stone. In a living room the size of Shepard's entire house Dewalt indicated a chair.

"Chief Shepard, if you'd wait here please. Mr. Cosentino wanted to see Mr. Bliss alone."

"I told you I was coming," Shepard answered.

"So you did! Mr. Cosentino regrets he won't have time for you this evening. His advanced years, his health…I'm sure you understand."

Shepard clicked his control up a notch to blanket the rising anger. "I'm investigating a murder."

Dewalt's smile never wavered. "So is Mr. Cosentino, through his agent here Mr. Bliss."

"Sorry, but given Mr. Cosentino's reputation—and yours—I find that kind of hard to believe."

Dewalt's lips began to turn down at the edges. His remarkably clear blue eyes seemed even bluer. "Mr. Cosentino is one of the area's most prominent landowners, businessmen and philanthropists. He has given more of his time and money to the well-being of the community than any other five men in his position you could name."

Shepard refused to back down. "He's the only man in his position around here I know of," he responded. "There's usually only one capo in a territory this small."

The soft tap of rubber on stone reached Shepard's ear. He stood with his back to the entry, listening as it came again, followed by a slithery sound he couldn't place. Shepard didn't turn. If Bliss had heard the sound, he made no sign, his eyes also on Dewalt, not the doorway.

Dewalt shook himself like a dog that had just climbed out of a river, as if Shepard's accusation provided momentary discomfort soon remedied. "I have no idea what you're talking about. Mr. Bliss, if you'll follow me please?"

He started out, but Bliss made no move to follow. Shepard pivoted to watch him, now able to see out into the entry. He heard a sound like a crab scuttling back out of sight beneath a rock, chased by the soft gliding, but could see no one.

"I think Mr. Cosentino would want Chief Shepard to join us," Bliss remarked.

Dewalt stopped, turned back. "Why?"

"For protection."

"From you?" He gave a frisky bark of a laugh.

Bliss' lips crumpled in his corrugated smile. "I've asked myself for days why Cosentino's so interested in solving this crime—why he'd become openly involved in a murder investigation. It wouldn't have anything to do with Mutual Holdings, would it?"

Dewalt looked puzzled. "Mutual Holdings?"

It hit Shepard then, and he saw a little way down the road Bliss traveled. "The Cannery Plaza development?" he added.

The steady taping in the entry drew nearer again, interspersed with the soft scrapes. Dewalt, too, must have heard the sounds from the hall, but he didn't acknowledge the fact.

"What about it?" Dewalt's voice stayed bland.

"Mutual Holdings owns the land where the hotel's being built." Shepard went on. "And Cosentino owns Mutual Holdings, doesn't he?"

Shepard could see Bliss giving him the surprised, but pleased nod of a professor who's heard a correct answer from a particularly backward pupil.

Dewalt opened his mouth to speak, saw something over Shepard's shoulder, rotated on his heel, and walked out of the room through a side door. He didn't utter a word. He never looked back.

Both Shepard and Bliss turned their attention on the doorway where a frail wisp of a man dragged himself into view, supporting himself on an aluminum walker. Clump, slide. Clump, slide. His fragility made Loren Holly look robust in comparison. A feather-light cloud of white hair floated on a liver-specked skull, its skin stretched tight. Did reaching the lofty heights men like Holly and Cosentino aspired to, require them to leave chunks of their flesh on deposit somewhere, a down payment toward a final accounting?

"How can I help you, gentlemen?" The voice sounded unnervingly soft and melodious and conspiratorial.

"Mr. Cosentino, I'm Daniel Shepard, Carmel Police Department. I believe you know Mr. Bliss."

Cosentino turned his gaze on Bliss, gray lips twitching. "Yes, I know Mr. Bliss." He dragged himself to an uncomfortable-looking straight-backed chair, turned with three precise placements of the walker, and eased himself down. He wore a white terry cloth robe and slippers.

"Forgive my appearance," Cosentino continued. "I'd expected Mr. Bliss much earlier. When I realized he'd been detained, I made preparations for bed."

"Sorry about that." Bliss' voice teetered dangerously close to Detective Lautrec. "We had some investigating to do."

Cosentino nodded. "I'm glad you joined forces. The sooner this terrible business is resolved, the sooner we can all get on with our lives again."

"The sooner your hotel can be completed?" Shepard asked.

"My hotel?" The soft voice sounded confused. "Cannery Plaza? That's Loren Holly's project. Not mine."

"The Sea Orchard Fish Company is a front for something that has nothing to do with fish. It's owned by Mutual Holdings. Alex Wagner was a front for Mutual Holdings."

"And you're the behind," Bliss completed with a crooked grin.

Shepard nodded. "There's always a paper trail, Cosentino. In time we'll find it."

Cosentino held out a hand. "None of this is relevant to Alex Wagner's death."

"He represented Holly Development," Shepard persisted. "He also represented Mutual Holdings. Both sides of the same deal were represented by the same man? I can't imagine why Holly, or Webb or one of them, didn't know that."

"Maybe one of them did," Cosentino replied quietly. He wiped at an invisible blemish on the walker.

Shepard digested this. "Maybe."

"Alex's conduct may have been questionable," Cosentino agreed. "But I'm certain it had nothing to do with his death."

Bliss strolled over to Cosentino, took out a handkerchief that looked none too clean, then knelt down and applied it to the spot on the walker Cosentino had been rubbing. "What about three million dollars?" he asked, concentrating on his work.

Shepard caught the angry look of distaste Cosentino gave Bliss' bent head. Bliss straightened, and stepped back, pocketing the handkerchief again.

The disgusted look transferred itself to the walker. "Three million dollars..." Cosentino echoed.

"Stashed for a rainy day," Bliss went on. "We figure he was skimming from both Holly and you—sorry—I mean Mutual Holdings. Did you want me to find the money without Chief Shepard's help? Was that why you asked me to investigate on my own?"

Cosentino's eyes bored into Bliss'. "If I hoped you'd bring me whatever you found in confidence, I was obviously mistaken, wasn't I?" He turned to Shepard. "This is all very interesting, but from what you've told me, you're farther from the truth into Alex's death than I thought. My interest in this case has nothing whatever to do with Loren Holly or Mutual Holdings. It's strictly personal."

"Explain it to us so we can understand," Shepard offered. "So we can get back on track again. Why are you so concerned about this murder?"

Cosentino's body gave a tired heave, then he raised his voice. "You'd better come in, my dear."

Shepard and Bliss looked again at the wide doorway to see who would next make an entrance. Shepard saw Bliss was as unprepared as he for who appeared. The woman walked uncertainly into the room, the eyes more haunted than Shepard remembered them.

"Gentlemen," Cosentino said in his soft voice," I'd like you to meet my daughter, Genevra."

CHAPTER NINETEEN

"When you came to see me that day, Chief Shepard, I knew I had to find out what had happened to Alex. I still loved him. I asked my father to see what he could do. He thought Mr. Bliss could help us…" Genevra Carroll's voice trailed off.

She sat next to Cosentino on the edge of another chair, her hand resting on the top of his walker. Her father covered her fingers with his. Shepard thought of a spider scuttling up on to a fly.

"The one good thing to come out of this is that I have my daughter back after all these years," Cosentino explained. "Genevra did not agree with certain business choices I made early in my life—"

Genevra shuddered. "You had a chance to turn your back on—"

Cosentino squeezed her hand tightly. It might well have been her throat, considering how abruptly her voice stopped. "That's family business, and has no bearing here." He turned back to Shepard and Bliss. "She had her name legally changed while she was away at college. She was good enough to continue to see her mother over the years until my wife's death, but she had no time for me."

"I'm here now," Genevra responded quietly.

He squeezed the hand beneath his own. "Yes, you are."

"Did Alex Wagner know you were his father-in-law?" Shepard asked.

"Of course. Other people knew. Close friends."

Shepard remembered the party where Genevra and Wagner had met. "Friends like Yale Gerringer?"

Genevra stared off into space. "He knew."

"So," Bliss nodded. "If a family member embezzled from you, it would be an even bigger insult, wouldn't it?"

"He didn't embezzle!" Genevra erupted to her feet, nearly knocking the walker over. "He was honest! I wouldn't have married him if I thought he was anything like—" She turned on Cosentino, eyes tearing. "—like you."

"You told me he changed in the last year of your marriage," Shepard continued. "What if that's when he started embezzling, but he couldn't bring himself to tell you?"

"No! You're wrong! You're wrong!!!" Genevra screeched, and dashed from the room. Shepard expected her to head for the front door, but he heard her footsteps on the stairs. Wherever she ran, it wouldn't be far enough. He felt for her, beginning to see what had wounded her so deeply. If she'd begun to suspect that her husband was a criminal like her father…worse, was a criminal working with her father, could she have killed him? Could the motive have been the theft of whatever innocence she'd tried to regain with her marriage?

Cosentino pushed himself up, leaned on the walker. "I don't know where he got the three million dollars. Since I have nothing to do with Mutual Holdings or Holly Development I don't care. I want the person who killed my son-in-law brought to justice for other reasons, but I see no hope that you can do that for me." Here he looked up at Bliss with a malevolence that sprang from deep inside the emaciated body.

"You, Mr. Bliss, have been a disappointment to me. I'd had reports you had certain talents that might have made you useful. I see now I was misled. You have learned little more than this…policeman…I no longer require your services. I'll find someone else to help me. I'm going to cancel your bail bond."

Bliss shrugged. "I've been in jail before."

"I know," Cosentino smirked. "You can't detect. You can't paint. You're not even a particularly successful criminal. Why you bother to go on living is a puzzlement to me."

Clump, slide. Clump, slide. Cosentino headed for the door.

Shepard called after him. "Cosentino, if you're thinking of sending Dewalt after the killer, don't. Not while I'm Chief of Police."

Cosentino did not look back, but he said, "I doubt that will be much longer." He disappeared from sight.

*　　　　　　*　　　　　　*

"What did he mean, I can't paint?" Bliss demanded angrily.

Shepard ignored him. "I couldn't see how Genevra would have the contacts to hire a hit man. Damn it, she grew up in a house with one!"

"Convenient," Bliss agreed.

They were on their way back to Carmel in a borrowed patrol car. Shepard scanned the dark trees on either side of Aguajito Road. Suddenly he slammed on the brakes. The car skidded to a stop on the narrow road.

"Are you trying to kill us?" Bliss roared.

Shepard pointed into the darkness. "You know what's on the other side of that hill?"

"I grew up here. Of course I do. Carmel Valley."

"Vista Colorado?"

Bliss shrugged. "One of those subdivisions near the mouth of the valley, I suppose. I've never actually hiked over the damn thing. I don't hike." He stopped. "That's where the driver of the van disappeared."

"Yeah," Shepard agreed. "I don't think in his condition Cosentino pulled the trigger himself, but Dewalt is short enough to fit in the shoved-up front seat of the van." He shook his head. "No. It doesn't track. When you were shot, Cosentino thought you were still working for him. Why would he want to have you killed?"

"He wouldn't," Bliss stated, his brow wrinkling like a basset hound. They looked at one another. "Therefore he didn't. Let me think now…I'd just begun one of my patented surprise charges to the net."

Shepard nodded. "I remember being surprised at how fast you moved."

Bliss gave him a sour look. "Thank you. I would've won the point, too. You were surprised. Wagner was surprised…"

"The gunman could have been surprised, too!" Shepard grabbed the microphone. "This is Chief Shepard!"

"Go ahead, Chief."

Shepard recognized Brad Kelly's voice. "Brad, has Greg Cowles reported in?"

"About an hour ago. He followed Bruce Wagner back to his hotel, and was parked outside."

"Thanks." Shepard slammed the mike back into its holster, and stepped on the gas. He started the light bar on the roof, but left the siren off.

Bliss grabbed the dash as they fishtailed around a corner. "Okay, they were shooting at Bruce Wagner instead of me, why? He was in Seattle when his brother died! Why would Cosentino want to kill him?"

Shepard tried to reason it out. "Suppose Alex has been skimming from Holly Development and Mutual Holdings for some time, but somebody finds out. So we get blackmail."

"The ten thousand dollar payments."

Shepard nodded. "But whoever the blackmailer is also knows Cosentino is behind Mutual Holdings, and sees a bigger potential payoff from him. So the blackmailer shops Wagner to the old man. Cosentino wants Wagner dead, both for dumping his daughter, and for stealing money, but the wrong brother is killed…somehow…"

"Oops…and you were going so well there for a while," Bliss said.

Shepard allowed himself a smile of satisfaction. "Coming from you that's quite a compliment."

"But there are problems with most of it."

"Yeah, I know."

"Number One: why would Cosentino get openly involved?"

"He knew my investigation would turn up his link to Mutual Holdings," Shepard proposed.

"But you haven't linked him. Not definitely. Number Two: if Cosentino wanted Wagner dead he would have sent Dewalt."

"Okay. So?"

"If you slow down, I'll slow down!" Bliss yelled.

Shepard had no intention of slowing down. If Bruce Wagner had been the intended target all along, they had one frustrated killer out there undoubtedly determined to try again.

"Of course Dewalt would be the one to pull the trigger!" Shepard yelled back. His hands slid along the steering wheel, easing the patrol car into a short stretch of straightaway.

Bliss spoke through clenched teeth. White knuckles almost popped out of his skin where he grabbed the dash. "Dewalt is a professional. He wouldn't have bothered himself with the craziness of the sand trap, and whoever he aimed at on the tennis court would be dead now. Number Three: you said the guy who drove the van had a cold. Dewalt doesn't have a cold."

Shepard pounded the wheel, then held on as they lurched around another tight corner, nearing Highway One. He knew they were finally homing in on at least part of the truth, but his overall theory flew in the face of too many facts.

"Bruce Wagner was holding something back tonight."

"Definitely," Bliss nodded.

"Maybe he knows a better reason for Cosentino wanting him dead."

Four minutes later they screeched into the park-like oval outside the Seascape Hotel. Shepard spotted the brown Ford parked near the street where it commanded a view of both the hotel, and the long mall that ran along one side. Shepard stopped the patrol car in front of it. They got out.

The Ford was empty. Shepard approved of the choice of location, but wished Cowles hadn't put the Carmel Police sign on the dash. He probably did it to avoid a ticket, but it pretty much defeated the purpose of an unmarked car. He made a decision. The young man was simply not cut out for law enforcement, and when things quieted down a little Shepard knew he'd have to break it to him.

Bliss looked around. "Where'd he go?"

"Maybe he spotted something. If Wagner left on foot, say down the mall, Greg would have had to follow on foot. Let's check Wagner's hotel room first."

They crossed to the entrance and went inside. The sprawling hotel catered to conventions, and even at ten o'clock at night a wide assortment of people with plastic nametags milled about the lobby. Piano music echoed from a lounge in the distance. He recognized the tune: "Send in the Clowns." Well, here we are, he thought.

Shepard got the number of Wagner's third floor room from the front desk. They headed up in the elevator.

They found the room at the end of a long hall, across from an alcove where an ice machine gurgled and clanked. A window nearby overlooked a row of chic office buildings. Shepard realized that Alex Wagner's law office was down there someplace. He knocked on the door. No answer. He knocked again.

"Chief?"

There was something in Bliss' voice that made Shepard spin. Bliss was looking into the alcove at a soft drink machine and one that dispensed snacks. A closed metal door stood between them and the ice machine. Bliss' eyes were fixed on the floor in front of it.

A small dark stain had spread out from beneath the door. Shepard hurried over to it. He didn't have to examine it to see that it was blood, already congealing. He took out a handkerchief, grasped the knob, and turned it. The door opened to reveal a small utility closet.

Greg Cowles sat on the floor in the midst of a clutter of pails and brooms. The entire left side of his head had been battered in. Bliss turned away.

Blood and hair covered a broken broom handle, cradled almost lovingly in Greg's lap. Shepard knelt and pressed his hand against the young man's neck. He couldn't pick up even the tremor of a pulse. Beneath his fingers the body felt cool and dry.

Chapter Twenty

Catherine Gonzales strode down the corridor toward Shepard, her ponytail bobbing. Now close to midnight, every law enforcement agency in the county had been alerted and an APB for the arrest of Bruce Wagner had hit statewide.

"I'm sorry, Dan," she with a small, helpless shrug. "I didn't know him, but—"

"I did," Shepard cut in. "Greg was an incompetent officer. It got him killed. But he wasn't a bad human being. I liked him."

She nodded. Shepard could see the sympathy in her eyes. It made him feel uncomfortable. His professionalism should be able to mask his feelings, but the death of a fellow officer, one under his command, sickened him.

Every cop faced the possibility of death in the line of duty. In the raging cauldron of the city the battle lines were drawn in blood, but Greg Cowles was the first policeman killed on duty in the entire history of the small Carmel department. Violence no longer respected such geographical niceties. These days the wolf howled at every door.

He fumbled for something more to say, but came up empty. Seeming to understand his distress and the difficulty he found expressing it, she stepped into the breach.

"Before I look at the body, do you want to hear my report on Alex Wagner?" she asked.

"Okay."

"Are you with me, Dan?"

"I'm with you. Shoot," Shepard replied with a trace of irritation.

She looked uncomfortable. "Dan, we don't have the right murder weapon."

Shepard stared at her as this sank in and kept on sinking.

"Because the wounds were too clean? You said that before."

She nodded. "Now I think I know why. There's a good chance a sand wedge was used, but not that one."

Shepard puzzled it over. "The killer brought his own sand wedge, killed Wagner with it, then smeared blood on Wagner's club?"

"I know it doesn't make a lot of sense."

"But then the killer would have had to make Wagner's shot for him as well. Wagner's blood was on the ball." He looked at her. "Wasn't it?"

"I'd say yes."

Shepard scraped at his close-cut hair with his hand. "Anything else?"

"Yes. The sand is wrong, too."

"The sand."

"What would you assume happened to Wagner after he was hit?" she prodded.

"He'd fall."

"The only sand on the body came from the ocean off Moss Landing. Hard to fall in a sand trap and not get some sand on your trousers."

"You said there was sand on the trousers."

"There was. Lots. But none of it came from the trap."

Shepard felt the universe begin to rotate. "The killer smashed in Wagner's head, then while holding him upright, made his shot for him? Or he changed his pants as well as his socks? I wonder if that was before or after he broke his legs for him. No, no. We can't keep piling on absurdities like this. We're looking at this all wrong somehow."

"There were green stains on his pants: both knees." she concluded. "But no, I don't think that means he was killed out on the course in full view of four witnesses, then carried into the trap so the killer could make the shot."

Shepard reflected. "If the killer was a golfer, anything's possible I suppose…Wait a second, you said the only sand on the body came from the ocean off Moss Landing?"

She nodded.

"You wouldn't happen to know how that compares to the sand on the ocean bottom below the Carmel Bay Country Club, would you?"

Catherine nodded again. "Most of the sand there is that white stuff they keep trucking in to replenish Carmel Beach. They get it from somewhere up in San Mateo. It's completely different."

Shepard grabbed her shoulders. "Cathy, Alex Wagner was the only person in that sand trap. He got those grass stains crawling away from it, then he was murdered someplace else. What was he wearing?"

She considered. "White or gray socks. Still some mystery there. Red shirt and blue pants."

Shepard smiled. "Red, white and blue. Very patriotic, don't you think?"

"I guess, but I'm still not with you."

"That's because you haven't seen Bliss' painting of the seventh hole. The sand trap looks like the mouth of a dead fish—"

"Sounds very fetching."

"With," Shepard concluded, "an American flag in its mouth, sticking up near the top."

The sun rose in her eyes. "Bliss did see Wagner! He saw the colors, but they barely registered in his composition!"

"Or in that mottled gray mess he calls his brain. Bliss, I've got you. You were a witness to a big piece of this, but only your subconscious knew it! Trained observer…He must have glimpsed Alex Wagner crawling away from the trap on his hands and knees! And from the position of that flag, Wagner crawled directly to the cliff."

"Where the dew was?" Catherine asked with a grimace.

Shepard groaned. "Right. He couldn't have crossed it on the ladder. We proved that. He didn't have time to construct a suspension bridge, and I refuse to believe he floated across on Aladdin's carpet. Still, I think we're close. Very close."

"Dan, I want this to be something, but there's also the blood on the sand wedge and the ball. If Wagner was murdered someplace else, say at the bottom of the cliff, the killer would still have to use Wagner's magic carpet to get back into the sand trap and make that shot. How would there have been time? I mean I'll barely buy Bliss being so caught up in symbols and imagery that what he was seeing didn't exactly penetrate, but would he have missed a second person sneaking along? Would there have been enough time for all of this? How could the killer have counted on having enough time? How could he or she be sure one of Wagner's golfing partners wouldn't stroll over to see what Wagner was doing down in there all that time?"

Shepard held out his hands. "I don't have it all yet. I doubt if Bliss does. But that's the beginning. It has to be."

"Is there anything I can do when I'm finished here?" Catherine offered, still not looking convinced.

"Yeah, the Sheriff's Department has the Sea Orchard Fish Company van. Can you go over the back of it? Look for anything that might prove it was used to transport Alex Wagner's body across the peninsula to Moss Landing."

"First thing in the morning. I'll call you at your office."

Shepard watched while she moved to examine the body in the linen closet. He turned his eyes away.

＊　　　　　　　＊　　　　　　　＊

The bus reached Cannery Row ten minutes late the following morning. Thousands of spectators descending on the peninsula for the golf tournament slowed traffic to a crawl on all the major arteries.

Bliss stumbled down the steps of the bus and on to solid pavement. He let the sign hang at his side for a moment while he looked around. The short heat wave had broken. A sharp breeze off Monterey Bay chilled further an already cool day. Omnipresent gulls wheeled overhead.

A handful of protesters trooped up and down in front of the Cannery Plaza construction site. Behind them workers slapped plywood over the skeletal frame of the hotel. Everyone looked as if they were simply going through the motions.

Bliss hefted his sign, cringing at the pain it caused in his wounded shoulder, and marched with a committed stride up to the protesters.

"Beautiful day for political advocacy!" He let the light of his smile sweep over each one as they passed. He counted seven in all, but no Jason Kiley. Seeing the suspicious looks he received from several of the activists, he raised his sign so they could read it.

The procession stopped dead in its tracks, all eyes riveted on his sign. Bliss ballooned with pride. He saw that they appreciated the uniqueness of his vision at once. It pictured in primary acrylics the Cannery Plaza hotel as a dead whale washed up on the beach. Astride the whale, recognizable to all that knew him, Loren Holly flayed the hide with a long flensing knife. He could see the message shouted by the powerful imagery affected them all.

A young woman with long, curly blonde hair and large blue eyes, stepped forward.

"What is that?"

"It is what it is." Bliss favored her with an indulgent smile.

The young woman nodded. "And what is that exactly?"

"You find the symbolism too subtle?" Bliss asked, beginning to reel in his lips.

"I can see the big thing's a watermelon. What is that? A seagull on top? Why is the gull smoking a cigarette?"

Bliss stared at her. It never failed to sadden him that when faced with true art so many people seemed immune, their minds deadened by a culture saturated with corporate logos and flashy advertisements designed to tell all and sell all with as little imagination as possible.

"Jason been around?" he asked.

Still staring at the poster the young woman shook her head. "Fat chance."

"Isn't he our fearless leader?"

"I don't know you," she replied, her eyes narrowing.

"It's Mr. Bliss," an elderly man interjected. He stepped forward, smiling. "I've always admired your..."

Bliss swelled again.

"...politics..."

Bliss' ego took a small hit, but he shrugged it off. A man may be known for many things, not simply what is most important to him.

"Thank you, sir."

"So you're Bliss." The young woman gaped. "I've heard of you." She looked back at the sign and nodded, as if at last understanding.

Bliss forgave her earlier ignorance. She couldn't help what mass culture had done to her.

She turned to the protesters. "Let's get it in gear, folks. Nobody will notice us if we just stand around."

With some reluctance the assembly line began to jerk forward again, a few still eyeing Bliss' sign. Bliss stepped into formation next to the young blonde.

"Why wouldn't Jason be around?" Bliss asked her.

"Because he never is, that's why."

"He was here last week when Webb and Romaine talked to you. The day of the news coverage."

"Of course. Jason always turns out for the media, then he leaves us to do all the real work."

Bliss frowned. "I knew he was a publicity hound, but I also remember him as being a very committed activist."

She nodded. "He was. Not anymore. Over the past few months he's changed."

Bliss stared so hard at her he veered toward the street and almost tripped over a fire hydrant. She grabbed him just in time.

"Just keep in line, Mr. Bliss. Picketing's a difficult skill, but I'm sure you'll get it in time."

"You're a very cynical young woman," Bliss observed.

"We're trying to save the planet. That could make anyone cynical."

"I'm trying to save it, too," he answered.

"Maybe you care, but there are millions—billions!—of people who don't give a good goddamn! We're not trying to save it for us, we're trying to save it for everybody, and not just human beings! God knows, considering all we're doing to destroy it, we deserve to be saved less than most other species!"

"Amen."

She looked at him as if trying to gauge his sincerity.

"What happened to Jason?" he asked. "How did he change?"

"Oh, one day we were all gearing up to stop this project dead in its tracks. We had petition drives organized, letters to newspapers, demonstrations planned…" Her voice trailed off.

"But you did all that," Bliss said. "I remember signing a petition outside the Carmel Post Office. The media covered your protest."

"Once. In eighteen months. Mr. Bliss, you're tuned in to activism. You notice things, but the people in the street—" Here she gestured at some window shoppers across the road. "—they probably think we're the bricklayers union on strike. Jason let this campaign fall to pieces, Mr. Bliss. He let it die."

"You know where I can find Jason?" Bliss asked, his jaw working.

She considered. "Friday morning? Friday morning's he does Mr. Gerringer's."

"The mayor of Carmel?"

"Yeah, Jason likes to weed for celebrities…"

Bliss continued to circle with her. He wanted to pay a visit to his bank, but decided he would first walk with the small group for a while.

*   *   *

The Carmel Police Station swarmed with activity: extra officers, double shifts, all to provide support for the massive security operations of the Pro-Am. Shepard guided Amy Ryerson into the relative calm of his office and closed the door, hoping there would be no additional crimes to investigate over the next four days. The tournament taxed the peninsula's law enforcement agencies to the limit.

Amy settled herself in the chair opposite Shepard's desk, a stack of computer printouts and faxes balanced in her lap. Her eagerness to be a part of the hunt shone through her distress at Greg Cowles' death.

"The dental records are a perfect match. We have photocopies from a Dr. Larrimer in Seattle. He's been Bruce Wagner's dentist for a long time. So," she concluded, "Bruce is Bruce and Alex is…dead…if you know what I mean."

Shepard found a smile he didn't feel. "Yeah. I get the drift. And Bruce Wagner was definitely in Seattle when his brother died?"

"Definitely." She nodded her head vigorously. "He was…ah…working on the wife of a prominent clergyman the morning Alex was murdered."

"Okay, what else?"

"One peculiar thing I noticed in the police report," Amy's voice became breathless. "They'd asked several of his colleagues and acquaintances if lately there was anything out of the ordinary in his daily routine, and one of them, a proctologist in his building, said no."

"That's peculiar?"

She nodded. "He said that up *until* the last few months he found Bruce Wagner's behavior very peculiar."

"How?"

"He would be a dedicated doctor, working all hours for weeks at a time, then he would get in these moods where he didn't seem to care anymore. He'd cancel appointments, go off on long lunches. He was driving his medical assistant crazy, this doctor said."

"How long had this been going on?" Shepard asked.

"As long as Wagner had the practice there." She checked her notes. "He moved across town six years ago. Said he needed a change of scenery or something."

Shepard sat up straight. "Six years ago…Great job, Amy." He pretended not to notice her blush of pleasure.

The phone rang. Shepard answered it.

"Dan? It's Cathy Gonzales. First, the Sheriff's Department wanted you to know they got a lot of fingerprints from the van. They're running them through the computer now. "I've got something for you, too. Do you remember a crate in the back of the Sea Orchard van?"

"About the size of a little coffin?"

"Yeah. That's the word all right. There were traces of blood on one lip of it and some fibers that look as if they match Wagner's blue pants. We found them stuck to a small piece of heavy gauge plastic wrap. Like a painter's tarp or something. Maybe they wrapped fish in it, but there was no other sign of plastic in the truck."

"Wagner's house is full of the stuff," Shepard put in.

"I'll get a sample. Dan, that crate explains the broken legs. One of two things must have happened. Either rigor had already begun to stiffen the limbs when Wagner was put in it and the killer had to break the legs to make him fit, or he was in the crate long enough for rigor to set in and the killer had to break his legs to get him out again. You want my gut reaction?"

"Definitely."

"Alex Wagner took his last ride in the back of that van."

"It makes a lot of sense," Shepard admitted.

"It'll take awhile for the blood to be typed and for a positive match on the fibers, and I want to go over Wagner's clothes again for wood fibers from the crate. Even if he was wrapped in plastic we may get lucky."

"You're very good at your job, Dr. Gonzales."

"Why, thank you, Chief. I've saved the best till last."

"You have my complete attention."

"I have a fingernail."

"Only one?"

"This one's special. I found it stuck on the edge of the crate."

Shepard clutched the telephone. "Tell me it wasn't Alex Wagner's."

"Nope."

"Then DNA matching—" Shepard began.

"Forget genetics, Dan. The way it was torn makes it easy to match. It didn't fit his. If you can find me a suspect before he has a chance to grow a new one, it could be the nail in his coffin."

He had barely thanked Catherine and hung up the phone when it rang again.

"Chief! Yale Gerringer!" The mayor's voice leapt out of the receiver. "You'd better get over here pronto! That crazy painter is attacking my gardener!"

CHAPTER TWENTY-ONE

Bliss sat on top of Jason Kiley in the gladiolas, both hands around his throat. The garden looked as if a tornado had hit it, cutting a swath through its very center that ended abruptly where the two men now struggled. Jason's boot heels dug into the rich earth as he tried to push the artist off him, but he failed to uproot Bliss.

Shepard headed toward them. Gerringer yelled from behind the screen on his front door.

"Stop them! I have a tee-off time in twenty minutes!" he yelled, his folksy sense of humor unable to cope with the potential destruction of both his gardener and his golf game.

Shepard reached the two men. Kiley saw him first.

"Get him off me!" he choked, eyes bulging.

"Are you about to add murder to your list of crimes, Mr. Bliss?" Shepard asked.

"I'm considering it."

"I don't think there's any more room on your rap sheet."

Bliss glared down at Kiley, his hands still tight around his throat.

"Start a new one."

Shepard put a hand on his shoulder. "Could you at least let go of him until you make up your mind?"

Bliss thought for a moment, then removed his hands. Shepard helped him to his feet. Kiley lay spread-eagled in the remnants of the flowerbed, his ponytail unraveled, rubbing his throat, swallowing a few times to make sure he still could.

Bliss pointed a long finger at him. "You betrayed a trust!"

Kiley struggled to his feet, brushing dirt and bits of dismembered plants from his clothes. "I don't know what you're talking about." He turned to Shepard. "Don't just stand there! Arrest him!"

"You're under arrest," Shepard told Bliss. Bliss just shrugged.

Shepard noticed that Gerringer had worked up the courage to come out into the yard. He stood a short distance away, watching with interest, his tee-off time momentarily forgotten. "You're taking this assault rather casually, aren't you, Chief?"

"No, sir," Shepard replied. "Mr. Bliss is under arrest. His rights have been read to him so many times, I'm sure he knows them by heart."

Bliss nodded. "I'm guilty. I don't need an attorney. I don't want bail."

Shepard held out his hands. "We could use more criminals like him, don't you think? Mind telling me the motive, Mr. Bliss?"

"He was suppose to save the planet, but somewhere along the line he got distracted by publicity...and retirement planning...but I'm not going to kill him because of that."

"Retirement planning?" Shepard asked.

"Yeah," Bliss scowled. "Seems he was buying a T-Bill a month for the past year, second day of each month, in regular denominations. Care to guess what size?"

Shepard's glance met Bliss', then he looked at Kiley who stared at Bliss, his eyes now bulging from surprise.

"Ten thousand dollars?" Shepard asked. The young man seemed to shrink inside his work shirt and denims.

"Ten thousand dollars?" Gerringer echoed him. "A hundred twenty thousand for the year? How does he make that much pulling weeds?"

Kiley glared. "I don't have to tell you anything."

Shepard stepped in close to him then, got right in his face.

"Two men are dead, Mr. Kiley. One of them was a Carmel police officer. I'm going to find the killer. Any reason you don't want to help me
do that?"

"No!" Kiley blustered. "I didn't kill anybody! Of course I want to
help!"

"Why was Alex Wagner paying you ten thousand dollars a month?"
Shepard demanded.

"So he'd sabotage the protest against the Cannery Plaza Hotel," Bliss
interjected with a sneer. "The peninsula's leading activist turns out to be
snuggled up warm and cozy with the people he's supposed to be fighting!"

Kiley wheeled on Bliss. "I didn't sabotage anything! And who the hell
do you think you are, anyway? Where's a middle-aged no-talent artist
with environmental pretensions get off attacking me!"

"I'm not going to kill you because you took bribes," answered Bliss,
his face an innocent mask. "Or because you care nothing about art,
although that would be justifiable homicide."

Kiley pointed a dirty finger at Bliss. "Did you hear that, Chief? He
threatened to kill me! Twice!"

"I've already arrested him for attempting to kill you, Mr. Kiley.
Threatening to do it seems sort of redundant."

Gerringer now stepped into the thick of things. "Alex Wagner was
bribing you, Jason?"

"I was a consultant!" Kiley replied. "Wagner wanted input on environmental impact."

Bliss snorted. "What kind of input costs ten thousand a month? No,
he hired you to put on a good show, but not too good a show, only
enough to get by, to make it look as if environmental interests were
being heard, but not enough to be any real threat to the project. You're
good at putting on shows, aren't you Jason? Came to love the cameras a
little too much maybe, maybe allowed money to corrupt what ideals
you had left, but hey, I'm not going to kill you for that."

Shepard could see the truth of Bliss' accusations in Kiley's eyes. Not only did the painter have an eye for detail, he knew something about character, too. He turned to Bliss.

"If you're not going to kill him for all those reasons, why *are* you going to kill him?"

Bliss' face took on a terrible countenance. It looked to Shepard like a basset hound metamorphosing into a werewolf.

"I'm going to kill you for what you did to Maggie Dennis," Bliss snarled. "I'm going to kill you because you with your greed and your vanity have no right to be in the bed of one of the finest women that ever breathed."

Kiley stared at Bliss in stupefaction.

"Huh?"

"And I'm going to kill you because you don't have a hope on God's green earth of understanding what I'm talking about."

Bliss took a step toward Kiley. The gardener stumbled backwards, falling on one of the few remaining clumps of gladiolas not decimated by the earlier brawl.

Shepard put a hand on Bliss' arm. "I'd really rather you didn't kill him, Mr. Bliss."

Gerringer stared down at Kiley, licking his lips and grimacing as if he'd just eaten something dank and rotten. "He killed Alex Wagner? Why? Did Wagner decide to stop paying?"

"I didn't kill anybody!" Kiley exclaimed, still watching Bliss and ready to bolt at the next sight of aggression.

"Where were you last Wednesday morning?" Shepard asked. "Say from six to eleven?"

Kiley blinked rapidly, brushing at the long hair that had fallen into his face.

"Wednesday…Wednesday morning…" His face became a war of conflicting emotions. "I…uh…I was with…Mag…Ms. Dennis…"

A growl rose in Bliss' throat, but he didn't move.

"Well," Gerringer said with a nod of decision. "Under the circumstances I'm afraid I'll be terminating your employment, Jason. I'm not sure what the law is in a case like yours. Accepting a bribe? Fraud? Maybe even blackmail, but…well…you understand…"

"Man, you are all such hypocrites!" Kiley burst out.

"I can't keep my foursome waiting," Gerringer said, making for his station wagon.

Kiley yelled at his back. "Fuck you, Mr. Mayor, sir! You would've done the same if you were me! When nobody cared or listened! Except you would never have been me in the first place! At least I tried! One slip doesn't destroy all the good I've done!"

The station wagon's engine caught. Gerringer backed out of the drive. Kiley looked at Shepard and Bliss.

"Yes, it does," Bliss said.

Bliss rode in silence on the way to the police station.

"I could put your actions down to an over-enthusiastic citizen's arrest," Shepard suggested.

"I'm not going to jail?"

Shepard rubbed a hand over his head. "You sound disappointed."

He could feel Bliss studying him. "You know, Chief, I'm a terrible influence on you. You're beginning to play as fast and loose with the law as I do."

Shepard laughed. "Nobody could ever do that, Mr. Bliss. You're the mountain. All the rest of us just stand in your shadow. But you did suggest to me once upon a time that justice was more important than law."

"Chief," Bliss echoed his laugh. "You'd better be careful. I could almost grow to like you."

"I'll try not to let it go to my head. Now, do you want to hear what I've turned up or not?"

"I can't wait," Bliss responded, settling back more comfortably in his seat.

Shepard recapped the forensic evidence that suggested the killer conveyed Wagner's body in the van, finishing with the fingernail stuck in the crate. Bliss listened without interruption, nodding occasionally as if the information neatly slotted itself into his own view of the case.

"So," Shepard concluded, "it looks as if Alex Wagner was taken from that sand trap, or left under his own power, and was then killed somewhere else."

"Doesn't explain the blood on the club or the ball though, does it?" Bliss mused.

"Ah, no. That's been pointed out to me."

"Nevertheless, I agree. You're on track at last."

Shepard scowled. "Oh, thank you very much."

"I knew you had it in you. Make a right turn at the next corner."

"Why?"

"Don't you think it's time we paid another visit to the murder scene?" Bliss asked as if it were the most obvious next move. Shepard had to agree. It was.

CHAPTER TWENTY-TWO

Shepard pulled the Ford to a stop in front of Alex Wagner's house. They sat there for a moment, staring at it.

"Why did Wagner sneak out of the sand trap in the first place?" Shepard asked.

"Holly was on to him. Maybe Cosentino, too. We suspect Wagner was playing both sides against the middle in the Cannery Row project, probably skimming from both pots. He had his three million. He must've realized somebody was on to him. It was time to disappear."

"Okay, fine," Shepard agreed. "But why like that? Why not just hop a plane to points unknown."

"Because then everyone would know. Somebody would come after him."

"We don't have extradition treaties with every country."

"I'm not talking about police," Bliss said, irritated. "You think Cosentino would care what country he ran to? You don't think with his international underworld contacts he couldn't track Wagner to whatever tropical hidey-hole he'd found for himself? Then all our local capo has to do is send Dewalt on a nice vacation. Wagner ends up hanging from a coconut palm."

Shepard nodded. "So Wagner had to disappear in a way that would take the heat off."

"Of course," Bliss agreed. "If it looked like he was dead, better if it looked like he'd been murdered, the investigation, even Cosentino might be sufficiently distracted. That's one obvious reason Cosentino wanted me to find the killer by the way, if he thought the murderer killed Wagner for the embezzled money."

"So Wagner plans a fake death."

"He couldn't resist the theatrical touch of the location, the miraculous shot. A way of thumbing his nose at Holly, I suppose. He didn't particularly need the embellishment of the impossibility of the crime, but once he decided on where he wanted to vanish from, he really had no choice."

"What about the blood on the club and the ball?" Shepard wondered. "Why was that necessary?"

"To make it clear he died, or was at least attacked, in the sand trap, and that he didn't leave it under his own volition. Once we theorize Wagner set that part of it up on his own, the blood is easily explained."

Shepard saw it. "He cut himself, smeared it on the club and the ball before sneaking away."

"Well, on the club at least…of course…"

"Quit saying 'of course'! I can see him sneaking away. Just as you saw him sneaking away!"

Bliss looked startled. "Me?"

"It's in your painting, Bliss! The flag in the fish's mouth!"

"What fish?"

Shepard closed his eyes. "Never mind. Focus on the colors. Red, white and blue. The flag you painted. The same colors as the clothes Wagner wore. Maybe you'd looked down for a second to mix a new color or whatever it is you do. You still managed to catch a glimpse of Wagner, but you were so caught up in your painting, you didn't realize what you were seeing."

Shepard stopped himself. "But that can't be, because that would only work if he left the trap in a hurry, and however he did it, it must've been slow and painful crossing that dew without leaving a mark."

"Red...white...and blue..." Bliss muttered. "How could I have been so blind...?" His brows huddled together, as if trying to comfort one another. "How can I call myself an artist? Maybe I'm not. Maybe I should give up..."

"No, no!" Shepard said in a rush, then realized what he was saying. "Well, maybe...if you think it's best..."

Bliss shook his head. "No, that would be selfish. An artist can't be concerned with his own petty needs. I have the rest of the world to consider. The world needs my art."

To that Shepard had no answer.

Bliss seemed to gather his wits. "You said something...he could not have left the trap in a hurry..."

"Right."

"Wrong. He would have wanted to get away from there as fast as possible. We've determined he couldn't risk an escape route that took so long the others might have walked over and seen him."

"But the dew—" Shepard began.

"The dew? Oh, bother the dew! Haven't you figured that part out yet?"

Shepard, feeling very inadequate, shook his head.

Bliss sighed. "We'd better go in then."

They got out of the car and headed for the front door. The once pristine garden already began to look a little seedy and rundown. Alex Wagner's carefully controlled world was at last coming apart.

"Has Bruce Wagner turned up yet?" Bliss asked as they reached the front door.

Shepard pulled out a key.

"No, but it's been less than twenty-four hours."

"He has to be found."

"He will be."

Shepard unlocked the door and they went into the darkened house. "Forensics found a piece of plastic wrap in the van as well as the blood and blue fibers."

Bliss nodded. "Less messy to transport a body. I believe I saw the rest of the roll used on the floor here in the garage."

Shepard remembered. The torn carpeting near the desk drew his gaze. "He was probably seated at the desk, going through his papers one last time. Somebody came up from behind him with a second sand wedge."

"Your people will probably find the murder weapon hanging on the wall of the garage," Bliss added.

Shepard went on. "So Wagner falls. The plastic gets blood on it. The chair tears the carpeting. No matter how thoroughly the killer cleaned, I bet we'll find some traces of blood on these files, or the desk and chair."

Shepard saw Bliss regarding him keenly. "Do we need to go look in the closets?"

"The closets?" Shepard thought for a moment, then smiled and shook his head. "For color-coded socks? No. Wagner sneaked away from the golf course, and came back here. He removed his socks because they either were soaked with seawater, or spattered with blood when he cut himself in the sand trap. In the darkened house with the shades drawn like this the killer took out a pair of socks he thought were white, put them on Wagner's feet, then replaced the golf shoes."

Bliss beamed, obviously gratified by Shepard's performance. Shepard felt moderately pleased himself.

"Naturally he'd want to preserve the illusion that Wagner had died in the trap with his spikes on," Bliss said. He wandered off in the direction of the kitchen. Shepard followed.

"The food," Shepard realized as the odor of decay welled up from the trashcan in the kitchen. "The food was stacked in the order he ate it. His last meal was a frozen dinner he must have had after returning from the golf course, not breakfast! That's why you asked what they'd all had for breakfast!"

Bliss sighed. "The observation is correct, but that wasn't why I asked the question. Remember I had not even seen the house then."

"But then why…?"

"Everything in it's proper place, Chief," Bliss cautioned. "Wagner would have wanted it that way."

They went through the kitchen door into the garage. Shepard noted again the roll of plastic on the floor and the bags of golf clubs on the wall.

"You're right," he said. "Wagner must have been killed with a sand wedge from one of these bags."

"Of course." Bliss ignored the look Shepard shot at him.

Shepard glanced at the ladder. "Two ladders. Same brand. One here, one in the ocean at the bottom of the cliff."

"Did you trace the purchase yet?" Bliss asked.

"No."

"It doesn't matter." Bliss scrunched up his shoulders to prove the fact. "You'll find out Wagner bought both of them, probably on the same day."

"Why two ladders?" Shepard asked.

Bliss shrugged. "If the first was damaged, or he had to leave it behind. Wagner was a very meticulous man."

"But the ladder didn't work. We proved that."

"How was he to know it wouldn't work until he tested it? He lugged one of the ladders out to the seventh fairway one night, reached the same conclusions we did, and instead of carrying it all the way back, chucked it into the ocean. He probably tried several methods of escaping from that sand trap before he hit on one that would actually work."

"And that was?"

Shepard could see Bliss reveled in the moment. He expected Bliss must be feeling the same kind of satisfaction as when someone admired one of his paintings. Then it occurred to Shepard that maybe Bliss had never had that experience.

"From the very beginning, if we ruled out magic and the supernatural, Wagner's disappearance from the sand trap seemed to require some sort of elaborate Rube Goldberg type of explanation. Martian tunnels, makeshift bridges that could somehow defy gravity. Giant slingshots even came to mind, as I recall."

Shepard corrected him. "They came to your mind."

"If you insist. Actually the answer was as simple as it could be, and it stared both of us in the face every time we walked into this garage."

Shepard's eyes flitted from corner to corner, but for the life of him he could not see an explanation of anything staring back at him.

"I need an expert opinion to be sure," Bliss informed him.

"Alright," Shepard sighed. "Where do we find the expert?"

"At the Carmel Bay Country Club, of course. Once I have the answer to my question I believe I can show you how Alex Wagner vacated that sand trap simply and quickly."

They made their way toward the front of the house.

"What about the miraculous golf shot?" Shepard asked when they reached the car. "Wagner did that, right?"

"Of course," Bliss responded. "He was the only one in the sand trap."

"How did he do it?"

Bliss gave him a grin that Shepard thought one of the most evil things he had ever seen.

CHAPTER TWENTY-THREE

Out on the course a foursome composed of pros Ben Crenshaw and David Peoples, actor Hal Linden and former quarterback Fran Tarkenton, teed off on the fatal seventh fairway. In the general manager's office back at the clubhouse all hell was breaking loose.

Chick Beal's dyed-black hair capped a sunburned face, his nose and forehead peeling. Shepard wondered if the man had ever heard of the ozone layer. Now, as the manager of the Carmel Bay Country Club faced Shepard and Carl Lorch, everything from the neck up went even redder than usual.

"You cannot stop play! This is the Ridgeway Pro-Am!"

"Murder is more important than golf," Shepard replied, keeping on his best behavior.

"Says who?" Beal shot back. "People are murdered every day. The Ridgeway Pro-Am is an annual event televised live in one hundred and fourteen countries. We've got former president Clinton out there! We've got the blimp!"

"You may also have the answers to my murder case. We'll be as low-key as possible, but I'm going to have a look at your seventh hole."

"Now, you listen—" Beal tried to interject.

"No, you listen, sir. A police officer was killed last night. One of my officers."

"Hey, I'm sorry about that, but that was over in Monterey, not—"

"He was killed by the same person who murdered Alex Wagner."

"You have any proof of that, Chief?" Lorch inquired. Shepard could hear the tone of carefully spun doubt in his voice.

"I will have." Shepard hoped his voice sounded more certain than he felt.

He could see Beal searching for more objections.

"I've already sent Mr. Bliss to speak to your head groundskeeper." Shepard said.

Beal stared at him. "Herman Bliss? That crackpot? He's out there loose in the middle of my tournament?"

"He's helping me."

"Son, I hope your retirement fund is all paid and current. What's he want with Bill Pinch?"

"He wants to talk to him about grass," Shepard replied, realizing again how shaky the legal ground felt beneath his feet.

"Grass." Beal glanced at Lorch, receiving sympathy and dog-like devotion in return. He gave Shepard a look designed to melt steel, then turned back to Lorch. "Get Yale Gerringer in here."

Lorch started for the door, but Shepard's words stopped him in his tracks.

"Sergeant Lorch works for me."

"Damn you, Shepard, you don't have any idea what's at stake here!"

"If you'll forgive me, sir, neither do you." Shepard started out. "Carl?"

Lorch hesitated, his watery eyes shifting from Shepard to Beal.

"Chief, you assigned me to the Pro-Am."

Shepard stared at him for a long moment, then decided he might as well burn a few more bridges while he was at it.

"I'm giving you a direct order, Carl."

Lorch looked torn between some withered sense of duty and a glimpse of the main chance. Shepard saw him toting up the score, but didn't wait to hear the outcome. He strode out the door hearing Lorch's voice behind him.

"I'll find the mayor, Mr. Beal."

Shepard searched for Bliss and the groundskeeper midst the throng of spectators that choked the club, and reflected that Lorch might end up chief of Carmel's police after all. Unless he could prove Gerringer, Beal and the entire town council were all tied up in a vast conspiracy to murder Alex Wagner and Greg Cowles only to remove Shepard, he didn't see his prospects for remaining in Carmel as very bright.

He found Bliss and Bill Pinch, a tall, gnarled man with a face tanned and lined by a life in the outdoors, standing near the maintenance shed. They sprouted like weeds from the sea of golf carts parked out of sight of the television cameras in an effort to foster the illusion that golf somehow required physical exercise.

"It's a hybrid of Kentucky blue grass and a Florida strain called Miami Short Stalk. Very flexible, non-brittle to take the pounding the weather and the sea can dish out around here. What we use for the roughs," he added for Shepard's benefit.

"Flexible?" Bliss asked. "Like a sponge?"

Pinch considered. "Well, it don't soak up like a sponge. We wouldn't want that. But it's sure springy like one, to hold its shape, don'tcha know."

Overhead the throb of huge motors reached them, increasing in volume. The blimp appeared over a corner of the maintenance shed. Against puffs of white cloud and a rich blue sky it swung out over the ocean, making a turn in a moderate breeze that would bring it back around over the course again.

"What about the length?" Bliss asked.

"We cut it shorter this year than last," Pinch went on, obviously flattered by the attention. "About three inches."

"Why'd you do that?"

"We got complaints. Golfers last year said the longer grass made the course too difficult. We already got ourselves a tricky course here, and the percentage of pros don't make par is pretty steep. It makes 'em look bad, don'tcha know, high scores like that. Pros aren't supposed to get high scores like that."

Bliss' face lit up like a pinball machine. "Chief, there was an outside chance, a minuscule chance I didn't know what I was talking about."

Shepard tried to make his own expression register surprise, but he saw the furrows in Bliss' forehead grow deep with suspicion. Bliss turned back to the groundskeeper.

"Can you bring one of the little portables out to the seventh green, Bill?"

Pinch looked uneasy. "We're not exactly supposed to be walking around in the middle of the tournament, Herman. Television cameras, don'tcha know."

"That's okay. All taken care of," Bliss assured him. "Just bring it with you. We'll meet you."

Shepard and Bliss headed off toward the course. They tramped through the trees, hearing out on the course the splattering of applause and an occasional whoop of appreciation over a nice shot. The deep-bellied throb of the blimp would grow and then recede as it criss-crossed the sky several hundred feet overhead.

When they emerged from the trees near the seventh green, they discovered Yale Gerringer, MacGregor, and two more security men waiting for them. MacGregor looked ready to explode. Gerringer appeared frazzled.

"Dan, you can't be serious," Gerringer began. "There are thousands of people on the course."

"I'm sorry, Mr. Mayor, but we're going out there," Shepard announced.

Beyond MacGregor and Gerringer, Shepard could see the gallery, flowing like a river of bright colors, along the edge of the fairway. A foursome was in the midst of holing out on the seventh green. Behind the hill to the left Shepard knew four more golfers would be lining up their next shots, flanked by hundreds of spectators, maybe more.

MacGregor shook his head. "I'm sorry, Chief, but I have orders to see that nothing disrupts this tournament. It means too much to the people of this community."

"That's right," Gerringer agreed.

"And the world," MacGregor finished with a lofty tone.

Bliss ignored them and headed for the fairway.

MacGregor and his men started after him.

"MacGregor!" Shepard called. The security man looked back. "You want to create a scene, we can have one. But if you want to keep this as low profile as possible, I suggest you go hold up the next foursome for a few minutes, allow us to do our work, and get out of your way."

MacGregor looked torn. He glanced at the mayor.

Gerringer looked uncomfortable. "Dan, I can't allow you to jeopardize—"

"Why didn't you tell me Genevra Carroll was Armando Cosentino's daughter, Yale?"

Gerringer shrank inside his clothes. "Cosentino...the businessman...?"

"Don't try it, Yale." Shepard pressed. "I don't care what your relationship is with Cosentino."

"I have no relationship—!"

"I want your support in this investigation. I want it now."

MacGregor glared at Shepard. "You're trying to blackmail the mayor!"

Shepard was about to retort, but Gerringer beat him to it.

"Now, Mr. MacGregor. I wouldn't characterize it like that. Mr. Shepard is simply reminding me of my civic duties. I appreciate it. The welfare of the people of Carmel..."

"Are you going to let them disrupt this tournament?" MacGregor demanded.

Gerringer shrugged. "I hope they won't. Chief Shepard says they won't. Not my decision to make…really…" Gerringer hedged. "This is private land. Not city property."

Still MacGregor hesitated, but he saw that Bliss had already reached the center of the fairway near the bowl-like depression. A female tournament Marshall in a subdued blazer and skirt hurried to cut him off.

"Shit." MacGregor sniffed loudly. He trudged out on to the course, followed by Shepard. Shepard stopped when he noticed Gerringer did not join them.

"I still have a round of golf to play, Dan," he said with a weak smile. "I'm afraid this isn't working out at all. You, I mean."

Shepard managed a philosophic shrug. "Maybe you're right, Yale. We sure seem to have a different set of priorities. Enjoy your game."

He left Gerringer in the shadow of the trees and trotted to catch up with MacGregor.

MacGregor sent his two men and the Marshall to prevent the next foursome from hitting their second shots, then he, Shepard and Bliss moved toward the sand trap. A gallery of close to a hundred people sat or stood in a semicircle around the back edge of the green. Luckily a yellow rope prevented them from getting near the cliff.

Bill Pinch appeared from behind the crowd carrying a gray metal canister about two feet long and eight inches in diameter. It sported a yard-long flexible tube with a nozzle at the end. Straps for carrying it on a man's back hung limply from the side.

Shepard immediately remembered where he had seen others like it: in Wagner's garage.

Pinch looked uneasily at MacGregor. "They said it was okay, Mr. MacGregor."

"Okay?" MacGregor sniffed again. "No, it's not okay, but we're going to get this farce over as quickly as humanly possible." He waved his arm. "Go ahead. Do whatever it is you're here to do."

Bliss indicated the stretch of grass extending from the sand trap to the cliff edge.

Behind them Shepard saw the golfers and caddies waiting. The gallery that had been filing past had slowed to watch. Those settled in at the seventh green also watched, aware that the drama they were seeing fell outside the normal schedule of tournament events. A hush seemed to have settled. The blimp tacked far out to sea, the throb of its motors only a low, ominous vibrato. Even the wind seemed to hold its breath.

"In here anywhere is fine, Bill. You don't have to do the whole section. Wagner had Mother Nature to help him last Wednesday morning anyway."

Pinch nodded, slipped the tank on his back, and adjusted the nozzle at the end of the hose. Water sprayed out in a fine fan. Pinch swung the nozzle back and forth over an area several yards square.

"It's later in the morning than it was when Wagner vanished," Bliss orated. Shepard could see he was in fine form. "But it's cool enough. There! See?"

Shepard saw. The thin mist of water on the grass looked almost exactly like a stray patch of morning dew.

"Okay, Bill, hold it for a second," Bliss commanded.

Pinch shut the nozzle and moved back. Bliss stepped down into the trap, marched to the edge nearest the ocean where the patch of wet grass began, and stooped down. Then with an agility that would have surprised Shepard if he had not seen Bliss climb that very cliff, or snag one of Bruce Wagner's ground strokes, Bliss scrambled out of the trap on his hands and knees. He scuttled toward the cliff, but at the end of the wet patch regained his feet.

Bliss hiked over to where he could see the golfers, caddies and security guards out in the fairway.

"Any of you fellas see me crawling around back there?"

The group shook their heads. Shepard realized the tall one with the silvery hair was Arnold Palmer.

Bliss pointed down at the marks his passage had made in the grass.

"See? The grass is already springing back into shape, thanks to that Florida strain in the hybrid, I'll bet." He received a confirming nod from Pinch, then went on. "But the trail through our dew is clearly defined. Impossible to miss. Okay, Bill."

Pinch stepped forward again and sent the fine spray out over the same patch of ground. Even knowing what had to happen, it amazed Shepard. It reminded him of those old cowboy movies where the out-laws erased their tracks with a piece of brush, only much more effective. As the mist landed on the scuffmarks left behind by Bliss they became as gray as the untouched grass.

Shepard walked over for a closer look. If Bliss had damaged some of the grass, Shepard could not tell even from a few feet away. When Pinch finally stopped spraying, the expanse of grass looked as pristine as when he applied the first coat.

Shepard looked up to find Bliss leering at him with a smug expression.

"Wagner didn't crawl. He moved fast, then used one of his sprayers from below the cliff edge. In a few seconds he was done. On the morning he disappeared Wagner had real dew to help set up his illusion. We have it most mornings this time of year." He received another confirming nod from Pinch. "And that's how Alex Wagner vanished into thin air in a matter of seconds!" he finished with a massive bow.

Pinch grinned and applauded. The gallery, several of whom were local enough to suspect what was going on, followed suit in a polite clatter of applause.

"Of course," was all Shepard could think to say.

Maybe the additional moisture from the sprayer got to the security man. Maybe it was the chill breeze the ocean again flung at them. Whatever, at that precise moment MacGregor sneezed.

Shepard and Bliss turned in unison to face him, and under their scrutiny MacGregor could not help himself. He sneezed again.

"That's a nasty cold you've got there, MacGregor," Shepard said in his most matter-of-fact voice.

MacGregor didn't brazen it out and blame the sea air or pollen. He must have realized his fingerprints were all over the van. The less salubrious blood typing of mucous from the tissues taken from the van would also damn him. The security man seemed to feel the weight of evidence smothering him like a wet Kleenex. He didn't try to explain or bluster. All he did was panic. And run.

CHAPTER TWENTY-FOUR

MacGregor put on a surprising burst of speed for a man in built-up shoes. His legs pumping like pistons, he fled across the fairway toward the distant trees. Shepard gave a shout to the security men with the golfers, but then realized the futility of trying to explain to them in a few breathless seconds that they were to tackle their boss. He ran after MacGregor. Behind him he heard Pinch ask Bliss if he was going to help.

"I don't chase," came Bliss' laconic reply.

MacGregor dodged past the startled foursome that included Arnold Palmer, running with the flow of spectators for the eighth fairway. Shepard pelted after him, glad for the discipline that had kept him doggedly churning up the sand along Carmel's beach every lunchtime.

Shepard raced past the group on the eighth tee just as actor Hal Linden swung his four wood, and sent a ball slicing out over the cliff into the sea.

"Sorry!" Shepard yelled as he plunged on. Linden, having no idea who Shepard could be, or why he was running past, just gave a philosophic shrug that seemed to absolve Shepard for sharing any guilt in the shot. Crenshaw, Peoples and Tarkenton stood and watched Shepard cut across the fairway, still pursuing MacGregor.

His lungs ached, breath coming in short gasps. The muscles in his legs bunched and complained, but little by little Shepard narrowed the gap between him and the fleeing man.

Shepard thought his luck had turned when he saw several men in discreet sports coats detach themselves from the throng around the eighth green and move to head MacGregor off. The man lining up a chip shot on the front apron of the green explained their presence on the course. Former president Bill Clinton watched his ball sail up and over the green, scattering spectators.

MacGregor flashed his I.D. wildly at the secret servicemen, shouted something, gestured back at Shepard, then again struck off at an angle away from the ocean. Shepard veered to cut him off, glad he wore his uniform, and hoping the secret servicemen didn't try to slow him up. Their duty lay with the former president who now looked over his next attempt to make the green. When they saw Shepard heading away, one of them spoke quietly into a small headset and they slipped back to their posts.

Shepard became aware of the blimp, now almost directly overhead. It sailed along at a high enough altitude so its thudding engines would not disturb play below, but Shepard saw no golf right nearby for the cameraman in the blimp to photograph. He had a sinking feeling the camera was broadcasting his huffing and puffing to one hundred and fourteen countries.

MacGregor now dashed along a paved path between the eighth and second fairways, making for the Carmel Bay clubhouse two hundred yards further on. Shepard closed the gap between them to less than fifty yards and closed it even farther once he too reached the pavement.

The diminutive security man might have made it to the clubhouse and managed to lose himself in the masses of people there, but just as he reached the point where the path met the boundary road that separated the first tee from the clubhouse he glanced back over his shoulder to gauge Shepard's progress.

A series of short white metal posts with chain stretched between them bordered the boundary road. MacGregor's right foot came down where pavement and grass met. His ankle twisted. He stumbled and hit the metal links with both legs. The chain swept his feet out from under him and he sprawled in a heap on the boundary road.

He tried to drag himself back up, but Shepard came pounding up, easily vaulted the low chain and skidded to a stop right beside him. "You were following Bliss in the Sea Orchard Fish Company van. You shot him out at the racquet club. You then abandoned the van up on Vail Way."

MacGregor, making no move to rise, shook his head.

"No, it wasn't me!"

"I'm going to advise you of your rights, Mr. MacGregor, but we'll be able to place you in that van, believe me. You have the right to remain silent. You have the right to an attorney—"

"I didn't shoot anybody!" MacGregor protested, at last scrambling to his feet, his immaculate trousers and blazer now scuffed and torn. Sweat streamed down his face.

"If you cannot afford an attorney one will be provided for you."

"I don't need an attorney I tell you!" MacGregor persisted. "I didn't shoot Bliss! Why should I?"

"Do you understand these rights as I have explained them to you?"

"Yes, yes, but—"

"Are you waiving your right to an attorney?"

MacGregor drew himself up as tall as he could and spoke in a determined voice. "Yes, I don't need an attorney. I've done nothing illegal."

"Trace evidence in the van suggests it was used to transport Alex Wagner's body as well."

"What?" MacGregor's eyes bulged. The sweat appeared to gush forth with renewed force. A fit of sneezing enveloped him.

"Are you sure you don't want an attorney, Mr. MacGregor?"

MacGregor considered for a long time before finally nodding. "Maybe you'd better phone Lester Brown after all."

Shepard reacted. Lester Brown. The attorney who had bailed Bliss out. Armando Cosentino's attorney.

He cuffed MacGregor's hands, checking each finger for the torn nail, but all of MacGregor's fingernails were intact.

*　　　　*　　　　*

"No, you cannot question him," Shepard said.

He and Bliss stood outside Chick Beal's office. Inside MacGregor consulted with attorney Lester Brown, who turned out to be a member of the club. His paging service found him ensconced in the Nineteenth Hole, the unimaginatively named bar less than a hundred feet from Beal's office. They were both under the watchful eye of Charlie Revere, one of the Carmel police officers assigned to the tournament.

Bliss waggled his head back and forth. "There's no symmetry in the composition! Is MacGregor a lizard? Did his fingernail regenerate itself?"

"Maybe he didn't kill Wagner, that doesn't mean he didn't take a pot-shot at you."

"Chief," Bliss cajoled. "You said yourself there were two people up on that ridge. You found the shell casings. If you search MacGregor's things you'll find the forty-five automatic, not the rifle that was used on me."

"You seem awfully confident about that."

"Of course I'm confident. MacGregor's on Cosentino's payroll. Why would Cosentino hire me to investigate, then hire MacGregor to kill me?"

"Maybe MacGregor can tell us that."

"Chief Shepard!"

Shepard turned to find Beal and Yale Gerringer advancing on him. Lorch followed like a dinghy dragged in the wake of larger boats.

"I'm sorry about the ruckus, gentlemen." Shepard said.

"Ruckus…" grumbled Beal.

Gerringer held up a conciliatory hand. "We'll sort that all out later, Dan. I'm here to congratulate you on solving the case."

Shepard gave Bliss a pained look. Bliss closed his eyes and lifted his shoulders.

"I never would have guessed MacGregor was the killer," Gerringer went on. "How did you figure it out?"

"Actually we haven't charged him with anything yet, Yale. He's definitely implicated in the case, but we don't know to what degree."

Beal groaned. "You mean you destroyed this tournament to catch the wrong man?"

"Lighten up, Chick." Bliss squinted in a fashion he'd often seen Gerringer's illustrious predecessor, Clint Eastwood, use to intimidate opponents onscreen and off.

"I'm not interested in anything you have to say, Deerslayer." Beal looked down his nose at the painter. Since he was shorter than Bliss this must have hurt.

"That was an accident!" Bliss exclaimed. "How many deer have you killed by building this club where they used to graze?"

"They still graze here, you putz!"

"You think they like Miami Short Stalk?"

"Gentlemen, please," Shepard interjected. "Can we get back on track here?"

"Yes!" Gerringer concurred. "I don't quite understand. If MacGregor didn't kill Alex Wagner, why did he run?"

"Oh, he is guilty of something, Yale," Shepard explained. "At least he withheld information from the police, obstruction of justice, beyond that we'll have to wait and see." It wasn't until he finished he realized he'd bought into Bliss' picture of MacGregor's innocence with little argument. "What's the damage to the tournament?"

"Everything's back on track," Beal admitted grudgingly. "The satellite feed picked up you chasing MacGregor, but only a few stations cut to it. They like to stay off disruptions like that at sporting events to discourage copycat behavior."

"I'm glad," Shepard replied.

Lorch flashed him what passed for a gratified smile as if to say, "I was behind you all the way, Chief!" Shepard looked right through him.

The door to Beal's office opened. A slender, balding man in glaringly bright golf clothes came out. He smiled at Shepard. "Mr. MacGregor reiterates he has done nothing wrong. Certainly he has neither killed nor assaulted anyone. He would like to cooperate fully with your investigation with the hope that any small breaches of the letter of the law can be forgiven."

Shepard shook his head. "I can't make any promises, Mr. Brown."

"No, no. I understand. So does my client. As I've said, he's prepared to cooperate fully, and is ready for your questions."

Bliss gave him a pleading look, but Shepard shook his head. Personally he would not have minded, but he couldn't allow Bliss to taint any evidence gathered in the interview.

Bliss seemed to understand. "Could I have a word with you in private, Chief?"

Shepard allowed Bliss to lead him aside.

"I need to take a little trip," Bliss began. "Only overnight. I'll be back in time for your singing debut tomorrow night."

"Mr. Bliss, I have a dead police officer and an investigation that is threatening to end my career. I don't think it would be appropriate for me to go ahead with the performance."

"But you have to!" Bliss pleaded.

"Why do I have to?"

"I expect my trip to come up with the name of the killer," Bliss answered in a matter-of-fact voice. "And the motive, but there's not much chance of finding any evidence that would stand up in court."

Without waiting for a reply he turned to the other men. "Chief Shepard is thinking about not making his debut tomorrow night. Please help me convince him it would be good for the morale of the town."

Shepard tried to get a word in, but Bliss steamrolled on. "Let's show the folks of this fine community they need no longer fear for their lives! The investigation's getting results after only a week. In a case of this complexity that's a remarkable accomplishment! Why, even though he's too modest to admit it, Chief Shepard expects to have this case wrapped up before Monday!"

Shepard stared at him, aghast.

"Dan, my friend, that's marvelous news!" Gerringer burbled.

Shepard held up a hand, shaking his head. "Mr. Bliss may be a little too overconfident—"

"Balderdash!" Bliss enthused. "Let's give him the support he needs and all turn out tomorrow for his debut! The first round of drinks are on…him!"

Shepard tried to defuse the situation, but it did no good. Gerringer and Beal, suddenly his best pals, crowded round, shaking Shepard's hand and slapping him on the back.

"That will be good news to all sorts of people." Brown met Shepard's gaze and held it.

By then Bliss had almost convinced Shepard the promises held more substance than cotton candy. The three men left them there, MacGregor apparently forgotten, and headed in the direction of the Nineteenth Hole.

Gerringer's last words echoed down the hall.

"I knew it was a risk, hiring an outsider…A major league outsider…but I knew if I was right we'd have ourselves a real take-charge Chief of Police…"

Shepard sighed. "I hate you, Bliss."

Bliss laughed. "That's fine, Chief."

"I really do."

"Chief, don't take what I said to our friends too personally. That stuff about how on top of the case you are. It was necessary. But you really do quite well given your limitations."

"What's this trip all about? I thought Wagner's death was all tied up in his double dealing on the Cannery Row project."

Bliss looked at him in surprise. "I'm disappointed in you, Chief. The project may have made the murder possible, maybe even inevitable, but beyond that it has nothing whatsoever to do with it."

Shepard felt more lost than ever. "Inevitable? Bliss, where are you going?"

"You really don't know?"

Shepard shook his head.

"Where it all began, Chief. I'm flying up to Seattle."

CHAPTER TWENTY-FIVE

Shepard tested a cassette recorder on his desk and adjusted the volume level. Amy sat cross-legged, pad and pencil ready. MacGregor's gun, a forty-five automatic as Bliss prophesied, was already being checked against the bullets recovered at the racquet club. Revere ushered in MacGregor and Brown, and seated them in two chairs facing the desk. He drew Shepard aside.

"Thought you should know, just before Brown came out to talk to you back at the golf club he called somebody."

"Who?"

"He tried to keep his voice down, but from the way he acted, I'd say it was somebody pretty important. Lots of 'Yessirs' and 'Nossirs' and so on. He mostly just listened."

Shepard nodded. "If you had to make a guess about who it was on the other end of the line, Charlie, what would that be?"

Revere grinned. "Armando Cosentino."

"Me too." Shepard smiled.

"Course I did manage to catch the number he dialed. I checked it after we brought MacGregor over here. It's Mr. Cosentino's."

Shepard laughed. "You didn't have to confess. You could've left me impressed with your deduction."

"I'd rather you were impressed with the thoroughness of my investigative technique, Chief. Detectives are supposed to be thorough."

"Detectives, huh? Okay, Charlie, I'll keep that in mind. Good job."

Revere stood with his back to the door. Shepard went around his desk, sat and turned on the cassette recorder. He gave the time, date and the names of those present, then leaned forward and fixed his eyes on MacGregor.

"Okay, Mr. MacGregor, do you now admit you were driving the Sea Orchard van on the morning Mr. Bliss was shot?"

"Yeah."

"You'd been following him for some time?"

"Two days."

"How did you come into possession of the van?"

"It was parked outside the Sea Orchard office. You know, on the wharf."

That, Shepard realized, explained why the killer had chosen the bay as the spot to dispose of Alex Wagner. To preserve the illusion that Wagner met his end at the golf course, the best place for the body to turn up would be the Pacific Ocean. Afterwards the killer could stash the van used to carry it right where it belonged. Otherwise he might have to abandon it, and if the body turned up, people might make uncomfortable connections.

Shepard also saw how MacGregor's borrowing the van threw a monkey wrench into the murderer's plan. Just when the killer thought he successfully covered his tracks, MacGregor commandeered the van to follow Bliss. That thrust it right back into the center of the case.

"How did you have access to it?" Shepard asked. "Where did you get the keys?"

Here MacGregor glanced at Brown. Brown gave him a bland look in return and nodded.

MacGregor went on. "They were given to me by a man named Victor Dewalt."

"Why?"

"He paid me five hundred dollars to…to look out for Bliss, but Bliss wasn't supposed to know anything about it. For some reason Mr. Dewalt had a pretty high opinion of Bliss. Don't ask me why. Anyway I was to see to it that no harm came to Bliss while he carried out this job."

"Kind of blew it, didn't you?"

"So did your man, didn't he? The one that ended up dead? I drove right past him while he was reading some magazine."

Shepard swallowed his impulse to comment. MacGregor was right. "Go on."

"When I saw where Bliss and that other guy were playing tennis, I looked around. The ridge seemed like the best spot to keep an eye on things, so I circled behind it and climbed up the other side."

"Did you recognize the man Bliss was playing tennis with?"

MacGregor nodded. "Almost crapped in my pants. He looked exactly like that attorney who was killed, Alex Wagner. Found out later it was his brother, right?"

"Right."

"So anyway I'm about halfway up the backside of the hill when I hear the first shot. I'm still hauling out my forty-five when I hear the second. And I want it on that tape that I'm licensed to carry that gun in my capacity as head of security at Carmel Bay. It's registered and everything."

"Okay, it's on the record. What happened after you heard the second shot?"

"Well," MacGregor continued, "I heard somebody come along the top of the ridge, blundering through the undergrowth like they were in a hell of a hurry. I let out a yell, got a bullet zipping by my head for my trouble and let off a couple rounds of my own."

"At who?"

"Just a shadow behind the brush."

"Big? Small? Male? Female?"

MacGregor gave his head a helpless shake. "I couldn't tell."

"What happened to him?"

"I don't know!" MacGregor protested. "Maybe he had a car some-where. "My cold was pretty bad then as I guess you know. I couldn't run worth shit. I realized how it all might look, so I made it back to the van and took off with you on my tail. That's the whole story."

"Why'd you abandon the van on Vail Way?" Shepard asked.

MacGregor tried to look nonchalant. "I ran out of road."

"Why'd you go up there anyway, MacGregor? Was it because you wouldn't have much of a hike to reach Armando Cosentino's home on Aguajito?"

"Chief," Brown's voice cut in like a knife through soft cheese. "Mr. Cosentino will freely admit he hired Mr. MacGregor to keep Mr. Bliss safe, a job Mr. MacGregor obviously performed inadequately. But he has no knowledge of Mr. MacGregor's actions on the day Mr. Bliss was shot, particularly any conduct of questionable legality."

Shepard saw then that Brown would protect Cosentino's interests even to the extent of throwing MacGregor to the wolves if he must. "Did you notice a crate in the back of the van, MacGregor? Smelled like fish?" Shepard asked MacGregor.

"Yeah, I saw it. Don't know if it smelled. I have a cold."

"Did you touch it? Go near it?"

"No."

Shepard told Brown he wouldn't hold MacGregor. The District Attorney would decide if any charges would be filed. Revere showed the two men out and Amy went back out front to her desk. Shepard brushed his hand over his hair. The familiar bit of melody that had been worrying at him since the case began insinuated itself into his thoughts. He hummed to himself and leaned back in his chair.

Wagner's plan for vanishing was the only premeditated part of the crime. How did the killer find out about it? Someone Alex told? Who would he trust enough? His brother? Was his next stop on his escape route Seattle to see Bruce?

How could Bliss insist the hotel project did not lie at the core of the case? It made the murder possible? Yes, Shepard could see that. The various people involved would have had the knowledge to commit the crime, and several had motive as well. But inevitable? Why was the murder of an embezzler inevitable? There were so many other more socially acceptable, not to mention less risky, ways of dealing with him.

Seattle. Two brothers who became estranged shortly after their mother's funeral. A tragedy at sea where Bruce performed heroically. He thought about the erratic behavior both brothers displayed over the years. Shepard remembered the moment he first saw Bruce Wagner at the airport. He remembered seeing an old movie from years ago about twins called the Corsican Brothers, and how linked they were. Could one Wagner affect the other's moods, even at long distance?

Or was the answer much simpler than that? He sat up, his feet hitting the floor with a sharp slap. His mind raced, the song knocked aside by a new idea. Could they have done it? Why? The thrill? The danger? A high so great Alex Wagner's experimentation with drugs had paled by comparison? It explained so much about the victim: his compulsiveness, why his marriage went sour, maybe even the embezzlement. Shepard suddenly saw with almost crystalline clarity what Bliss sought in Seattle. The truth gleamed like a two-edged sword that cut both ways. Now at last he understood why the killer wanted both brothers dead.

*   *   *

Bliss' feet scuffed across the concrete floor of the warehouse as he made his way down a cross aisle, a canyon of crates stretching high overhead. To his right he could see the glow of light from what should be the office. Outside a foghorn moaned.

After landing in Seattle that afternoon, he'd gone straight to the library to scan back issues of the local newspaper on microfiche, going over page after page dealing with the ferry boat disaster. Some of the clippings matched those taken from Alex Wagner's safe. On the night of February fifteenth six years before, the ferry had been on its regular route from Seattle to Port Washington when it veered off course in the fog and struck a rocky shoal. It sank in less than thirty minutes. Many of the survivors made it to a nearby island, little more than a cluster of rocks jutting up out of the bay.

Bliss found Bruce Wagner on the passenger list and another Wagner named Lucinda, identified as his mother in a later story that focused on Bruce's heroic efforts to save lives. Bruce insisted his mother had not been on the ferry that night. Bliss thought he now understood why.

He went back and forth over the passenger list, comparing it to the names of the dead and injured. All the bodies from the tragedy had been recovered. No names matched any of the suspects in Alex Wagner's murder. Armed with the list he next made some phone calls back to California until he at last made the connection he knew must be there.

One of the casualties was named Dolores Muñoz. As with many other professional women these days, she undoubtedly chose to retain her maiden name even after she married. Manager of a commercial bank in California, she had been in the Seattle area on business, according to her office. Married with three children. She'd been traveling to Port Washington to sightsee the following day.

Bliss came around the corner of one aisle and spotted the small office cubicle just ahead. As he drew nearer he saw a lone figure, feet propped up on the desk: a Chinese-American man in his late thirties, powerfully built.

Bliss knocked on the window. The man looked up, a startled expression on his face.

"Derek Chow?" Bliss called.

The man nodded, got up. "Mr. Modigliani? Come on in. Coffee? It's a bitter night out there."

"Thanks," Bliss responded with a grateful nod. "I could use some."

Bliss glanced around the room while Chow poured coffee into two cups from a machine on a low bookshelf. Lining the walls were pictures of his family on what looked like hundreds of separate vacations.

"You sure seem to get around," Bliss commented.

Chow smiled. "Well, night security work doesn't give you much chance to see the world. I get claustrophobic, so when vacation time comes I'm outta here." He indicated a pile of travel brochures on the bookshelf. "Sometimes it helps just to read about all those places, you know? Plan where we'll go next?"

Bliss noticed an open book on the small wooden table that served as Chow's desk. "Principles of Anatomy?"

"Yeah," Chow looked embarrassed. "I'm taking courses at the university in the afternoons. Me as a doctor, right? It was really my wife's idea, but I'm getting into it."

Bliss wished him luck. "Thanks for seeing me on such short notice."

"Haven't talked to a reporter in a long time. I thought the ferry sinking was old news."

"I'm doing a follow-up," Bliss explained in what he hoped passed for a journalist's determined manner. "Where the survivors are now." He glanced again at the medical book. "How it has affected them."

Chow handed Bliss a cup. "I've got the same job I had then. The same life. Maybe that'll change soon, who knows?"

"You were one of the heroes. You swam down over and over in freezing water, pulling people out of the wreck."

"I'm a good swimmer. They needed my help." He shrugged. "I did what I could."

"Papers at the time said you and that doctor, Bruce Wagner, did a lot more than anyone to minimize the casualties."

Bliss saw Chow's expression darken. His whole body tensed. "Yeah, that's what they said alright."

"But he wasn't much of a hero really, was he?"

Chow looked wary. "What?"

"Wagner I mean," Bliss persisted. "You sure didn't think much of him from one interview I read."

"He didn't want to help!" Chow blurted out. "He said he had to look after his mother. She looked okay to me. There were a lot of others who needed him more!"

"But he did help the injured, didn't he?"

Chow nodded. "I guess. That's what they said later."

"You disagree."

"From what I could see he could've done a lot better, but people told me I didn't understand these things. Finally I shut up." He indicated the book. "Now that I understand more, my opinion hasn't changed. Why are you so interested in Wagner?"

Bliss smiled. "I'm not. Really. Not anymore. I'd rather find out about another visitor you must have had."

"Who?"

"Dolores Muñoz's husband?"

Bliss watched with satisfaction when Chow looked startled. "Yeah, he showed up not too long after the accident, wanting to know anything I could tell him. I think in some way he just wanted to share her last moments. He really loved her. I told Betty Ann—that's my wife—I felt bad. I should've whitewashed things I guess, but I was still so angry…"

"You told him Wagner could have saved her, but botched the job?"

"Yeah, he must've panicked or something. She still had a pulse when I brought her up, but there was some debris or something lodged in her throat. He tried a tracheotomy on her; hit a major artery or some-thing…I mean I know the guy was just a gynecologist and they're right when they say I probably couldn't do any better, but I saw him. I saw his eyes. He looked flat out lost and scared." He stopped. "Say, how did you know about him? The husband I mean." Chow asked in amazement.

"I didn't. For sure. Until now. He had to have gotten the truth from someone, and in all the reports I read, you were the only witness quoted who disagreed with the general consensus that Bruce Wagner was a hero."

"Hero!" Chow exclaimed. "That isn't the title I would give him!"

The foghorn moaned again like the ghost from that sunken boat six years earlier, a ghost crying for justice.

"What, then?"

Chow slammed down his cup. "As far as I'm concerned he's a murderer."

CHAPTER TWENTY-SIX

Ramblin Rick's Bistro was a popular hangout tucked at the end of a narrow passageway between a leather shop and an art gallery. In any other town the passage would be an alley. In Carmel people called it an arcade.

Huge burgers, homemade fries and a beer menu far more extensive than its wine list endeared Rick's to patrons tired of the nearly empty plates of nouveau, nouvelle and New Age cuisine practiced on the tourists in the trendier local restaurants. Rick's consisted of a large bar area with a restaurant beyond. At one end of the bar a low platform served as a stage for local musicians.

The Monterey Peninsula attracted as many musicians and composers as it did artists and writers, and Rick's featured an eclectic range of music on different nights from jazz to classical enjoyed by a packed house most nights of the week. Sunday, Karaoke night, was really the only chance you had to avoid the crowds.

Friday nights gave Rick's a chance to introduce new talent to its clientele. On this Friday a baby grand piano and a microphone on a stand stood in the middle of the stage. Shepard sat on the bench in front of the piano, arranging his music and trying to look relaxed. He now knew why Bliss manipulated him into performing. Bliss had obviously coerced Ramblin' Rick, a bear of a man with a full black beard, to be a part of the conspiracy. The artist probably owned this building, too.

A quick glance at the faces of his audience gave Bliss away, but now it was too late for Shepard to do much about it. Every face was familiar. Everyone in that room, except for Rick himself and his staff, was somehow, however remotely, connected to Alex Wagner's murder. Bliss had arranged a mass gathering of the suspects like an Agatha Christie novel.

Since returning from Seattle that morning, the artist had avoided Shepard's phone calls, yet from the look of things he'd been hard at work pulling every string he could to pack the house.

Loren Holly entered with his wife, an elderly woman so wizened she looked like the mummified remains of a human being. She made Holly look huge by comparison, and that, Shepard reflected, could be one reason he married her.

Holly cornered Shepard. "Is this some new kind of extortion? Are we being forced to attend your concert?"

Shepard assured Holly he could leave if he wanted to, but was not surprised when after much grumbling Holly allowed that he might stay to find out what Bliss was up to.

"I'm hurt, Dan," Yale Gerringer said. "I already told you I planned to come. You didn't need to send Bliss to coerce me."

After delivering his half-hearted protest, Gerringer retired with Maggie Dennis to a table near Holly and his wife. The mayor had become quite meek since their final argument on the golf course.

Bliss even had tried to persuade Cosentino to attend. A polite but firm Victor Dewalt arrived to inform Shepard that Mr. Cosentino rarely socialized. Mr. Dewalt however expressed his delight in the invitation. He escorted Cosentino's daughter, Genevra. She looked haggard and more haunted than ever. They sat near the bar, Genevra drinking heavily. Dewalt nursed what looked like a single glass of ginger ale.

Jason Kiley lurked near the entrance, probably hoping to make a quick getaway if Bliss came after him again. Shepard thought Bliss' wrath would more likely focus on the mayor who had made a waving and hand-shaking entrance with Maggie Dennis on his arm.

The manager of Carmel Bay, Chick Beal, showed up, as did his groundskeeper, Bill Pinch, although not together.

Leonard Romaine and Ben Webb entered together. They'd won their battle with the Planning Commission only that afternoon. The hotel project was proceeding full steam ahead. Both looked as if they were in a mood to celebrate, but uncertain if they were in the right place to do it.

Shepard's glance swept back over the crowd. Catherine Gonzales sat at a table near the back with Amy. Both had promised to come to lend moral support and backup harmony if necessary. They waved.

Significant in his absence was Bliss.

Shepard spoke up over the conversation in the room. "Listen, folks. This is obviously not a simple concert here, but I want you to know that however you were forced into coming, the Carmel Police Department can't force you to remain."

No one said a word.

"You're free to go," he insisted.

No one moved. Finally, Shepard saw Kiley step aside in the door. Three men walked in. The first was Bruce Wagner. Behind him came Charlie Revere and the artist.

Shepard allowed himself a small feeling of satisfaction. Certain he knew why Alex Wagner died, he also realized the most likely place where Bruce might hide: his brother's house, trusting the investigation to concentrate elsewhere. After all it was the one place on the peninsula to which he had his own key.

Wagner, Bliss and Charlie threaded their way through the scattered tables and approached the stage. Shepard could see Wagner walked with a pronounced limp. When the three men reached him, Charlie spoke first. "Things were pretty quiet at the house. Mr. Wagner did a good job of staying away from the windows. When I saw Mr. Bliss arrive and try to get in, I thought I better take charge. I would have taken them both to the station, but since Mr. Bliss said he was coming here to see you…"

"No problem, Charlie," Shepard told him.

The gynecologist glowered. "Am I under arrest, Chief Shepard?"

"You knew a police officer had been attacked, Wagner. You fled the scene. There's an APB out on you."

"I didn't know he was dead, Chief. I swear it."

"Maybe he wasn't," Shepard pointed out. "Maybe he died when you didn't help him."

"I didn't see it. I only heard it. A scuffle outside my door, then the sounds…those awful sounds of something hitting…the body falling…I ran. I admit it. I climbed out the window, dropped to a roof below. I sprained my ankle, tore ligaments…Behind me I heard the door of my room burst open. I dragged myself across the roof, expecting to be shot down then and there, but no bullet came."

"The killer's marksmanship leaves a lot to be desired," Bliss grumbled, rubbing his shoulder. "Beating people's heads in appears to be a more successful modus operandi."

Wagner gestured at Bliss. "You have a lot of explaining to do, Chief Shepard. Allowing this artist to pretend he was a detective! How could you allow him to impersonate an officer of the law!"

"I regret that minute by minute, Dr. Wagner. But I'm placing you under arrest for fleeing the scene of a crime and obstruction of justice." Shepard looked at Bliss. "And as the evening progresses I suspect there may be more charges. Charlie, find Dr. Wagner a seat close to the stage here."

Shepard saw Romaine and Webb move to join Holly at his table. The room quieted in expectation.

Shepard looked at Bliss. "Everybody here you need, Mr. Bliss?"

"Me, Chief? They came to hear you sing."

"Don't be coy. You arranged this party."

"Send them home," Bliss challenged.

"I tried. Nobody will go."

"Then they're all here of their own free will."

"That's debatable, but they're all too scared or too curious to leave."

"Then the stage is set. Do me one favor. Have that young officer with the freckles go stand behind Holly, would you?"

Shepard nodded, beckoned to Charlie and gave him his instructions. As unobtrusively as possible Charlie first exited the room at the rear, only to re-enter a few seconds later to lean casually against the wall behind Holly.

Shepard moved away from the piano and faced the audience. The noise in the room dropped as if someone had switched off a radio.

"Ladies and gentlemen," Shepard began. "Mr. Bliss, whom most of you know, has been assisting me in the investigation into the death of Alexander Wagner. However you may feel about the propriety of an amateur working in conjunction with the Carmel Police force, I want to say that without Mr. Bliss this case would never have progressed as far as it has."

Bliss seemed to grow a foot taller, the gratification written plainly on his face. Shepard thought that if this had been an auction for one of Bliss' paintings he could not have looked more pleased.

"Is it solved then, Chief?" Gerringer spoke up.

"I'm going to turn the floor over to Mr. Bliss now, Yale. After he's finished, you can decide that for yourself. Mr. Bliss?"

Bliss lumbered forward, every eye in the place fixed on him. "Thanks, Chief." He turned to face his audience. "Alex Wagner was a complex human being, a man of seeming contradictions, obsessively neat, yet ethically sloppy. He didn't plan on embezzling three million dollars from the Cannery Row project—"

He ignored the excited buzz that arose in the room. Holly slammed his fist down on the table in front of him, nodding triumphantly to his wife and the two men seated with him.

Bliss went on. "He would probably have been content in his life as it was. It offered unique opportunities for excitement and sensation that even drugs and extra-marital affairs couldn't match. But then someone discovered his secret. Not that he was embezzling money. He wasn't yet. Not even that he was playing both ends of the Cannery Row deal against one another, or that he was bribing those necessary to bribe to see the project went forward without a hitch."

Shepard saw Kiley glance at the nearby door, but the gardener made no move toward it.

Leonard Romaine spoke up. "Mr. Bliss, and Chief Shepard, I want to go on record as saying neither Mr. Holly nor any other members of his organization was aware of any bribery."

"What about the embezzlement?"

Romaine nodded. "It was under investigation, and we'd begun to suspect Alex's relationship with Mutual Holdings as well."

"I don't need to bribe anybody!" Holly thundered. "Cannery Plaza is a good project! Good for the community and good for the environment! It's good!"

"And good for your wallet, too," Bliss observed. "One day when the last cypress tree is a fond memory and this entire peninsula is one gigantic mall, that'll be good, too, won't it?"

"Stow the politics, Bliss," Ben Webb warned him.

Shepard turned to Bliss. "We're here to catch a murderer."

"I haven't forgotten," Bliss growled.

"What was this big secret Alex Wagner was hiding?" Webb asked.

Here Bliss looked down at Bruce Wagner. Wagner would not meet his gaze. "The same secret his brother here has spent the past few days rigorously trying to protect. For who knows how long, probably since they were kids, Alex and Bruce Wagner have played a game. At first it was harmless enough, I suppose, although it must have always had its darker side. But in later years it became reprehensible and finally, six years ago, it proved fatal."

Bliss paused one final time for dramatic effect. The silence stretched on and on. Right then Shepard could have beaten his head in with a sand wedge.

Bliss continued at last. "They changed places." He held out his hands. "Swapped identities. Not only once or twice, but all the time. The first few times it was probably prompted by the kind of mistaken identity that always happens with identical twins. Later on the thrill of role-playing, of acting out the life of another, must have become irresistible."

"It was," Wagner said quietly. "And I want to say that we never meant to harm anyone."

Genevra Carroll leaped to her feet. Dewalt tried to restrain her, but she broke free and charged Wagner.

"You son of a bitch!" she screamed. "It wasn't erratic behavior or mood swings! I was living with two different men! You shared my marriage! Sometimes I was in bed with the man I had married, the man I somehow fell in love with, and sometimes it was you! You shared me!"

Shepard saw the look of disgust on Maggie Dennis' face. She hadn't known, but now she realized that both men had shared her as well.

Dewalt led Genevra back to her seat with surprising gentleness.

Bliss' gaze bored into Wagner. "You lied and betrayed as a matter of course, a way of life. No wonder your brother found it so easy to manipulate the Cannery Row deal and then steal money from it. A small step for someone who had grown up in a world of lies."

"No one was supposed to get hurt. We made a pact," Wagner persisted, but his voice carried little conviction.

"That pact was broken six years ago, wasn't it?" Bliss asked him. "The night a ferry between Seattle and Port Washington foundered. A doctor was desperately needed. Your mother thought there was one on board. She volunteered your services. Only she didn't know. You'd fooled her, too. You were down here playing lawyer. It was Alex Wagner who was on the ferry who was forced to play doctor for real."

"It was a freak accident," Wagner said, his voice trailing off. "How could we foresee—"

Bliss cut him off. "Your mother guessed the truth at some point." Wagner nodded. "And the horror of what you two had done killed her."

Here Wagner pulled himself upright, glaring at Bliss with a look of contempt. "Oh, don't be so melodramatic. She had a stroke. Period. People don't die because of dramatic revelations or broken hearts except in Victorian novels."

"Maybe," Bliss agreed with surprising equanimity. "But it was never quite the same after that night, was it?"

"No."

"You continued to do it though. To trade places."

"We tried to stop. Alex got married." He didn't look at Genevra. "But it was an obsession. We knew it was wrong of course, but we couldn't stop...You're right; it was thrilling, more than thrilling to pretend to be someone I wasn't. To live another life, outside it, looking in like God almost. There's no way to explain. There's no way for anyone to understand."

"Your lives were molded to make the switch as easily as possible," Bliss went on, relentless. "Clothes, even food methodically arranged. Lives ordered down to the last detail, so there'd be as few slip-ups as possible. But it was never perfect. Those around you sensed something was wrong. Alex's wife. Your colleagues."

"They never guessed," Wagner said with a hint of pride.

"Someone did," Bliss countered. "Last year your brother began embezzling enough money to make his escape. Did he warn you?"

Wagner shook his head. "We...switched...less often...That was all. I thought he was becoming tired of the game again like the other time. I was afraid he was going to stop. And he was! He was going to run out on me! We'd been playing for forty years! How can you turn your back on a commitment like that?" Horribly, Wagner burst into tears, hiding his face in his hands.

"So you don't know who killed your brother, and has tried to kill you twice?" Shepard asked him.

Wagner shook his head, tears still flowing. "I found those clippings when I searched our safe and guessed what must have happened." He looked up at Bliss. "A relative or something? One of the people Alex tried to help on the ferry?"

"One of the people he murdered," Bliss corrected. "By pretending to be a doctor. A man named Derek Chow, a true hero that night, guessed your brother's lack of medical knowledge failed to save more than one person. We're only interested in one death here tonight. That of a woman named Dolores Muñoz."

Again Shepard scanned the room, looking for a reaction to the name. He could see none.

"Alright, Bliss," Yale Gerringer spoke up. "Who was she?"

"Your wife, Mr. Mayor."

Shepard gaped at Bliss in amazement. The room fell so silent you could hear a jaw drop.

Next to Gerringer's table the executives from Holly Development gawked at him. Maggie Dennis shrank back as if she'd just discovered her date was a werewolf. Shepard suspected Bliss savored this particular reaction to his words the most. Charlie Revere shifted slightly to now lean in his direction.

The mayor and Bliss gazed at one another for a long moment.

"They have your fingernail, Yale," Bliss said in an almost apologetic voice. "It was torn off when you stuffed Wagner's body in that crate. I'm told they can do wonderful things these days with DNA matching."

"Mind if I take a look at your hand, Yale?" Shepard asked.

Gerringer looked for them, flicked at the middle finger of his right hand with his thumb, then stuck the finger out defiantly at Bliss. "Fuck you, Herman."

Bliss stared at him, expressionless.

"What about this sick bastard?" Gerringer indicated Bruce Wagner. "There wasn't enough evidence to prove Alex Wagner killed Dolores. After all this time what could they charge Bruce with? Accessory before the fact? It wouldn't begin to atone."

Gerringer directed this at Shepard. Shepard moved forward to stand next to Bliss.

"Maybe not," Shepard answered. "I imagine you've researched this case more thoroughly than most."

"I have."

"Before you say anything else, I'd like to give you your rights."

"I know them, Dan," Gerringer sighed. "I waive the right to legal counsel. I admit I killed Alexander Wagner."

CHAPTER TWENTY-SEVEN

Gerringer flashed a wry smile in Bliss' direction. "I underestimated you, Herman. You're a very dangerous man."

"Thank you," Bliss nodded graciously.

Gerringer looked back at Shepard. "At first I thought Dolores' death was simply malpractice, maybe negligent homicide after talking to Mr. Chow," Gerringer continued in a calm, conversational tone.

Shepard saw Wagner turn to stare at him.

"Do you know what you've destroyed?" Wagner asked.

"Half-destroyed," Gerringer amended. "Both you and Alex were responsible. Your brother, playing doctor, ended her life. You made it possible for him. At the time I thought you were responsible, but I knew the case would be almost impossible to prove in court."

"Did you know about Alex?" Bliss said.

Gerringer shook his head. "No, only that there was a brother. A twin. I asked around in Seattle, turned up some oddities in Bruce Wagner's behavior, including an erratic golf game. Although I understand his tennis game is better."

"Not much," Bliss muttered.

Gerringer smiled crookedly at Holly, Webb and Romaine, but the three men just stared blankly back at him.

"I decided to find Alex Wagner," he continued. "It only took a few months."

"When did you realize they'd switched places the night your wife died?" Shepard asked.

"Not long after that," Gerringer said. "I arranged to retire early from my company, but beyond that I had no plan. It was on another visit to Carmel I ran into the man I thought was Alex at some friends'. There was something different about him. I followed him home, watched him for several days, then followed him back to Seattle on a plane and watched him walk right into his other life. It was eerie. I suppose we passed the real Alex in a plane that day, headed south to renew his life."

"I liked Carmel, had friends here. I suspected at that point it was Alex Wagner who killed Dolores. I didn't think of revenge. I wanted justice. I wanted Alex to pay. So I retired here."

"Why didn't you kill him then?"

"I tried only a few months later," Gerringer responded. "I poisoned him the night I won the mayoral election for the first time. I botched it so badly he just thought he had ptomaine from the crab dip. I tried again a few months later. I tampered with the brakes on his car. They went out on a level stretch of highway. He pulled to the side of the road and called AAA.

"After that I became more cautious. I didn't want to go to jail, how would justice be served by that? Then I realized the switch the night of the accident wasn't a one-time thing. They swapped places every few months or so.

"In those days I was only interested in killing Alex. I didn't want to get the wrong one. For a long time I didn't try again. I was too scared. But all the while the rage grew inside me, squeezing me..." his voice trailed off.

"Something changed eighteen months ago," Bliss prompted. "What was it?"

Gerringer sighed. "Somehow Alex found out who I really was. He came to several parties at my house. I was always careful to keep pictures of Dolores out of sight, the letters and mementos, but you know the kind of man he was. He probably went through my things, my private things, and found...her...I guess that's when he spooked and started embezzling."

Shepard put another piece together and glanced at Genevra Carroll. "That would be when his marriage started falling apart, too."

Genevra riveted her attention on Gerringer, the expression on her face a strange mixture of shock and relief.

Gerringer went on. "By scaring him I managed to create my own opportunity to get closer. What I didn't realize is that at first he was embezzling to buy me off! He came to me one night. A settlement he called it. That's when I knew the truth. He had to die. I don't think you can pay for life. It is given or taken away."

"When he saw you wouldn't be bought off, he decided to make a run for it?" Shepard asked.

"Yes. But he didn't know how I followed him everywhere, watched as he started to plan his disappearance. I realized he was handing me a perfect alibi on a platter.

"As Mr. Bliss said, while everybody thought the murder occurred in that sand trap, I was safe. I knew when Alex planned to return home. I'd seen him time his route from the seventh hole along the beach to his house."

Bliss glanced at Shepard. "I believe I mentioned it was shorter that way..."

Gerringer shrugged. "I went to his house and waited for him."

"Why are you confessing, Yale?" Shepard asked him.

"You'll find this hard to swallow, Dan, I know, but I'm a very moral man. While I still believe both Alex and Bruce Wagner deserve to pay with their lives for taking my wife from me, I heartily regret killing your officer. He was at the wrong place at the wrong time. He saw me there at the Seascape the night I went to kill Wagner. I couldn't let him stop me. I'm sorry."

"That still doesn't explain why you're confessing in front of all these witnesses," Shepard persisted.

Gerringer held up his hand. "You have the motive. You have the fingernail. I have three wonderful children, Dan. Karen, Becky and Donald. And they have children. And while my actions are going to cause their families immeasurable pain, I'm going to do everything in my power to expedite the criminal process. I'll plead guilty, cooperate in every way that I can. Hopefully the trial will be swift, my tenure on the front pages brief, then some new sensation will capture the media's attention, and they'll be free to pick up their lives with the least amount of disruption.

"If only I knew Dr. Wagner here felt the same way about justice. I fully expect him to fight whatever charges are brought against him."

"I have a right to defend myself," Wagner said. "Any guilt is Alex's alone."

Gerringer looked upset. "Yes, you may get off scot free. And if I were a better shot, I'd end it right now."

At those words Charlie Revere stepped up behind Gerringer, but the mayor raised his hand.

"I'm not armed. You'll find the rifle I unfortunately wounded Mr. Bliss with in the trunk of my car."

Charlie politely asked him to stand up and patted him down anyway. The young officer nodded to Shepard.

Gerringer turned to look at Shepard. "I think that about covers it. I can go into the gory details later, how I used the Sea Orchard van to get rid of him, and so on. In my trailing after him, I'd picked up quite a bit about Mutual Holdings and the Cannery Row hotel. I hit him from behind. I suppose you'll think that makes me a coward. Maybe I am. I regret I couldn't look into his eyes, and tell him why he was dying, but I'm not a very good murderer I'm afraid. I thought he might somehow get the better of me, if we were face to face.

"I'm ready to go, Chief. I'm sorry I didn't get a chance to hear you sing."

Charlie took out handcuffs and glanced at Shepard. Shepard shook his head. Charlie led the mayor out.

When they passed Dewalt, Shepard saw him murmur something in Gerringer's ear. Whatever it was, Gerringer stared at the little man, then allowed himself a look of almost relief as he glanced one final time at Wagner.

Shepard guessed what it must be. A promise to see justice done. Wagner had more than one debt still due to the Cosentino family. Shepard realized he would have to do everything in his power to see that Bruce Wagner survived to reach trial. He disagreed with Gerringer. He thought they could put Bruce Wagner in prison as an accessory at least in Dolores Muñoz's death. After that he'd be beyond protection. Cosentino would ultimately reap his final vengeance.

As soon as Charlie exited with his prisoner, a wave of noise swept over the room. Bliss turned to Shepard.

"You sure you don't want to sing, too, Chief?"

Shepard laughed and shook his head. "Not after being upstaged like that, Bliss. Carmel will have to wait awhile before my debut."

Bliss grinned. "I'll be here when you do."

         *   *   *

Shepard debuted at Ramblin' Rick's two weeks later and not on Karaoke night. His first set was very safe, very middle-of-the-road, and the response was at best polite. For the second set he branched out a little, got bluesy, and even presented some of his own stuff, including an as yet unfinished number based on the melody that had first started haunting him on the seventh fairway at Carmel Bay Country Club almost a month earlier. He called it "Impossible Bliss," but hedged when asked the title and said he was still working on that as well.

The evening's sole moment of unpleasantness occurred between the sets when a female patron of uncertain age and equilibrium accosted Bliss. She must have been very drunk because he seemed to strike her as a possible romantic liaison for the evening.

"My dear lady," Bliss informed her in his most pompous voice. "I did not come here looking for love. I'm here to listen to Chief Shepard sing."

"Oh," she splurted. "So you think you're too good to go out with someone like me, do you?"

"Of course," he replied, shocking her into silence.

The second set went a lot better than the first. Shepard had been around enough to know this was usually the case. A few rounds of drinks can loosen up the stiffest room in no time at all. Still, they really did seem to enjoy what he was laying down, and it pleased him.

It looked as if it could take years to clean up the fallout from Alex Wagner's death. Yale Gerringer's children visited him at the Monterey Country Correction Bureau. They and their families announced they would stick by him to the end. The close, loving family stood in stark contrast to the Wagners and their bizarre game.

Bruce Wagner remained in custody under heavy guard, awaiting extradition proceedings that the city of Seattle had filed. Authorities there charged him as an accessory in the death of Dolores Muñoz and three other victims of the ferryboat disaster. Shepard didn't think Cosentino would make a move until everything had cooled down, but he wasn't about to take any chances.

There were also several civil suits pending against Bruce Wagner and his brother's estate. How large the prize would turn out to be in the end was anybody's guess. Bruce was Alex's heir, but Holly Development filed suit against the estate, claiming it was composed in the main of money embezzled from Holly. Holly also sued Mutual Holdings, but the court was having difficulty finding anyone to serve the papers on. If Cosentino held the strings of Mutual Holdings, an army of attorneys were still unable to prove it. Genevra Carroll moved back to Santa Cruz, once again estranged from her father. Shepard did not know why exactly.

Jason Kiley left the area for greener pastures. No proof could be found that the ten thousand dollar payoffs were anything other than the "environmental consulting fees" Kiley claimed.

The Pro-Am was a tremendous success both for Carmel Bay Country Club and the city. Chick Beal had heartily endorsed Shepard at the regular weekly council meeting, and for the moment at least his job seemed secure.

Shepard looked out over the audience at Ramblin' Rick's, and found only a few familiar faces this time. Cathy Gonzales, Amy, Charlie Revere, and Stan Durbin were all there. He felt a small twinge of guilt. Who was watching after the town tonight?

After wheedling the name from Bliss the previous weekend, Shepard had driven over to Salinas to see the wealthy landowner the artist claimed had bought a sculpture of his. Sure enough, there it was: a rusting metal monstrosity towering nine feet above a field of ripening strawberries. Dressed in ragged clothes by the farmer, it terrorized the local crow population. The farmer swore the thing even drove off insects. His strawberry crop certainly seemed to flourish.

Shepard lifted his hands from the keys on his last song and smiled at the applause, led enthusiastically by his officers and Bliss. The artist stood near the bar, slapping his hands together and whistling as loud as he could. When the crowd turned back to their drinks and conversation, Shepard began to gather up his music. Bliss wandered over.

"They liked you," Bliss admitted.

It sounded like a simple statement of fact, but Shepard saw the emotion beneath it. For Shepard music, his art, was just a sideline. It made him feel good to be able to produce something that pleased others as well. He realized Bliss would kill to have that same satisfaction. Bliss' talent for observation was uncanny. He had a vision worth expressing.

Shepard knew Bliss had far more he wanted to say with his art than Shepard did. But somewhere deep down inside the man Bliss must sense he lacked that vital spark that would ignite the vision and transfer it to canvas. He could dream the dream, but the talent to share it seemed always to elude him.

Bliss seemed to sense something in his face gave away more than he was accustomed to revealing. The corner of his mouth scrunched up and the shrug he gave was so big his right ear almost reached his shoulder. "Not my kind of music of course."

"Of course." Shepard smiled.

"My tastes run more to symphonies. Lots of instruments playing, that sort of thing. Music with meat on its bones."

"Come clean, Bliss."

"I beg you pardon?"

"The case isn't over and you know it."

"Chief, I swear I don't know what you're talking about."

"The golf shot! How did Wagner do it? I figured out the motive at least. Even though I thought the killer was Leonard Romaine."

Bliss looked surprised. "Romaine? Why?"

"Well, when we learned Wagner wasn't killed until some time after leaving the golf course, that destroyed the three best alibis in the case, those of his golfing partners. I remembered Romaine was a widower and when it became clear the killer must have lost someone in the ferry accident..." He stopped. It had sounded good to him at the time.

"You would have caught up eventually," Bliss assured him.

"But what about the miracle golf shot! Wagner wanted to leave Holly and the others with a parting shot, and boy did he ever! But how could he be sure the ball would go in the hole?! You promised to tell me!"

Bliss looked nonplussed. "Good lord, I didn't think it was necessary! You saw everything I did, more than I did as a matter of fact! There was more physical evidence about that small point than anything else!"

"What physical evidence?"

"The goop on the green…the broken thermos Wagner tossed off the cliff…"

"Whoa! Slow down! The birdshit? You're telling me—"

"Chief, I'm really disappointed in you. What did Wagner have in his freezer?"

Shepard stared at him. "His freezer? Frozen dinners alphabetically arranged so his brother would never leave anything out of place and nipples and things, ice…cubes…wait a minute, there was also cream in the refrigerator…" His mind clicked over a notch. "A thermos, molds for making round ice cubes…"

Bliss held out his hands.

"Are you telling me he made a golf ball out of white ice?"

"What else? We already know he needed to cut himself to put blood on the club and the ball. What stopped him from popping over to the club before the match—they were the first foursome every Wednesday like clockwork remember—and planting the bloody ball in the cup? He probably left the thermos in the trap along with the plant sprayer to re-do the dew. He wouldn't hit the ice ball of course. That would splatter it, but I'd say a careful toss in the direction of the pin would be all he needed.

"The others would see 'the ball' fly out of the trap and drop toward the green. Remember too they didn't see it actually hit, at least Webb didn't describe it that way and nobody bothered to contradict him. The ice ball broke up and began to melt leaving only that bit of crystallized goo I found. The ball in the cup completed the illusion."

"I hate you, Bliss."

Bliss laughed. "You said that already. A lot of people do, Chief." He leaned in close to Shepard. "Say, that scuffle I had with Kiley…"

"He left town before he could press charges. I think we can let it slide."

"Oh, that's fine. I truly appreciate it…"

He started to turn, but swiveled back.

"About that other little misunderstanding…the indictment for breaking and entering? I don't suppose there's anything you could do about that?"

Shepard ran his hand through his hair. "It's not a traffic ticket, Bliss."

"I know that, Chief. I know that," Bliss replied. "But it was all in a good cause…the investigation and so on…"

"I'll see what I can do."

Every wrinkle on Bliss' face seemed to smile. He nodded and turned away. Shepard waited patiently. Bliss took one step, two, three, four. Then he whirled and trotted back up to Shepard.

"There was one more thing," Bliss admitted.

Shepard nodded. "Somehow I knew there would be."

Bliss held out a crumpled piece of paper. Shepard took it.

"What's this?"

Bliss looked embarrassed. "My expenses? Seattle? I stayed in a very cheap motel."

Shepard glanced at the amount. "Under the circumstances I think I can get a payment authorized."

"Thanks, Chief. I've got to be going. Work, you know," Bliss confided.

"I hope now you'll return to…what you do best…your art?" Shepard felt very proud he managed to say that with a straight face.

"Art is my life," Bliss acknowledged with a solemn nod of his shaggy head. He started off, but he turned around. Shepard saw that devil of a glint in his eye. "Until you need me again of course."

With that he headed toward the exit. The drunken woman swooped to cut him off.

"Not so fast, stretch," she clamored. "You think you're so high-and-mighty?"

"Yes," Bliss replied. "With good reason."

"If you're too good to go to bars looking for a little companionship, what do you do for a love life? What kind of dating do you do?"

"At my age? Carbon."
He slouched out the door.

The End

About the Author

Lee Sheldon was twice nominated for Edgar Awards from the Mystery Writers of America. He was a writer-producer in Hollywood, writes and designs computer games and online entertainment, and is working on a book about storytelling and character development in video games. His website is anti-linearlogic.com.

1-58348-021-8

Printed in the United States
100175LV00004B/337/A